The Running Horses

The Running Horses

FRED GROVE

Doubleday & Company, Inc.
Garden City, New York
1980

All of the characters in this book
are fictitious, and any resemblance
to actual persons, living or dead,
is purely coincidental

ISBN: 0-385-14741-4
Library of Congress Catalog Card Number 79-7625
Copyright © 1980 by Fred Grove

The Running Horses

Chapter 1

Lee Banner followed the blood-bay filly with approving eyes. He was prejudiced—wasn't every hopeful horseman about his own?—but experienced judgments other than his own agreed that Cindy was a walking picture. That blazed face and those white socks on her hind feet, and that left eye a pale blue. Fifteen hands high. Good muscle. Good bone. Good balance. So natural and graceful, the way she moved. That was the main thing, her fluid motion. Like a piece of silk on the Oklahoma wind. Did he dare dream again? He wondered and felt both a hanging back and a longing.

He whistled shrilly and she tossed her head and fixed him with an alert look. He whistled again and she frisked up to the gate as he held out a handful of pellet feed. Although she was a pet, he hadn't pampered her. Spoil a horse and you built your own trouble, like spoiling a child that later couldn't cope with life's hard knocks. Running horses needed a lot of schooling and handling, a lot of human company. That helped keep them calm before a race and improved their manners in the starting gate, where a clean break could mean the slim margin between winning and losing.

He didn't need a watch to tell him it was feeding time. His little band of broodmares and foals, which he liked to think of as a family, waited at the other pasture gate for their suppers. Followed by Doc, the ranch's black-and-white mongrel watchdog, he walked across and slid the bolt and let them in.

The mares had a regular pecking order, but beware the one that tried to break it. Sometimes they reminded him of little old ladies at a supermarket, shoving with carts to reach the checkout stand first. Cinder Sue, the oldest, and Cindy's light-bay mama, was on the lead as usual. She was barren this year.

As the matrons trailed for the barn, the one called Dixie cut out of line to go ahead. At once Cinder Sue wheeled and squealed and bit at her.

"Cut that out—you two!" Lee yelled, amused, shaking his head.

Dixie, quickly buffaloed, returned to second in line. That little colt of hers sure looked like a dandy.

Because Cindy was nearing racing age as a two-year-old, Lee kept her in a pasture separate from the others to avoid getting her kicked and possibly injured. That could happen. A horseman was already assured of his destined share of bad luck without creating more through carelessness, for he was allotted a full measure as certain as God made sunshine.

He came back and opened the gate for Cindy. She romped past him.

"Sassy," he called after her.

His barn of concrete blocks—built with his own hands, the family helping on weekends, the front painted red, the sides white, the peaked roof bright blue, with a broad breezeway separating the stalls—sat on a sandy slope that bottomed on bermuda and oat pasture and scattered cottonwoods. In summer and warm autumnal afternoons, the horses enjoyed rolling in the cool sand. There was also a circular break corral, recently completed. About one third of his fencing was pipe, done little by little as time and money allowed. Underground lines linked the sweet-water well and tanks in both pastures. Someday he was going to have automatic waterers in each stall. Such was progress in a do-it-yourself operation.

He turned along the breezeway, past the tack room and its pungency of leather and liniment, to the west end of the barn to the feed room. Morning and evening, he fed oats and a mixture of sweet stuff with vitamins and minerals, and sometimes mash, followed by alfalfa hay. A man was performance and money ahead to feed the best. He began to fill the feedboxes.

Land Rush, his quarter horse stud, a clear bay with black points, was making a racket of lordly impatience in his stall.

"Mamas and babies first, old horse," Lee reminded him. "Where are your manners tonight?"

Next, he threw down alfalfa, closed the feed room, and coming to the front of the barn, shook Bull Durham into a brown paper and rolled a cigarette while he considered the broad pasture across the road. It was as level as a floor except for the little draw about midway that you wouldn't notice from the road. He needed more pasture. Trouble was, that high-powered Oklahoma City lawyer wanted $5,000 an acre. He shook his head at the inflated figure. That kind of money just wasn't around. Feed was high, too. Inflation, when was it going to slow down? Serena's job in town as a teacher and counselor paid for a good deal of the little ranch's upkeep. Lee supplied the rest—filling in odd times at the feed store, or with county road crews running a grader, or sometimes working rodeos—he and Land Rush, who contributed modest stud fees during the breeding season from early in the year into summer.

An impulse took Lee to the corral gate, Doc tagging along, and down the lane to the wooden sign facing the road. The once-bold lettering of red on white had faded more than he realized. It read dimly:

RUNNING QUARTER HORSES
Home of
LAND RUSH (AAAT)
(Rushing Man—Oklahoma Lady)
Fee, $500
Live Foal Guarantee
Lee Banner, Owner

I'd better touch that up, Lee reproached himself. This place is beginnin' to look like a sharecropper's.

Not many horsemen brought their mares to Land Rush's court. Mostly men of modest means. Friends and their friends. Few of them had gambled nominating money for the big futurities in New Mexico. Few had the money. It took some $2,500 to pay a colt or filly through to the All-American Futurity Trials at Ruidoso. Took money and faith—and luck to get them that far. Although Land Rush's get had done well on the small Oklahoma tracks, and he was the fifth leading sire last season at Sallisaw's Blue Ribbon Downs, he wasn't well known. His wasn't a glamorous name. His career, though AAAT, had been too brief.

Only last week a visitor, noticing the sign, had driven in out of obvious curiosity. Right away he let fall, not without a certain patronizing manner, that he had recently "gone into the racing game," hired a leading trainer, paid $50,000 for a filly scheduled to make her debut at Sunland. Whereupon, Lee wished him luck, and whereupon the other intimated that $500 sounded like a cheap stud. Not enough class to attract top mares.

"Class! Well, let me tell you something, mister. Land Rush still holds the three-fifty record at Blue Ribbon Downs—ran on down there in 17.45, which is just a hair off the world's record. Sallisaw's not Sunland or Raton or Ruidoso, or out there in California at Los Alamitos—but speed is speed, wherever you find it."

The man opened his mouth to speak, but Lee silenced him with: "Land Rush was unbeaten as a two-year-old—ran top triple A—speed index 111—was headed for the All-American trials—going great guns till he went down in a three-horse tangle at Columbus, Texas, on a muddy track. I should say unbeaten till then. Garbaged his right knee. I brought him home. He never ran again. I thought too much of him."

"No offense meant."

"I understand," Lee said, cooling down. "Just wanted to set the record straight. Now, Rushing Man, his daddy, went back to Peter McCue, and Oklahoma Lady to Oklahoma Star, who was by the Thoroughbred Dennis Reed. You've heard of Oklahoma Star?"

The man gave him a blank look.

"Well, Oklahoma Star just ran a scored one furlong in eleven seconds flat. He beat the great mare Slip Shoulder, and Kate Bernard, among others. Rushing Man outran everything in northern Oklahoma but Leo, and he ran nostril to nostril with him. A dead heat at Pawhuska—three hundred yards. Everybody's heard of Leo, probably the greatest quarter horse broodmare sire."

"Oh, yes."

"You're welcome to come in. There's coffee on the stove."

"Thanks . . . uh. I'd better get along."

And as the visitor drove away, Lee thought of the postscript he might have added to Land Rush's story: End of a dream. A dream for a stakes horse that came by only once in a man's lifetime. Lee hurt every time he thought about it.

He was at the house, beginning to think about supper, when he heard the car coming from the direction of Norman. There was no mistaking the groan of that old motor, still going after some 100,000 miles. He waited by the porch, feeling the lift of anticipation.

In moments he saw the tan Falcon make the curve where the blacktop road turned to follow the grassy flood plain of the South Canadian River and come deliberately on, like a tiring old Thoroughbred, Lee thought, entering the head of the stretch, being jockeyed and paced for the charge to the wire.

Serena was late. She drove in and stopped, turned off the ignition. The old car seemed to sigh its relief, then expire.

Lee walked around to the driver's side and opened the door, while Serena gathered up the usual stack of papers for evening grading. Arms loaded, she stepped out and gave him a quick kiss.

Serena Banner's high-boned face wore a wide-eyed, hopeful look, as if she thought people would do what she wished, which they often did. She was thirty-eight and looked younger, her light-brown hair just beginning to show gray, which she made no attempt to conceal, and her large eyes were smoky black, set wide and deep, a feature passed on by her part-Chickasaw mother. Her slimness made her look taller than she was, and she had long, tapering legs and high, firm breasts. Cool and practical, she had pulled Dixie's baby out of her when Lee was gone that night last spring. Lee was proud of her and her two degrees from the state university, earned over the years, mostly summers, between clerking at a variety of jobs, whereas he had barely finished high school.

With a university-educated family, Lee had become self-conscious about his lack of higher learning and his use of cowboy grammar around company until daughter Nancy took him aside. "Daddy," she said earnestly, after classmates had spent a Sunday afternoon at the ranch, "you know so many things not found in books. I have professors who'd give a great deal to know what you know about nature . . . taking care of horses and training them to run their best distances . . . what you know about the different native grasses and planting things. How to braid a pretty quirt. How to build a good fence. How to build a good barn. . . . Mom and I love you just as you are. You're a natural man."

"In the rough." Lee had smiled back, touched.

Serena was saying tiredly, "Another teachers' meeting."

"Another Thank-God-It's-Friday, huh?"

"An emergency meeting," she said, unsmiling, "with the PTA and some parents. Had a girl brought in this morning by her minister and mother, an eighth grader who's been on speed and smoking pot. She said others in her class had tried drugs. The main problem is how to stop non-school juveniles from selling to grade school kids."

"I'll tell you how to stop it. Knock some heads together. Get out the old hickory stick and lay it on heavy."

"The situation is far more complicated than that, Lee. Too, some of the kids are selling to other kids."

"Today's kids are spoiled, Serena. You know that. They have too much. They don't have enough to do. Nobody wants to work hard anymore."

He saw that tolerant expression, backed by exasperation, come into her eyes. They had been over the subject before. She said,

"We left things open for a follow-up, but we found the parents simply could not believe that this was happening. They think if they let the problem alone it will go away." She struck an attitude of defensive pride. "However, our city is no worse than a lot of others, better than most. It's a nationwide problem."

Without rebuttal, he took the papers from her and they went into the house. She sniffed delightedly. "You've cooked dinner!"

"A pot of stew. Been on since morning. I hope it's done."

"I could eat it raw."

He placed the papers on the coffee table, talking over his shoulder. "Nancy called at noon. They're fixin' to get ready for a party at the dorm tomorrow night. So she won't be out." He frowned. "She's decided to change her major again."

"What is it this time?"

"Education."

Serena flung him a pained look devoid of surprise and sighed. "From home ec to history to education."

"She's only nineteen. I figure she wants to be a teacher like her mama."

"You'd take up for your baby no matter what."

"Seems to me I remember another baby who jumped around a lot while I was ridin' all them mean bulls on the big rodeo circuit. Had to marry her to settle her down, way she kept chasin' after me."

"As usual, Mr. Clean, you are talking like a male chauvinist. When, as a matter of fact, it was *I* who settled *you* down. Though I'll be so generous as to give part credit to the Brahma bull that stepped on you in the National Finals."

He flinched in mock pain. She was laughing at him with her eyes. That was one of her appealing ways, that sense of humor. She could laugh when laughter was needed. She could take teasing and she could tease back, and when she did he caught the same unquenchable liveliness of the pretty, small-town girl he had married twenty-one years ago.

"Oh, I don't know now," he went on. "Man gets tard of purty barrel riders bunchin' up around him all the time." He was reaching for her as he spoke, slipping an arm around her waist and pulling her to him, still teasing. "Or maybe I felt sorry for that poor little country girl with the calf eyes that kept draggin' her rope for me."

She was about to let him kiss her when he said that. She pulled back, feigning pique, turning her face away, and all he could manage was a peck on her cheek.

"You're spoiled," she said, finally looking at him, quirking her mouth.

"And you're mighty devilish. But I like that."

"I'm hungry, Lee." She kissed him then, fully.

"So am I. Let's eat. If the stew's not done, just tell that cook to dig out his bedroll and drift."

Washing up for dinner, he grimaced at the weathered face he surveyed in the bathroom mirror. He was forty and he looked it, he thought, contrary to the old saying that horses kept a man young, noting the sun wrinkles and the creases and his thinning hair, white blond against his deep-bronze skin. His ash-gray eyes had acquired crow's feet at the corners, and his left shoulder was lower than the right one, thanks to that Brahma bull. At least he could see that he wasn't picking up tallow around the middle; older he got the leaner he seemed to stay, despite the way Serena cooked up a storm on weekends. But that blamed bald spot! Wetting the comb, he carefully parted his hair on the left side and drew his cowlick over the telltale sparseness.

They ate in hungry silence for a while. The stew was done. Then Serena asked, "How's Cindy looking?"

"If I ever saw a filly with go on her mind, she's it. Cal came over this morning and we worked her against his old gelding. You know, lap-and-tap start, old style. She breaks real good, Serena. Keeps her head straight. Stays balanced. Runs straight. Comes out firing like she means it. Catches on fast. But she can learn just so much here. Needs a few races. Before long I'll take her down to Wildhorse Downs . . . see what she can do. That's a nice little track, with starting gates. Smoky Osgood keeps talkin' up a poor-boy match race. But she's too young yet. I don't want to risk her."

"If you think she has real potential, maybe we should have nominated her as a yearling for the All-American?"

"Guess I'm superstitious after what happened to Landy and Cinder Sue. All the bad luck they had after we paid their early nomination fees, then had to drop out. No . . . this time we'll wait and see, and when the time gets close and if she still looks sharp, running triple A time, we'll plunk down late money to make her eligible for the trials."

"About when would that be?" A frown laced her forehead as she finished her dinner.

"June fifteenth or August fifteenth. The two dates you can supplement a nominee."

"You're talking about a very expensive gamble, Lee. Thousands of dollars."

"I know. And that August deadline costs twice as much as the June date. But that late you know pretty well what your horse can do—or might do."

"Where would you get all that late entry money?"

"From the bank. I think J.B. would loan it to us, if we had a fast horse. Could be, Cindy will earn some between now and then."

"That's a gamble, too." Thoughtfully, she pushed back her plate and folded her hands in her lap, a kind of weariness moving into the smooth face. "Sometimes I wish we'd get out of the horse business and stay out."

"It's not just a business, Serena."

"What is it then, pray tell?" Her voice had taken on a sudden edge.

"Why . . . it's way more than that." He hesitated and fell to wondering, looking within himself. "For one thing, it was something to come back to after we quit the rodeo circuit, something to tie to. We both enjoy horses. They're more than running machines, the good ones. They respond to schooling, they can tell how you feel about them by your touch and your voice." He was talking in a rush now. "Someday you hope you'll have a great colt or filly that goes on up there. Landy was on his way when he got hurt. A real stakes horse. Cinder Sue had some bad luck,

but she showed me plenty of class and heart. . . . It's more than
a business to me. It's a dream as well. Some men climb mountains or get in little boats and sail around the world and get their
pictures in the papers. Me, I want a horse of ours to win the All-
American. That's my dream."

"Well, you can't dream away the money it takes, Lee. It's insa-
tiable. Our feed bills drain us every month, and there's always a
vet bill. We have Nancy living in a dorm at the university. She
had bids from several top sororities. But we couldn't afford it.
We can't even afford a used car for her."

"I can't see that she needs a car." They had been over that before also. Lee was adamant.

"Nevertheless, if she had one she could come home more
often. Your pickup is shot and my old car . . . I just hope it lasts
another school term. We have to have transportation. Call horses
whatever you like—but to me they're no more than an expensive
gamble or hobby that keeps us forever strapped." To his astonishment, she rose abruptly and left the table to stand by the
fireplace, her back turned to him.

He regarded her for another startled moment, then got up.
"Heck fire, Serena, you know Cindy has to have her chance. It's
only fair to her. She's bred to run. All that speed on both sides."

"So was Land Rush. So was Cinder Sue."

He stepped toward her and held out his hand, a gesture of reassurance.

Before he could touch her, she said, very low, "Guess I'm a little tired tonight," and went to their bedroom and closed the door
behind her.

He let her go, unable to deny her straightforward words. True.
True. Every one. Yet . . . Angry at himself for what he was pow-
erless to change this moment, he wheeled through the kitchen,
across the back porch, and outside, striding rapidly for the barn.
Doc materialized at his feet, on guard at his usual post by the
corral gate. Lee stroked the old dog's head and ruff, murmuring
nonsense to him. Doc whined and licked, followed Lee inside
the corral.

After looking in on Land Rush, Lee turned Cindy back into

her pasture and the broodmares and the little ones into theirs. Only the stud was stalled at night. Lee had wondered if he shouldn't take the precaution of keeping Cindy in the barn after dark, in case some drunk stopped along the road and took pot-shots at fence posts.

He paused, his pulse quickening, listening to the rustle of the horses, catching the lighter steps of the youngsters, feeling every hoofbeat. A rhythm there, a running rhythm. A flow of sound. A going away now. A faint drumming. Their dark shapes dimming as they raced for the open pasture, blurring like smoke against the dark line of the cottonwoods yonder. Running horses.

Lee Banner liked this time of year best, summer hanging on and fall creeping in, the afternoons warm, the evenings cool, a full moon silvering the land, so bright a man might read his newspaper in the yard. A footloose breeze purred across the South Canadian like a benediction, for this was grass country, this was horse country. His Grandfather Banner, a Texan, had homesteaded here in the Run of '89, tearing horseback across the river, jumps ahead of a pack of land-hungry settlers, to drive his stakes and hold off a later claimant at gunpoint. Lived in a dugout that first winter. And somehow Lee's father had hung onto the old place during the Depression; and now, Lee thought, we're hanging on, too.

The house loomed before him, a sturdy, simple, one-story frame his father had built himself in the 1920s and painted white, a color Lee had kept. He had modernized it, piped in water, insulated the walls and attic, and built on the back porch for Serena's washing machine. Together they had carpeted the living room and the two bedrooms.

He walked on, Doc close at his heels. For a moment back there he had forgotten his troubles.

When he returned to the house, Serena was sitting on the sofa in her pink robe, grading papers. She glanced up but did not speak. He settled in his chair, picked up the morning newspaper and scowled at another editorial opposing legalization of pari-mutuel betting.

No, Lee fretted to himself, let all this Oklahoma and Texas

money go to the New Mexico tracks, especially out to Ruidoso. Here in the so-called Bible Belt, they still associated horse racing with the old-time notion of black-coated, gimlet-eyed gamblers, whiskey drinkin' and fightin', and now they claimed the Mafia would move in if betting was legalized. Yet Oklahoma and Texas sent more fast runners to the New Mexico stakes races than all other states combined, and Oklahoma runners had stood most times in the winner's circle of the All-American. Their names almost as familiar as those of his own little band: Decketta, Savannah Jr., Rocket Wrangler, Easy Jet and Easy Date, Possumjet, Bugs Alive in '75, and right here in Norman the Jones family had won it all with that long-striding, walking picture filly, Laico Bird.

It was, he concluded, enough to disgust a horseman. Norman was surrounded by horse farms; others downriver in the vicinity of Purcell and Wynnewood. Stallion stations, the big outfits were called. Outfits standing big-name studs carrying money lines that would make a banker run for cover. Winners of big futurities and derbies, now commanding stud fees to match their reputations. Well, if Cindy could run, and he honestly believed she could, and if bad luck didn't play a hand, more top mares would be calling on Landy after next racing season, once news got around as to her breeding.

All this going on, he brooded, in fact an industry at work, employing many, many people, and about the only time the newspapers even mention a top running horse is when one wins the All-American. He set about finishing the newspaper, wishing to break the silence, but not knowing what to say.

He must have dozed, because when he stirred and looked around, Serena had gone to bed. He laid the paper aside, watched the ten o'clock news and weather—another clear day forecast—turned everything off and stumbled through the darkness to the bedroom.

Serena lay on her side, her back to him. He started to touch her as he always did when he was the last to bed, a good-night touch, thought better of it, and undressed.

Lying down, he struggled to organize his thinking. Maybe he

should get a steady job in town, though offhand he didn't know where that might be. Maybe he could get on at Tinker Field, join the herd of commuters. But if he found a full-time job, he would have to hire a man to look after the place in his absence. Horses had to be fed, stables mucked out, fences kept up. With the big-city crime wave overflowing to the outlying areas, it was wise to have someone around even during daylight. They could clean you out. Had one horseman, downriver; took horses and furniture. Hire a man, he brooded, if you can find one. Trouble is, nobody wants to work hard anymore. Hell no, they'd rather draw welfare and live on less. Or was it more?

He tossed and turned. Maybe he should sell off all but a few of his horses, keeping Landy and Cindy, maybe Cinder Sue and Dixie? That option fled the instant it came to him. He just couldn't do it. There were the little ones coming up—just babies, really—the two little fillies and Dixie's dandy little colt that Lee wanted to register as Dixieland. And there were the old mares. He owed them plenty, for they had given so much. In turn, wasn't he obligated to them? The answer was obvious. You owed debts to horses that had been good to you. You paid the debts. Truth was, he wanted them to live out their days on the place where they were foaled. And Cindy? She deserved her chance as a running two-year-old. But taking a full-time job would require placing her with a trainer and campaigning her by long distance. Some worrier trainer with a stable of runners and she would be just one of the bunch. No, he determined, if she's going to run I want to train her and campaign her myself . . . if we can manage it. I want to be there.

On that hopeful resolution he drifted off into a fitful sleep, aware there were no easy choices. You just hoped the bank would carry you if you hauled your horse to the track wars.

He woke to feel Serena beside him, the covers thrown back. Moonlight was a silver mist filming the room. He touched her. Serena was naked, faced to him. Stirring, he felt her hand move across his chest and around him as she laid her head against his shoulder. Desire plunged through his drowsy surprise. He turned

his head and pulled her closer, almost roughly, and buried his
face in the curve of her neck, loving the scent of her.

"I was terrible tonight," she whispered.

"Just honest, was all." He kissed her. Her cheeks were wet.

"I couldn't sleep," she said.

"I haven't much."

"You work so hard."

"No harder than you."

"Your horses are your life, and tonight I would have taken
them away. How selfish of me!"

"We all get discouraged at times. . . . Look, Serena, at the
moonlight. It's a beautiful night."

"Yes. I love you, Lee. No matter what I said."

"And why do you suppose I passed up all them rodeo
queens?"

He kissed her hair, her eyes, her cheeks, her lips. He stroked
her back, her thighs, the feel of her like satin.

They said no more. All her loveliness was there for him, made
lovelier in the half-light. He felt her caressing him, needing him
as he needed her. She lifted her face to him and her arms went
around him, as if locking him to her forever.

Now they lay in the softest of light, hands clasped, in warm silence. Lee was near sleep when all at once she said, "I just
remembered something."

"What?"

"That blue pickup."

"What blue pickup?"

"I've seen it every day for the past three days. I saw it this
morning when I drove to school."

"Where?" He still wasn't much interested.

"Parked beside the road at the south end of the pasture. Two
men. They kept looking across the pasture."

"Our pasture?" he asked suddenly, thinking of his horses.

"I mean the big pasture across the road."

"So?"

"They drove off when I came by."

"Maybe they want that piece of land as much as we do." He

chuckled softly. "Except maybe they can afford it. Maybe they want to start a horse ranch."

"If they're horsemen, why haven't they stopped here?"

"Did you see what they looked like?"

"Nondescript. In their late twenties or so. I wouldn't say they looked like horsemen, and I wouldn't know them if I met them face to face. But I did jot down their license number. It's an Oklahoma tag. Cleveland County."

"Go to sleep. I'll keep an eye out."

A dream or reality—that roaring? He broke out of deep sleep, upon him the approaching roar of a plane, so low he feared it was going to hit the house. He threw a protective arm across Serena. As he did, the plane passed over, its blast filling and vibrating through the old house. Lee jerked upright, hearing Serena's startled, "That plane—so close!" She sat up. "He must be in trouble."

"He's gunning the motor now, he's climbing. Sounds all right. If he's looking for a place to land, there's the university field."

"He's coming back," Serena said wonderingly, after moments. "He sure is."

The roaring intensified. Seconds later Lee heard the pilot cut the motor. "He's coming down—then he is in trouble." When the plane passed over again, Lee went to an open window where he could see across the road to the big pasture. The plane was gliding down, whistling wind, landing lights on. He saw it touch down, very fast—too fast, it seemed, but smoothly. Now it was slowing. About midway of the pasture it rocked. Of a sudden it dipped and he heard a loud *crrruump* as it nosed over and stopped. Lee knew what had happened. The pilot had hit the draw.

"I'm goin' over there," he said, getting up and grabbing trousers and shirt.

"Lee—be careful."

"Maybe he's hurt. You call the sheriff's office. Get somebody out here."

"All right."

Stomping into his boots, he ran outside and down the lane to the road and across to the fence. Slipping between the strands of barbed wire, he ran toward the glare of the landing lights several hundred yards away. At least the plane wasn't burning.

Running nearer, he saw two men standing beside the wreck and heard an accusing voice, "Thought those dumb bastards said this was level all the way."

"You fellas hurt?" Lee called, coming fast.

They jerked around. "We're all right," one said, waving him off. "You can go on back, man." The taller of the two, he wore an open-neck, casual suit and a beret. Everything about his face, the Fu Manchu mustache and the beard and the high Roman nose and the long chin, combined to give him a beaked look.

Just then the second man, who was bent over, holding his right shoulder, let out a groan.

"You *are* hurt," Lee said. "Come on to the house. We've already called for help."

"Called?" The tall man again. He and the other stood very still, and the injured one said, somewhat hastily, Lee thought, "Just a bruised shoulder. I'm okay."

He didn't sound okay, he didn't look okay, bent over like that, but he could take it. Of indeterminate age, hatless, balding, he had the battered features of a street fighter: flattened nose, puffy mouth and eyes. Short-legged, thick-chested, he wore a gray sweat shirt, jeans and white sneakers. Now he straightened, forcing himself.

"We've got help coming," the tall man said easily. "Was having motor trouble coming in, so radioed ahead to Westheimer Field. No need for you to stick around. Thanks, anyway. They'll be here any minute." His voice, low and controlled, had a reed-like quality.

"Well," said Lee, shrugging off the contradiction, "you're welcome to come to the house if you like."

"Thanks, man. We'll wait here. No problem."

Lee left them, walking slowly, his mind lingering on the vague wrongness back there, and reminded himself that it was none of his business. He'd offered to help.

He wasn't far from the fence when he saw a car tearing along the road from town, lights flashing, siren howling. He started running and saw it round the turn. At the same time he caught sight of a second car's lights topping the ridge above the flat. It was coming like a scalded cat. He ran to the pasture's wire gate, jerked the top wire loop free and threw the gate out of the way. Standing at the road's edge, he flagged down the sheriff's car.

"Where's the crash?" a young voice yelled from beneath a big white hat. The radio was bleating off and on, its gabble a flat monotone against a background of continuous scratching.

Lee recognized Undersheriff Bob Caldwell. "Over in the pasture. Two guys. One's hurt a little. Said they didn't need any help. Said they'd radioed ahead to Westheimer. Had motor trouble."

"How do I get over there?"

"I left the gate open."

"Get in, Lee."

Lee was stepping in when the other car whipped past. Lee looked. A pickup. A blue Chevy pickup. By then young Caldwell was gunning through the gate. He bulled for a hundred yards or more.

"Over to your left," Lee hollered. "There . . . see it? Hey, they've turned off the landing lights. That's odd."

The patrol car's headlights found the plane, a crippled silver bird with its bill stuck in prairie sod. Caldwell tore faster, braked hard, left the lights on target, and both men scrambled out and across to the wreck.

Lee checked to look around. There was no one here. On the road a car horn was blowing *ta-ta, ta-ta* over and over. He circled the plane and told Caldwell, "They're gone."

"Uh—oh. I don't like the looks of this, Lee."

The car horn stilled, started up again, *ta-ta, ta-ta*, faster than before, insistent. Lee could see lights on the road north of the house. That pickup . . . had to be. With his thought, the vehicle blasted off at a tire-screeching run, headed north. He said, "I'll give odds our two friends just left in that pickup that passed you when you stopped on the road."

Flashing a light, Caldwell climbed inside the plane. Ducking low, moving toward the rear, he passed from Lee's view. A moment, a very long moment, and he yelled, "No wonder they took off—this crate's loaded to the gills with marijuana!" He came out swiftly, on the run toward the patrol car. "I'd better get on the horn—and fast."

"Wait, Bob. Serena's got the license number of the pickup."

Chapter 2

Lee was at the barn Saturday afternoon when Serena called from the corral gate, "Bob Caldwell's on the phone."

Lee came outside, leaned the pitchfork against the side of the barn and took off his gloves. "Did he say what he wanted?"

"It's about last night."

"That's not hard to figure." He was frowning as he joined her.

Caldwell's crisp voice vented an unusual elation. "Howdy, Lee. Thought I'd better bring you up to date. The Highway Patrol picked up four guys in that blue pickup early this morning on I-35 in Oklahoma City, thanks to the tag number Serena took down. We arraigned 'em in district court a little while ago, and they're being held in county jail in lieu of bond. Associate Judge Abernathy set the preliminary hearing for two P.M. Monday." His voice took on emphasis. "Now catch this—there were eight hundred pounds of packaged marijuana in the plane, plus a quantity of heroin."

"Heroin?"

"Yes—heroin. Five pounds of it. Doesn't sound like much, offhand, but that amount happens to be worth a cool million bucks on the street, and the marijuana comes to an estimated eighty-five thousand street value. Lee, this may be one of the biggest drug busts in Oklahoma history, and we've had some big ones."

"Oh, boy."

"The heroin is uncut stuff—in rock form. It didn't come from the third or fourth man down the line, but from the trafficker who brought it over the border—straight from the labs in Mexico. All nice and neat in sixteen five-ounce cellophane packages—ready for the dealers across the state. We figure the marijuana is from Oaxaca, a southern Mexico state. Landing here is part of a trend toward use of smaller cities as relay points, especially for heroin, because of stiffer enforcement in large cities. . . . Good thing you folks called when you did. Another few minutes that blue pickup would've been gone with the load. He was right behind me, coming out of town. I figure the plane was early, else the guys in the pickup would've been there waiting."

"Glad we could help a little."

Caldwell went on in a somewhat hesitant voice. "We've got a problem here, Lee. Sheriff Avery and I have been talking to the district attorney. He says that since no drugs were found in the pickup, we can't make anything stick. Can't tie it together, you know. Right now we've got the foursome charged with possession and intent to distribute. See what I mean?"

"I see," Lee said, feeling his first real unease.

"Now, what we need to know is, can you identify the two men with the plane?"

Lee didn't reply for a moment. He could feel himself wanting no further part of this. "Guess I could," he said finally.

"I mean positive identification. You'd have to be certain."

"I saw their faces. I talked to 'em."

"Great! This will give us what we need, though I figure we'll have to let the pickup pair go. Don't believe Judge Abernathy would say we have grounds to hold 'em for trial. They could claim they just happened along or something."

"Even though we heard 'em honking?" Lee replied with a nervous little laugh.

"Right. Even though we heard 'em honking. Lee, I realize this is asking a lot, that it means getting you involved. Are you sure you want to do this now . . . appear in court?"

"I don't hanker to, but I will," Lee said, aware that Serena was watching him, wide-eyed and intent.

"Thanks, Lee. It's the only way we can come up with a strong case and make it stick. You will be our chief witness. . . . Here's something else. The plane, a Cessna 177, is Mexican registered. . . . Their lawyer said he will arrange for bail Monday. He's some slick bird out of the city named Schuman, already bellyaching about their rights. I wonder if he's ever thought of the countless number of ODs they're responsible for, or the school kids whose lives they've messed up? . . . Another thing. One of the suspects was packing a .357 Magnum handgun, no less, but was subdued before he could use it."

"Which one was that?"

"The tall, skinny guy."

"The one with the Roman nose? The cool *hombre* with the Fu Manchu?"

"You do know him, then. Great! Remember the other man's description?"

"Heavyset. Short. Bald. Looks like an ex-fighter. Flat nose. Hurt his right shoulder in the crash."

"You're doing fine, Lee."

"Now I'm going to ask you a question. Who are these people?"

"The tall one says he is B. C. Green, of Albuquerque. The other guy claims he is Duke Dolan, also of Albuquerque. They carry New Mexico driver's licenses. The photos on the licenses match, but so what? They're not talking. . . . See you at two P.M. Monday, Lee. No—be there early. Judge Abernathy always starts on the dot. Again, our thanks to you both."

"All right, Bob."

Lee hung up and looked at Serena. She was taut and pale, quite pale. She said haltingly, "So you're going to court? You're going to testify?"

He tried to shrug it off. "Bob wants me to lend a hand, that's all."

"*Lend a hand?* It's far more than that. No mere gesture."

"Serena, that plane carried a million dollars worth of dope. Bob says the state won't have a case unless I identify the two men with the plane. He asked me to do that at the preliminary hearing Monday afternoon before Judge Abernathy. I told him I would. If I don't, they go scot-free, to fly this stuff in over and over again."

"I don't want you to testify."

"I can't back out now."

"Those people . . . people like that . . . you don't know what they might do."

"I can take care of myself."

"I'm thinking of Nancy, too. People like that . . . you read about it in the papers. Theirs is another world from ours."

"I know that."

"I don't want you involved, Lee. I want you to think about us." Her voice had a shaken quality, uncommon for her.

"What about your school kids, Serena? What about kids all over the state? What about *them?*"

"Please, Lee. Stay out of it."

He patted her shoulder, awkward about it, and walked out of the house and back to the barn, Doc at his heels, thinking, Serena's right, which was why he hadn't told her about the .357 Magnum.

He let Land Rush out into the corral and the stud broke free, always eager to go despite that lumpy right knee. He could hardly gallop. It hurt Lee just to watch him, to think how far he might have gone.

Lee Banner forced the thought down and deliberately resumed cleaning out the barn.

Bob Caldwell was waiting for him at the head of the stairs when Lee climbed the second floor of the Cleveland County Courthouse some fifteen minutes before two o'clock. Caldwell—crew cut, dark, intense, early thirties, cowboy boots and tan trousers, plaid shirt and silver bolo tie—held out his hand and said, "Thanks for coming, Lee. This won't take long. Just the patrolman, myself and you—you're last. Wait out here. We'll give you the high sign when the district attorney is ready for you."

Lee, seeing the crowded hallway, drew the undersheriff aside. "Bob, I want to make something clear. I won't have my family drawn into this in any way. I won't have Serena taking the stand if the case is bound over. I won't have her subpoenaed. None of that. Understand?"

"Lee, I can't promise. That's up to the DA. But I don't think that will be necessary. You're our key witness."

"I mean it, Bob."

"I know how you feel. We're also prepared to give you and your family protection if necessary."

"Protection! Figure it'll come to that?" Lee was suddenly uptight.

"Just routine. See you in a little while." Caldwell went down the hall to the elevator.

Lee rolled a smoke and waited, uncomfortable in blue suit, white shirt and maroon tie, worn at Serena's insistence. A highway patrolman also marked time in the hallway. The other witness, Lee supposed, looking about. There was the usual scattering of courthouse loafers, mostly senior citizens, and over by the entrance of the district courtroom a photographer waited, his eyes on the elevator down the hall. Apart, a group conversed in guarded tones, likewise watching the elevator. The men wore platform shoes, sport shirts, funky hats, beads and dark glasses, their young, restless women in butt-tight slacks and low-cut blouses. No bras.

Lee had to smile a little at himself. He was old-fashioned about women and readily admitted it. Serena got on him frequently about his conservatism. He had blown his cool when Nancy came home braless from the university at the end of her first semester. She still went without, and he still opposed her abandonment. Still, he thought, he shouldn't complain as long as she made her grades and stayed out of trouble.

There was a stir, a sudden milling, then a hush, and he turned with the others, seeing Caldwell step from the elevator, followed by four prisoners: the two with the plane coming first, sided by a deputy and Sheriff Claude Avery, stout, florid, earthy, in his fourth term and a cinch for No. 5, if he sought it. All the prisoners were handcuffed except the man called Dolan, who carried his right arm in a sling.

The photographer, camera ready, stepped alertly forward, sighted, and a bulb flashed. At that Dolan started a left-handed swing at the photographer.

Sheriff Avery grabbed him on the upswing and yanked him back as he might take a fractious mule by the bit.

Grinning, the photographer sighted again. A bulb flashed. He stepped clear, his grin spreading. "Got you in there, too, Sheriff."

The man called Green struck an amused pose. Hurriedly, the photographer obliged him.

"That's enough," Avery barked, displeased. "Move along."

The procession filed on and as it passed into the courtroom, the group followed as one, the women swaying sinuously, suggestively, on the arms of their older men. Lee read swaggering arrogance in them all. He had expected that, but what disturbed him and disgusted him was their unmistakable allegiance. And the girls . . . they looked so young, no older than Nancy.

After a deputy closed the doors, he heard the bailiff's voice and the creak of wooden benches and the scrape of feet as the spectators stood for the judge. Court was called into session. A murmur of voices followed.

Before long the patrolman was called. He came out after a few minutes. Caldwell took the stand next. Lee caught bits of his testimony, detailing the contents of the plane, setting the time and the place. His testimony ran at length, and then Sheriff Avery was at the door, motioning for Lee.

Sworn in, hat in hand, facing the courtroom, Lee saw surprise shuttle across the faces at the defense table.

District Attorney Ben Russell rose, brushed back a lock of obstinate iron-gray hair, and strolled toward the witness chair, his voice friendly and assured.

"State your name to the court, please."

"Lee H. Banner."

"What is your occupation, Mr. Banner?"

"I raise running quarter horses."

"Where do you live, Mr. Banner?"

"Northwest of Norman about five miles."

"Were you home last Friday night?"

"I was."

"Did a plane land near your place that night?"

"It did . . . across the road from our house and was wrecked."

"Did you run over there to render help if needed?"

At once the defense attorney, a leanly built man with an outthrust jaw and a mass of jet-black hair, was on his feet, shouting, "Objection! Your honor, the district attorney is leading the witness. Putting words in his mouth. Let the witness speak for himself, without prompting."

Judge M. M. Abernathy, young and somewhat nervous, pounded for order. "I shall have to ask you to lower your voice, Mr. Schuman. . . . Rephrase the question, Mr. Russell."

"Of course, your honor." And to Lee: "What course of action did you take after the plane came down?"

"I ran over there to help if I could."

"What did you find?"

"The plane was nosed over in a little draw in the pasture. Two men were standing beside the plane."

"Did you speak to them?"

"I did."

"What did you say?"

"I asked if anybody was hurt, if they needed help. Invited them to come to the house."

"What was their response?"

"They said they were okay, for me to go back. That help was on the way . . . said they'd radioed ahead to Westheimer Field they were coming down because of motor trouble."

"Because of motor trouble?" Russell repeated, pursing his lips. "Did the plane sound in trouble before it landed? That is, was the motor sputtering or cutting out?"

Schuman pounced on the question. "Objection! If the court please, this witness is a horseman. Not a trained flier. Not qualified as an expert on airplane engines."

"Mr. Russell," Abernathy asked, "do you intend to link this up?"

"I do, your honor. To show the purpose and intent behind the night landing."

"Very well. The witness will answer the question. Was the motor sputtering or cutting out?"

"It was not," Lee said. "It sounded all right to me when the plane passed over my house the first time and when it circled back for the landing." Suddenly remembering, he spoke on impulse. "And when I ran up to the plane, I heard one of the men say, 'I thought those dumb bastards said this was level all the way.'"

And the courtroom, silent until now, rippled into instant laughter, and as Schuman shouted objections, Abernathy gaveled for order and spoke sharply. "The witness will henceforth confine his testimony to the question. The court will strike the last. Continue, Mr. Russell."

The DA was smiling. "Mr. Banner, you have testified that you saw two men by the plane. Did they appear injured in any way?"

"One man was holding his shoulder, but he said he was all right."

"Did you think that odd?"

"Yes, I did."

"Objection, your honor! He's leading the witness again."

"Objection sustained. Continue, Mr. Russell, but limit your questioning to what the witness saw and what was said. Not what he thought. Not the state of his mind."

Nodding, Russell asked, "Would you know the two men by the plane if you saw them again?"

"Yes, sir."

"Are they in this courtroom?"

"They are."

"Please point them out for the court."

"One is the man with his right arm in a sling," Lee replied, pointing toward the defense table. "The other is the man on his left, with the Fu Manchu mustache."

"You are positive?"

"I am," Lee said firmly.

Schuman was on his feet, waving his arms. "Objection! Objection! This is absurd and totally illogical. How could the witness describe two men seen momentarily in the dead of night?" He took a belligerent stance. His voice fluted even higher. "The defense challenges the credibility of this witness."

Russell pivoted on him, his face flushing anger. "The witness is merely testifying to what he saw."

Suddenly both were roaring at each other, and Abernathy pounded for order. When the voices subsided, he turned to Lee. "Mr. Banner, the court reminds you that you are under solemn oath. Can you clarify that statement?"

"Yes, sir. First of all, the moon was full. Like daylight. And the landing lights on the plane were still on."

Schuman flung Green a startled, open-mouthed reproach, and sat down.

As if letting that point sink home, Russell paused, then asked Lee, "Shortly after this, Undersheriff Caldwell arrived on the scene, did he not?"

"Yes, sir."

"Describe for the court what ensued."

"We drove to the plane. But the landing lights were off and the two men were gone. We could hear a car honking on the road. I figured it was the pickup that had passed the patrol car . . . that the two men went off in it."

Schuman, screaming objections, howled, "If the court please, the witness cannot *figure* anything."

"Objections sustained. Continue, Mr. Russell."

"What happened next, Mr. Banner?"

"Bob Caldwell searched the plane. He said it was loaded with marijuana. Next morning when he called me, he said the marijuana totaled out eight hundred pounds. He said he also found five pounds of uncut heroin."

"We have no further questions, your honor," Russell said, triumphant. "Mr. Banner is our last witness."

"The witness is excused."

Lee felt a giant lift of relief. Walking past the defense table, he came face to face with the man who called himself Green, and a coldness ran over him as he met the eyes, as hard and flat as a piece of marble. Downstairs in the sheriff's office, he rolled a brown-paper smoke and waited, cognizant that this was just the beginning.

Twenty minutes later Caldwell breezed in smiling. "The judge bound Green and Dolan over for district court trial, released 'em on fifteen-thousand-dollar bonds each. Naturally, they pleaded innocent."

"Fifteen thousand?" Lee echoed. "Seems mighty low for a haul this big."

"Drug cases are common these days."

"But not this big, you said."

"True. But we presented enough evidence to hold 'em for trial —that's the thing. He let the pickup pair go, which we expected."

"When's the trial?"

"Be on the fall docket, coming up soon. I'll keep you posted."

"I can hardly wait," Lee said, displaying a twisted grin.

He walked from the courthouse to his battered pickup, before him still, like frozen images, the combative courtroom figures: the district attorney wheeling on Schuman, and the latter's mouth-curling savagery, and Green and Dolan, if those were their names, their expressions of contempt never changing—contempt for the court and what it stood for—so damn sure they were going to get off till he had identified them. Well, he had said his piece and he would have to say it again, next time in front of a district court jury. He dreaded that and wished it were over.

The sagging pickup door hung. He slammed it harder; it closed. The motor caught on the third try and he drove north through busy traffic, then turned west and took the overpass across I-35, always relieved to put behind him the increasing congestion of what used to be a quiet university town.

At home he changed into workaday jeans, shirt, boots and hat. It was too early to feed and he liked to feed at the same time every day, which was one of the secrets of keeping horses healthy.

The sound of the Falcon drew him to the porch door. Serena was home early. She got out rather hurriedly, arms burdened as always, but paused when she saw him. He went out to her. The kiss, the usual kiss, that also hurried.

"How did it go?" she asked, trying to sound casual.

"Okay," he said, and filled her in on the results without particularizing. "I was on the stand just a little while."

"Was that all?" She seemed surprised.

"That's it."

"I just hope it is, Lee." Her honest eyes narrowed, straight upon him, full of concern. "What I mean is, was anything said to you?"

"You mean . . . by the other side?"

"Yes. I mean a threat."

"Why, no. Not one word."

"There's still the trial."

"It will be over then." He grinned a reassurance he did not feel. "Why don't you think about supper while I dab some paint on our horse sign before feedin' time?"

"I just wish you weren't involved."

"We won't be for long," he promised, and added a little pat on the behind of her neat pants suit.

He spent an hour on the sign and fed the horses, and when he came to the house, Serena was busy in the kitchen. He began washing up for supper. Just then the phone rang and he heard her call, "Honey, can you get that? I'm making a salad."

Drying his hands, he hurried to the low table by the old-fashioned hall tree, picked up the receiver and said, "Hello," expecting to hear some ol' boy calling about a horse.

The friendliest of voices answered, "Mr. Banner, sir?"

"Yes, this is Lee Banner."

"You're just the person I'm happy to talk to, Mr. Banner."

Another sales call, Lee guessed. Somebody out of the city selling awnings or siding or storm windows, or tickets to the Policemen's Ball. "I'm not interested in anything right now," he said mildly. Why be nasty over the phone when the other man was only trying to make a living the hard way?

"I'm not selling anything, sir. Just calling for a couple of friends."

"Friends?" Pleasant and professionally courteous, the voice was not one that Lee recalled hearing previously.

"Old friends, Mr. Banner, sir."

Lee was beginning to resent the runaround, the spurious *misters* and *sirs*. "What do you want?"

"I was waiting for you to say that, Mr. Banner."

"Cut out the mister stuff. What is it?"

"I respect you, otherwise I would not address you in that manner. I'm calling for friends who are in serious trouble on account of you."

"Now, just how is that?"

"I want to be perfectly frank about this. Straight from the shoulder, sir."

"Who the hell are you, anyway?"

"My name is of no concern, Mr. Banner. I want you to know that I've checked on you and that I am impressed. You're a hard-working man. Former rodeo star, now in horse raising and horse racing, both of which are chancy ventures, are they not?" Before Lee could break in: "As I said, I want to be frank and fair. It comes down to this. I could make it worth your while—very worth your while—if you could forget you saw those two men at the plane."

For a moment, Lee was too dumbfounded to speak. Then his anger erupted. "Buddy, you're barkin' up the wrong tree."

"I know what you're thinking, Mr. Banner. Instead, I wish you would think of what I have in mind for you as a gift. Could you, for example, use five thousand dollars? Hard cash? Unmarked money? Conveniently left in your mailbox?"

Lee slammed the receiver down and turned away to find Serena standing in the kitchen doorway.

"What was all that about?" she asked.

He dismissed it with a wave of his hand. At that instant the phone rang again. He snatched up the receiver and the same smooth voice said, "Just consider it, will you, Mr. Banner? Thank you, sir."

That was all. The phone hummed in his ear.

"Lee! What is it?"

"Some guy . . . wrong number. Keeps calling back." He took a step toward the living room, his breath coming short and tight.

"Lee," she persisted. "I want to know."

"I told you."

"You didn't. You're trying to protect me from something, and you're not very good at lying. It's about the trial, isn't it?"

He looked at her. They had been honest with each other, always, else they couldn't have come this far. She was more than his wife, she was his pardner and friend. He sighed and said, "It was a bribe offer so I wouldn't testify against Green and Dolan. Five thousand dollars."

"Oh, Lee." She touched a hand to her throat.

"Probably some crank who was at the hearing. What do you say we eat supper?"

Chapter 3

Two days passed without further word from the caller, and Lee welcomed the consuming routine of keeping fences in shape, hauling feed, cleaning stalls and paddocks, fumigating to control flies and working with Cindy. It was worming time, so Thursday he had the vet out to administer doses of vermifuge through a tube.

Once Serena said, "I think you ought to tell Bob Caldwell about that man's call."

"What could he do? No way to trace it."

"Just the same, he ought to know."

"We'll see."

"You still think it was a crank call?"

He hadn't at the time and he didn't now, but he nodded and said, "Else we'd heard again by now."

Friday noon he was fixing lunch when the phone rang. He answered it, expecting to hear Nancy saying whether she could come home for the weekend, and tensed when the overcourteous voice spoke:

"Hi, Mr. Banner. This is your friend with all the money."

"You're no friend of mine. Who are you?"

"Just say I'm an intermediary. Now that you've had time to

think over my offer, I am hoping you will listen to another very generous proposition."

"I'm not interested."

"Even if I raise the ante?"

Lee's first reaction was to disconnect, but he stayed on in hopes the man might yet make a slip. "I said I wasn't interested," Lee replied, maintaining a calm voice.

"Would ten thousand interest you, my friend?"

"Look. You're wasting your time. Don't call me back."

"Now, Mr. Banner. We're all reasonable people. All I'm asking is a favor for my friends. This could be the easiest money you ever made or ever will, and no questions asked. Like I said before, cold cash in your mailbox or wherever you want it—unmarked, in any denominations you want."

"Guess you're working for that shyster Schuman." Lee hung on.

Easy laughter pealed. "You're talking about S. S. 'Slick' Schuman, one of the Southwest's leading criminal attorneys, Mr. Banner. That would be a logical guess, certainly, sir. But no—I'm just your friendly intermediary, trying—"

"You're not mine," Lee cut in.

"Trying," the unabashed voice went on, "to reach a common ground of agreement for both sides."

"If you're open and above board, like you claim, why not come by here and talk about it?"

That touched off a humorless "Ho-ho." Behind it, Lee visualized a loose-mouthed, fleshy-faced man given to dramatics. One fact he did know now, it wasn't Schuman's ridiculing voice. "Mr. Banner," the man all but cooed, "you can be foxy. You've been around the track, as they might say in your business. However, as much as I'd like to visit with you in person, I can't do that. In place of that, listen to this. I have been instructed to go no higher than ten thousand. On my own I will go up to twelve—my final offer."

"Makes no difference. I'm not interested."

The voice hardened suddenly. "If you don't take it, it could be the biggest mistake you ever made."

"Whoa, now. Exactly what do you mean?"

"I mean I'd hate to see such a nice man as you make that mistake, Mr. Banner."

Lee let go. "You threatening me?"

"I'd rather not put it in those words. You see, Mr. Banner, you've cost my friends a bundle—a big bundle. Valuable merchandise lost. Probably a confiscated airplane worth seventy thousand. Plus bail money. Plus attorney's fees. Slick Schuman has no bargain rates. Plus the strong likelihood of prison terms. Bruno is very unhappy about all this, and Bruno never forgets anybody who's crossed him."

"Bruno? Who's Bruno?" That was a slip, Lee knew.

"Er . . . I respectfully decline to answer that. The question is —for the last time—will you accept the offer or not, Mr. Banner, sir?"

"Go to hell!" Lee hung up, thankful that Serena wasn't here. Boiling mad, he dialed the Cleveland County Sheriff's office and asked for Caldwell. The undersheriff was out. After a brief delay, Sheriff Avery took the call.

"What is it, Lee?"

Lee told him, in terse detail, to which Avery replied wearily, "It's an old game, threatening a witness. I'll pass the word to the DA."

"Tell him I've got a double-barreled shotgun and I intend to use it on Slick Schuman and that bunch if they come here on the prod."

"Take it easy, Lee. Probably all bluff. I wouldn't be too quick to blame Schuman. I'd say it's the defendants acting on their own. Meantime, I'll send a patrol car by your place now and then. Or I could put a deputy out there full time."

"A deputy would only upset my family. Been enough of that already. You know, I'm dumb, Claude. Why didn't I say I'd take the bribe, then have you fellows catch somebody putting the money in my mailbox?"

Avery's slow chuckle drifted over the phone. "Let's not get fancy. We're not on 'Kojak.' No, Lee, you handled it just right, and you can testify to the bribe offer in court. Russell says we've got the case won as it now stands. On top of that, we found out the plane was stolen in Arizona. Tucson authorities have a hold order on these birds when we finish with 'em. . . . Listen, the trial has been set. Heads the docket a week from Monday. We heard just before noon. Bob was to call you this afternoon."

"That's a relief. I want to get this over with, Claude."

"I know how you feel. Don't worry. And I'll assign a patrol car out your way."

"All right," Lee agreed reluctantly.

Afterward, he stood long in thought, conscious of the old house creaking in the early fall wind, feeling its comfort and strength and all that had happened here, the sad times, the hard times, the good times. The house was like a living, breathing presence, not only a reminder of the past, but of the promise of the future and of life going on. Now, he thought, everything here is threatened, maybe even my family.

A hot wind seemed to whirl up through Lee. Striding to the bedroom, he took the double-barreled 12-gauge shotgun from the closet and strode to the back porch. Rummaging, he found a box of shells in the relic Hoover cabinet. He had never kept a loaded gun around the house, not till this moment. He punched in the loads, set the safety, and leaned the shotgun behind the cabinet, braced between boxes so it couldn't fall, where he could reach it quickly coming out on the porch.

The sheriff's patrol car made a deliberate pass by the house that afternoon, and again shortly before dark, honking each time, and it was the honking that drew Serena from the bedroom to the doorway.

"Lee," she called, "that looks like a sheriff's patrol car. Come here."

He came to the doorway. "It is. I called the sheriff's office this morning, like you suggested. The car is Claude Avery's idea, not mine."

"Was there another call?"

"Oh, no," he lied, keeping his eyes on the moving car. "I still think that was some crank. So does Claude. Nothing to worry about."

Her voice curious, she asked, "Then why did he send a patrol car?"

"Just a precaution."

"Did he say if the trial's been set?"

"Week from Monday."

"And you didn't tell me!"

"Been busy. Slipped my mind. There's nothing to worry about."

"Nothing to worry about—yet the sheriff sends a patrol car, and I noticed the shotgun's not in the closet." She held those dark, straightforward eyes on him, searchingly, and he saw them change from questioning to apprehension.

He said, "The shotgun is on the back porch behind the cabinet, and it's loaded. I put it there today."

"Another precaution, I suppose?"

"That's all."

"Lee," she said, her smoky gaze widening, deepening, "this bothers me. These are violent people. I don't want to admit it, but I'm afraid. I feel it."

"An Indian afraid? A mighty Chickasaw?" He was trying to tease her out of it.

"I'm afraid for all of us. I really am, Lee."

He took her in his arms and held her close, frustration sharp in his throat. After a bit she stirred and said, "I feel better now."

Tuesday afternoon Lee saw a sea-green Mercedes sedan turn in and stop. Closing the corral gate, he waved and went out to the car.

A man got out smiling. A strapping-big man. A business type. Lee sized him up. Dark suit of expensive cut, blue shirt, dark blue tie. Conservative western hat. Clean-shaven. In his comfortable forties. Rather bold brown eyes. A heavy-boned face. He held out a big hand. "Guess I've come to the right place."

Lee grinned. "Let's hope so."

"Name is Moss. I'm from Tulsa. I'm looking for a top quarter horse to cross on some Thoroughbred mares."

"I'm Lee Banner. Like the sign says, I'm standing Land Rush. He's got running blood, top and bottom of his pedigree, and his speed index at three hundred and fifty yards is one eleven."

"I've heard of Land Rush. Reason I'm here."

"Glad to know that. By the way, there are some plenty top sires in your area. Gallant Jet stands at Wagoner. Sir Winsalot at Miami. And Bayou Bar holds court at Chelsea."

Moss nodded. "I see you keep up."

"I try to. Oklahoma has a world of good sires these days."

Moss was taking in the place, particularly the barn area. "You have a nice layout here, Mr. Banner."

"Thank you. We try to improve it as we go along. Now, these Thoroughbred mares of yours. I'd be interested to know their breeding."

"They're"—Moss hesitated—"they're . . . Wichita Oil mares."

"Wichita Oil? Some high-powered blood there. Believe he's by that French stud, Prince Taj, who goes back to Nearco on his dam's side. I'm not sure about Wichita Oil's dam, but I think it's Royal Butterfly by Royal Note."

"Don't ask me," Moss said, looking mystified. "I got these three mares in a deal not long ago when a friend sold out. As you've probably guessed, I'm new at the racehorse business."

"Looks like you've made a good start. Good foundation mares. Would you like to see my horse?"

"Indeed I would."

They strolled that way, Moss intent on the surroundings. Doc, at his post by the corral gate, rose and growled low at the visitor. Lee spoke sharply, silencing him, and explained with a grin, "This is his territory. Figures it's his job to protect everything beyond this gate, especially Land Rush."

Grumbling, Doc followed them while Lee showed Moss the well-kept ten-stall barn and attached paddocks, and last, with pride, the bay stallion.

"He's as gentle as an ol' kid horse," Lee said, going up to Land Rush in the paddock, snapping a lead strap on his halter, "and he passes that on to his offspring. Generally, they're well-mannered in the gates and they like to run."

"Calm temperament. I like that. All right if I lead him around? I mean, do you think he'll let me?"

"Go right ahead. He'll step along with you. No trouble."

Without hesitation, Moss took the rope and led Land Rush around and back, around and back. Nodding, he said, "He could be just the sire I need. I like his conformation."

Moss might be new at the horse business, but he wasn't afraid of a stud, like most people. He seemed right at home. "This horse," Lee pointed out, "is heavy-boned, square and wide through the chest. He's got a short back with a long underline and a long, well-rounded hip. The fastest horses have these long hips, that long muscle. Too, you want powerful forearms, short cannons, and good muscle in the stifle and gaskin areas, like this horse. It's the individual that counts in breeding."

Lee stopped talking to release Land Rush. Usually, a visitor would want to know all about Land Rush's track record and breeding before he agreed to bring his mares to court and for keeping. Moss was gazing about again, apparently more interested in the layout of the little horse ranch than in asking questions, so Lee recited the facts, ending with the career-terminating spill at Columbus.

"We don't scrimp on feed, Mr. Moss. We feed the top grain mixture and the best quality alfalfa and prairie hay we can buy. We clean the pens daily and fumigate every other day for flies. One mare to a paddock. After feeding in the morning, the mare is turned out on oat pasture. Green pasture is good for breeding. We plant oats around the first of December. That way we have green pasture when we need it in January, February and later. We're on a natural slope here, which helps drainage and cuts down the mud problem. Our vet is Dr. Vaughn Drake. He's tops."

Lee ceased speaking. Heck fire, wasn't the guy interested in the type of care his mares would receive?

Suddenly, Moss quit his looking. "I see. I'm impressed, Mr.

Banner. Yes, sir, you have a nice layout here. Well kept. Modern. When should I truck my mares over? Next few weeks?"

That was sudden, Lee thought. He said, "It's early yet. The breeding season starts around the middle of February. Personally, I like my foals to drop in late February or early March. You don't want a real late foal. The earlier youngsters have a big advantage in growth and maturity over the late ones."

"I'll let you know," Moss said, taking his eyes off the premises again, and stuck out his hand.

"Better call me early in December," Lee said. "If I start booking up, I'd better call you, if you want to leave your number?"

"Won't be necessary. I'm in and out a lot. I'll be in touch early."

Lee felt a dropping off in the agreement at the last moment, and decided he'd probably never hear from the guy. That happened often. No follow-up. Not even a business card.

They left the paddock.

At the corral gate Doc growled when Moss passed through. The Tulsa man turned, not without irritation. "Don't believe your dog likes me."

"He's the same with all strangers. Get back, Doc."

Nothing more was said on the way to the Mercedes. Moss got in, started the engine, waved a "see you," and drove off in the direction of Oklahoma City.

Lee watched him go, a little puzzled, recalling how suddenly the man had agreed to bring the mares over, and then how he had seemed to back off. And he hadn't even asked about the mare charge, which was a modest four dollars a day. Well, some people had more money than horse sense.

Chapter 4

Saturday was cloudy and humid, presaging a change, and a rainstorm struck around midnight, howling and gusting until the old house groaned. Lee's first thought was of his horses. But after he had listened awhile, the wind tired and the whimsical rain settled to an off-and-on drumming. He lay back relaxed, thinking what the moisture meant after the late summer dry spell. Just before he fell asleep, he thought he heard Doc bark a couple of times. That, no more. Probably at a hurrying varmint, for the rain had let up again. In rough weather Doc slept at the barn. When Lee woke later, all he heard was the dripping off the house.

Up early, because he always fed early, he came outside to a perfect morning: clear, bright, cool, grass smell like incense on the river valley breeze.

He first sensed that something might be wrong when he didn't see Doc at the gate, impatiently waiting, overjoyed to join Lee on his rounds at the barn.

Puzzled, Lee looked hopefully to his left along the line of the corral fence, then toward the barn. Doc wasn't in sight. Looking right, down the fence line where it made a right-angle turn, he saw a motionless black-and-white shape. No! No! He ran over there.

It was Doc, of course, down in the fence corner. Lee crouched and touched him. Doc was rigid, stone-cold. There were no visible marks, just mud. Lee stood and looked down, grief and the protest of disbelief clashing within him. Seeing the white muzzle tore at him. Doc was getting old, sure, but . . .

Lee turned slowly away and on to the gate and inside. The broodmares and their foals were waiting at the pasture gate. At this hour Landy would be trumpeting for his breakfast. This morning he was not. *Was not.*

That meaning reached Lee gradually, belatedly, and then swiftly became the strangest of alarms. He sprinted through the mud to the barn. By now Landy would be making a racket in his stall. Lee looked. Landy wasn't there. A sickness tightening his chest, Lee ran to the paddock gate and looked.

Landy was down and he lay so very still.

Lee knew before he tore at the gate and rushed there that his horse was dead, and he was. It was almost more than a man could stand, more than he could believe, but his unwillingness to accept what his reason told him was true suddenly left him. All he could do was gaze down, while the river breeze played with the black mane, rustling it as if life yet remained.

Feeling overtook Lee, washed over him. His face quivered. Great tears began sliding down his face. He was choking, scarcely able to breathe. You grew up on a farm and expected stock to die sometime, for that was the cycle of life. But not this, not now. When a good horse was still in his prime as a sire, had years left to pass on his speed and heart, his class and disposition.

Step by step, he circled his horse and could tell nothing. As on Doc, no marks. Lee used to take Doc along when Land Rush was running, and the dog would sleep at the stall door, on guard. Take Doc away and the horse would pace up and down, become a nervous stall-walker. When Doc returned, he quieted down. Old friends.

Thinking of Serena now, Lee started to the house. At the paddock gate an oddness arrested him. The gate was ajar when he ran in, wasn't it? It was. He remembered. He hadn't slid the bar to open it. No. Hell, no. He hadn't left a gate open since he was nine years old, when his father cured him of that carelessness with a deserved licking. Rage began to rise in him, every muscle tightening as his mind cut back to last night: *Doc had barked at something.*

He moved fast. Grimly scanning the ground around the gate, he found the muddy shoe tracks, partly washed away, but tracks beyond all question, tracks that led him past the paddock and on to the pasture fence south of the barn. They had gone out that way. Turning back, he followed the incoming tracks to the corral gate—Doc's post.

Dry-eyed, grim, he reconstructed what had happened. Aided by the cover of the storm, they had slipped in this way, down the lane, past the house. Doc, hearing them, had left the shelter of the barn to guard the gate. That was when Lee heard him bark. After getting rid of the dog, they had gone to the paddock. The picture was complete except for how they had done everything. Lee bowed his head, feeling the lash of guilt. Why hadn't he got up when he heard Doc bark?

The full impact of his loss struck him like physical pain. His great fury seethed, building by the moment, but now he had to take charge of himself and tell Serena. Sick at heart, he found his way to the house.

Serena was fixing breakfast. She always fixed a big breakfast on Sunday. The television was going. A resonant voice was giving a brief news summary. Lee stood still, fumbling for the evasive words that refused to come. The newsman signed off and a smiling gospel group came on, singing "When We All Go to Heaven."

His very silence must have caused her to turn and ask, "What is it?"

He got a grip on himself. There was no easy way. You just said it. "I don't know how to say this," he began, his voice cracking. "Something's happened. Doc and Landy—they're both dead."

Her eyes flew wide. She was dumbfounded for the longest of

moments, unable to move, unable to believe. And then all at once her face crumbled and she fell sobbing against him.

As soon as he could, Lee made the necessary official calls.

Dr. Vaughn Drake, the veterinarian, and Bob Caldwell arrived almost together. They shook Lee's hand. For a bit, nobody said anything.

"I want an autopsy on both my dog and my horse," Lee said, and told them about discovering the shoe tracks.

"Whatever you say," nodded Drake, a slim, pale, systematic man, several years younger than Lee.

"Has anybody been snooping around?" the undersheriff asked.

"Nobody I've seen. Had one visitor this week. Man from Tulsa. That was on Tuesday. Said he had some Thoroughbred mares he wanted crossed on a quarter horse stud. He sure looked the place over, but that's not unusual. They always do."

"Could be your man. Came here to case the layout. Did he give his name?"

"Just Moss. No first name. He was driving a green Mercedes. I didn't think to take down his car license. No reason to."

Caldwell regarded Lee with further sympathy. "Hope you had some insurance."

"I didn't. Couldn't afford the premiums, I thought. Never figured anything like this would happen to a healthy horse. If I had, it wouldn't make it up."

He led them to the dog, and after an interval there, to the corral gate, where he pointed out the incoming tracks, and then on to the paddock. While Drake busied himself, Lee showed Caldwell the outgoing tracks and said, "Let's see where they lead to."

"I'd say three sets of footprints," Caldwell said as they scouted across the spongy pasture. "See, here's where they spread out. It's three, all right. One man was heavier than the others. See how deep his tracks are? You know, Lee, I'll bet one of these bastards was a jackleg vet."

Lee nodded, his mind swinging back to the so-called Tulsa man, who had said he was new at running horses, and yet how at ease he was handling Landy. What if he was? Maybe the man had saddlers. And what could you prove now?

The tracks pointed toward the road, angling away from the house. At the barbed wire fence the undersheriff halted, eyeing the grassy slopes of the bar ditch. He pointed. "A car pulled off on the shoulder there. Look at those deep ruts. Damn near got stuck. Looks like they had to push out."

"There's something shiny in the bottom of the ditch, Bob. Let's see what it is."

They eased through and Lee's anger flew wildly at the litter of bottles and the syringe in the grass. He shot a knowing look at Caldwell, who whipped out a handkerchief and gingerly began retrieving. "Doubt we'll get any clear prints off these, but Vaughn will sure know what it all means."

They hastened back across the pasture, already drying out fast in the wind and sun. From here the old place was framed in tranquil focus, like a print across Lee's eyes: the modest little house, the neat barn and paddocks, the network of fences, the mares and foals, feisty Cindy romping in her private pasture— horses as yet unfed, he was reminded. The river off there as bright as a new ribbon after last night's needed rain. Everything seemed so much smaller today. And how still it was! Lee's earlier emotions, a numbing mixture of shock and grief, wrath and bewilderment, had drawn down to a heart full of dull pain and cold, cold rage.

Drake took one look at their findings, spread out on the ground, and declared, "Hell, they doped him to death. I'll verify everything at the clinic. But that's what it looks like, Lee. I'm finished here. Now, I need to see further about your dog." He shook his head. "My, how I hate all this." He trudged off through the mud.

Standing beside Caldwell, Lee said, "I guess you know what I'm thinking."

"I know and I can't tell you how bad I feel, Lee. I got you into this. I can't forget that."

"Sometimes a man has to stand up. I don't blame you."

"Problem now is proving anything."

"It will all come full circle someday. I believe that."

Caldwell's understanding eyes rested on Lee. "I hope so."

"And you can bet I'll be on hand for the trial."

Presently, Drake and Caldwell left, promising to call back later in the day.

Lee fed his horses, glad to be alone, glad to have chores to do, and afterward turned in finality to the paddock. Now this moment between a man and his horse: "Pardner," Lee Banner said, "I hope where you are the grass is always green, the water is always sweet, the straightaways are always smooth." Bending down, he gently clipped the black forelock and slipped off the halter and took them to the tack room to keep alongside Land Rush's racing bridle and his racing plates, worn the day he set the 350-yard record at Blue Ribbon Downs.

That done, Lee went to the house to be with Serena.

Early that afternoon the yard started filling with neighbors' pickups and cars. No one knew quite what to say. Land Rush's murder was like a death in the family, besides a death in the family of running horses.

Lee felt better seeing his friends. There was Cal Tyler, a spare man of fifty, wearing a curled-brim hat that seldom came off, a long-sleeved shirt open at the neck, Levi's, Texas-made boots, and a silver-buckled belt across his board-flat middle. The skin of his angular face was leather-brown and tight, and his blue eyes moved amicably from man to man.

Smoky Osgood was there with Cal. His paunch, more noticeable because of his short stature and bowed legs, pushed against a bronze belt buckle that depicted "The End of the Trail." His somewhat prankish face, as genial as a traveling horse trader's on the lookout for a swap with "boot" or a match race, was unusually solemn today.

"Is there anything we can do?" Cal asked Lee.

"Thanks. Not a thing right now, but later you and Smoky might help me with Landy. I'm waiting on Doc Drake's official autopsy report." He took a long breath and sighed. "All I can seem to think of is that this is the end of our breeding program."

"You've still got some mighty good horses," Smoky encouraged. "Cindy's coming along, and I sure like the looks of that little colt of Dixie's. He's a comer, mark my words."

Lee tried to smile. "Trouble is, there's nothing quite like the original. There's coffee in the house. Why don't you boys go in? Serena will be glad to see you."

Another pickup entered the yard and Doug Adams got out, head hanging. Riding since his early teens, he still resembled a choir boy with his smooth face and believing eyes and shock of straw-colored hair, worn full and over his ears, like the university students whose cars he serviced and worked on at the West Lindsey Street filling station. He had been aboard Land Rush in all his races, including the Columbus spill, when he suffered a concussion and a broken collarbone. Hurt and angry, he held out a horseman's hand. "Bob Caldwell called me." His voice sounded hollow, hurt.

"I didn't have the heart to tell you," Lee apologized. "Not yet."

Doug's feelings blazed. "I just wish I could do something about this. He was a real honest horse. Always gave his best. Had all kind of guts."

"We'll know more later today, Doug, when I hear from Doc Drake. Go in and have some coffee. It'll help Serena."

Later, they all sat around and visited and drank coffee and inevitably the flow of talk shifted to Land Rush. "He might have been another Go Man Go but for that crazy accident at Columbus, the kind that often seems to happen to the extra good ones," Cal said, looking up at the framed photos over the fireplace mantel: Land Rush as a leggy foal with Oklahoma Lady, Land Rush as a yearling, Land Rush crossing the finish line when he set the 350-yard record, and the proud winner's circle of Lee, holding the new champion's bridle, and a beaming Serena beside Lee, and Nancy, a sun-grinning youngster in shorts, blouse and rakish billed cap. "He had speed and heart and he was always a sound horse—good bone. Don't recollect that he ever shinbucked once. One reason, Lee's a good leg man and he brought Landy along in a very slow manner. No yearling futurities, you can bet that." Cal rolled a smoke. "I'll never forget Landy's first out. Lee had him down at Ardmore in a little match race. He was the calmest horse I ever saw . . . seemed half asleep, almost bored. But when the gates flew open, he exploded like a bat out of Carlsbad. I thought Doug would lose his seat, but he hung on. And the few times that horse didn't get off just right, his overpowering finish made up for it. Farther he went, harder he ran."

"He was always easy to handle," Smoky added. "A kid could've led him around with a piece of twine. He always seemed to anticipate what you wanted him to do."

"Guess his disposition made it easier for those people to do what they did," Lee said. "But I wouldn't of had him any other way. You want a sire to pass that on. . . . Cal, do you and Smoky remember the first time I put a stock saddle on him? He not only threw me, he threw me plumb over the fence."

Everybody got a chuckle out of that.

They were gathered outside as the day wore on, while Lee waited for the phone calls, when a blue-and-white sports car dashed up. In it was Nancy, driven out by a young man. Clad in sweater, jeans and sneakers, she ran over to Lee. "Oh, Daddy! I've been out. Mom just got me at the dorm. Rick brought me."

Nancy looked like her slim mother, which proved, Lee had joked more than once, that the distaff side of the family was the dominant force in any union, not the sire. Her hair, worn straight and long, was also the color of her mother's, light brown, and her eyes were dark and her eyebrows and long lashes were black. Her nose was perhaps a wee bit short; no matter, she was a pretty girl and well formed. She was beginning to cry.

He put his arm around his daughter. What could you tell the young ones, whose hurt always seemed the deepest? He couldn't find the needed words. Some people always knew what to say.

"Daddy, who would do these terrible things? And why?"

He shook his head. "Sis, why don't you go in and help your mother? Take Rick." He moved past her to the car. "Thanks for bringing Nancy out, Rick. Come in." As the young people entered the house, Lee thought, Guess she needs that car after all.

Caldwell called. "We couldn't lift a print off any of that clutter. Wiped clean, besides rained on. Those guys were pros, Lee. Left us nothing to go on."

"You're talking about hard evidence. The motivation is plain as a mule's kick. Threats—now murder. I don't intend to stand still about this."

"Ben Russell will bring it all out when you're on the stand," Caldwell said, a note of caution in his voice. "It will strengthen our case plenty. We've got more than enough now for a conviction. I realize that can't make up for what you've lost, but it will be some satisfaction." When Lee didn't answer, Caldwell said, "See you Monday."

"You can bet I'll be there."

Lee hung up, his depression mounting, like a bad dream from which there was no waking. Before he could turn away, the phone rang again. He snatched at the receiver, his pulse jumping, hoping, half expecting to hear, *Mr. Banner, sir.* Instead, Doc Drake's efficient-sounding voice spoke:

"I've got it all pinned down, Lee. They fed him barbiturates through the jugular vein. A gosh-awful amount. I can't say precisely how long the dosing took, but I estimate they did it gradually over a period of an hour or more, maybe two hours. Not too difficult to do with a gentle horse and for somebody used to handling horses and who knew how to locate the vein."

"I see."

"About your dog," Drake continued, yet hesitant. "They tossed him a bait of ground meat and strychnine. He didn't suffer very long. Strychnine works so fast hardly anything can be done in time. In these cases the dog becomes rigid, undergoes convulsions, has great difficulty standing and breathing. It's over fast."

"I see."

"I'm terribly sorry, Lee. Wish I could help some way."

"You've found out what I wanted to know, Doc. I'm obliged to you."

A reporter came to the house. Lee held back nothing, including the autopsy reports, and dug out a photo of Land Rush as a racing two-year-old.

"Mr. Banner," the young man said, "I covered the preliminary hearing the day you testified against Green and Dolan. Do you see any connection between that and what's happened here?"

"That's pretty obvious, though I can't prove it. I was also offered a bribe over the phone not to testify, but I can't prove that either or who offered it."

"Whew! A bribe." Some fast note-taking, then: "How much?"

"Twelve thousand was the last offer. That was a week ago last Friday."

"Was your stallion insured?"

"He was not. Not a dime. So it can't be said that it was done for insurance."

"How much would you estimate his value?"

"Hard to say. He was our whole breeding program, and beginning to be recognized as a speed quarter horse sire. Of his twelve starters this year, his third crop of foals, ten were Register of Merit winners. I turned down thirty thousand dollars for him last June. He wasn't for sale at any price. I wish you would say that he was unbeaten till he got hurt as a two-year-old, and that he still holds the record at Blue Ribbon Downs for three hundred and fifty yards. Ran it in 17.45. I'd appreciate that."

"I will," the young man said, impressed. "I didn't know he held a track record."

"Not many people do," Lee said, releasing a particular bitterness. "Oklahoma newspapers don't pay much attention to quarter horses till one jumps up and wins the All-American, the richest horse race in the world. But that's the fault of horsemen as well. We ought to holler louder. Let people know what we have right here in our state. I believe they'd be proud if they knew."

After a look around, the young man went away, promising, "I'll call the AP on this, too."

The afternoon was spent when Cal and Smoky drove off, the last to leave. By this time all essential details had been carried out. The stall-walker and his friend rested in the main pasture, side by side.

Lee stood awhile in the stillness of the yard, a tautness upon him. A fire burned inside him, deep, deep, and he doubted whether it would ever go out. He paced to the empty barn and back, still resisting, still refusing to accept what had happened.

Serena came out of the house, a look of inquiry on her drawn face. "We wondered where you were." Her eyes searched his face. "Are you all right?"

He bunched his lips, nodding.

"I've asked Rick to stay for dinner. He offered to take Nancy back this evening. She has an eight o'clock in the morning."

"Good." He glanced at the muddy tip of one boot. "You know, I've been thinking. You're right. Nancy does need a car."

"It can wait."

"I'll look around next time I'm in town."

She took his hand and they strolled out to the road. In the stillness, distant sounds were magnified: the roar of a truck on the interstate to the east. Cattle bawling across the river.

The sign loomed before them. They regarded it at length, like weary travelers come to a crossroads. "I want to keep that up for a while yet," he said.

"I think you ought to for as long as you like."

He turned suddenly, catching her grave sweetness, struck by the guilty insight that he had been mostly concerned with his own feelings today, not fully realizing hers. He threw an arm around her and they held each other in silence.

Long after Nancy and her boyfriend had gone, Lee lay awake thinking, while Serena slept within the circle of his arm. Always close, they had been drawn closer today. Throughout the day he had held himself in around his family and neighbors. Now he could be honest with himself. Caldwell's words kept spinning through his thoughts: *Left us nothing to go on.* Which meant the law could do nothing. But Lee Banner could. In the storm of his mind he found added respect for his Grandfather Banner, who had defended what was rightfully his when someone tried to take it. Lee couldn't sleep. He merely dozed and drifted, always returning to what had happened. Now and then warm tears rose to his eyes. The law could do nothing. But Lee Banner could. Tomorrow was Monday—trial day. He longed for it to come.

Lee arrived before nine o'clock. Among the knots of people stringing into the courthouse he searched for Schuman and Green and Dolan, and did not spot them. If he had Schuman figured right, the defense attorney would challenge a heap of jurors today before a jury was seated and the trial got under way. Lee went in and took the stairs to the sheriff's office, in his ears the hum and shuffle of the crowded hallway on the courtroom floor above.

Caldwell was hurrying from an inner office when Lee came in. "Just tried to call you," the undersheriff said. His crew-cut hair seemed to stand up like quills above his tense face. His voice had a dragging quality. "It's all over for a while," he said, his eyes avoiding Lee's.

"What do you mean?"

"Green and Dolan have skipped out—jumped bond. Schuman called Ben Russell from the city a few minutes ago."

Lee stiffened, raw anger raking through him. "That figures—after what happened." He chopped his fisted hand downward. "Boy, did they get off easy. Forfeit a little measly bond money, then fade out."

"We've got out an all-points bulletin. The bonding company will be on the lookout, too."

Lee's mouth thinned to bitterness. "You don't think they pulled out just this morning, do you, Bob? Why, they're long gone by now. Been gone!"

"All we know is that Schuman said they'd checked out of their motel when he called this morning. He was going to drive them down." Caldwell's face was becoming more flushed and apologetic.

Lee wheeled for the doorway.

"Hey! Where you headed?"

"To the city—to see Schuman. He knows damn well where they are."

"Now, don't go charging off, Lee. Not that I blame you. You're not packing a gun, are you?"

"I don't need a gun. I've got my hands."

He did not simmer down until he was at the outskirts of

Moore, five miles north of town on the interstate, when it occurred to him that he didn't know where Schuman's office was. Pulling off, he drove into a filling station to check the Oklahoma City directory. There was only one Schuman listed under attorneys, out on Classen Boulevard.

Twenty minutes later Lee swung into a parking lot that flanked a modernistic office building. The directory in the lobby pointed him to the second floor. He opened the office door to meet the upraised stare of a plump, fortyish woman, hair an overdyed red, whose eyes, weary and worldly, belied the round face you expected to be pleasant and was not.

Two young white men waited on a chrome-and-leather divan. They stared curiously at Lee through pink-tinged sunglasses. Their reddish-hued eyes, beneath long strands of hair, seemed to be appraising him from behind foliage. On the wall above them hung a large picture of the Statue of Liberty. Otherwise, the room was severely plain except for the green carpet, which felt as thick as a stand of spring bermuda under Lee's boots.

Lee asked, "Schuman ·in?"

"He's on the phone right now. These two gentlemen are next. Mr. Schuman doesn't see anyone without an appointment."

"He'll see me," Lee said, and broke past her desk for the frost-paned door beyond.

She rose like an ascending blimp. "You can't go in there!"

Lee's hand was on the doorknob. He flung the door open and charged in, swinging the door closed behind him.

Like the woman said, Schuman was indeed on the phone, talking animatedly, with gestures, from the depths of a maroon-colored leather chair. He slapped down the receiver and blurted, "Who're you?" followed by a flash of recognition.

"Where are they?" Lee shot back, glaring down at him.

"Get out of here."

"I said *where are they?*"

"Get out or I'll call the police."

Lee reached across the desk and grabbed him by the front of his shirt and jerked him to his feet. "Answer me."

"I don't know." Sweat began to bead on the long face.

"Answer me." Lee shook him the way Doc used to shake barn rats, until Schuman's eyes joggled. He mumbled, "Th' motel said they checked out early Sunday."

"Sunday? Only you didn't let the DA know till this morning. Where'd they go? New Mexico? Old Mexico? Arizona?" Lee shook him again.

"I swear I don't know. I don't."

Lee, his eyes boring into Schuman's, felt the edge of his fury dulling, for he saw fear and no covering guile. Schuman was telling the truth. He didn't know. His eyes said so. Lee sensed that much was true. He slammed the man down into his chair. "Here's a little message to pass on to your friends. They killed my dog and they killed my horse—that's murder. You tell 'em Lee Banner is looking for 'em—and will keep on looking."

He longed to smash the man. Somehow he didn't in the end. He walked out.

Chapter 5

By this time November had come, bringing crisp nights and the hint of early winter, but the days continued sunlit and warm; and the horses were livelier than ever, the old broodmares tearing off across the pasture, manes streaming, their stork-legged youngsters beside them, eager to run, eager to romp and play. Cindy, in her private domain, the liveliest of all, her blood-bay coat flashing. Often the horses sunned themselves on the sandy loam, not unlike winged creatures resting between soaring flights.

Lee Banner would watch for long moments, and then turn once more to his dull chores, occupying himself with tasks that could have waited, aware that he had begun to doubt himself. For the first time in his life he had lost his hold. He seemed without direction or purpose. He had, he realized, slipped into a kind of miserable inertia, a resistance to irrevocable change that bordered on depression. He hadn't called Cal or Smoky, and when they invited him to go look at a horse or to a sale, he had begged off, giving work as the excuse. Understanding, they nodded and told him to come over when he could.

Serena, he suspected, had asked them to come by.

One evening she asked him point-blank, "Lee, when are you going to put Cindy in training?"

He looked away, evading an answer.

"You used to say she's bred to run, that she deserves her chance."

"I know."

"Well . . . ?" Her smile encouraged him.

He had no reply.

"As a start, you could have her knees x-rayed . . . to see if they're closed."

"Yes, that would need to be done."

She sat down beside him and brushed at his cowlick. "*Would?* Lee, honey, when are you going to come out of this?"

"Out of what?"

"This way you are—this mood you're in. You won't even let your friends help you. You won't let me."

He said, "A man has to carry his own load."

She dropped both hands to her lap. "I've seen you ride mean bulls when you should have been in the hospital. I've seen you smile away hard times and cold winters, and shrug and say, 'Just remember, Serena, that spring will come every year.' Remember?"

He nodded.

"I've seen you take hard licks and get discouraged, but I've never seen you quit like this."

"Quit?" He jerked a half-angry look at her.

"Yes, quit. You've given up. You won't face up that Landy's gone. You've locked yourself in. You won't try to cope."

"Cope, hell. That's exactly what I have done. I've been doing a lot of thinking, Serena, and I've made up my mind. I'm not going to campaign Cindy. If we put her on the track, something will happen to her like what happened to Landy at Columbus."

"Every horseman has bad luck at times. We're not the only ones. Look at Cal and that fine Bug colt he lost from colic."

"Only we don't have to keep on taking it. You were right back there when you said get out. So I've made up my mind. We're selling out. All the horses. Lock, stock and barrel."

"Lee!" Shock sprang her eyes wide. "You can't mean that."

"Afraid I do, Serena. I don't want to take this anymore. I'll get a steady job somewhere."

She inched away from him, hands pressing against her knees, her face alien to him, an expression he had never seen before. She got up and left the room. He wanted to call her back, but was silent, knowing he could not. Why had he said that? It had leaped out of him unthinking, needing just the right moment to touch it off, words he wished he could recall the instant he spoke.

There was no making up of lovers that night and they no more than spoke at breakfast. Difficult days followed.

On this morning a continued hoof rumble caused Lee to check his rounds at the barn and look. Cindy was dashing back and forth, long, sweeping runs, from one end of the pasture to the other. Watching, he waited for her to break off. But she persisted, capricious, full of herself. Drawn to her pasture gate, he had the guilty reminder of not having hand-fed her for some days. This cool, bright morning she was like a child inviting him to play, showing off, cavorting out of sheer enjoyment and energy.

He opened the gate and walked slowly toward her, observing her with mounting interest. She was filling out, growing fast. She romped past him, her flying mane a banner, and bore off into a dust-raising turn, her two white-socked feet flashing. As she came about, slowing, he suddenly found himself joining the game. He clapped his hands sharply and she broke again, coming faster, on the gallop, and frolicked past him, arching her pretty neck, kicking up her heels. When she wheeled near the fence and hesitated, he clapped again and made as if to run with her. Again she broke, and he heard himself shouting, "Come on! Run, Cindy, run!" and as she rushed by, he heard unusual laughter, high and loose and joyous, and was startled, because the laughter was his own. His first since that bad day. Inside him

rose an unexpected sense of release, of rediscovery, even re-
prieve.

When she turned again, and checked, about to halt, he whistled. She flicked her fox ears, watching him. He whistled again.
This time she came to him.

"You tryin' to tell me something, Miss Feisty Britches?" he
said, digging into his jacket pocket for a handful of feed.

Her knees were closed enough to stand training. On that go-
ahead, Lee started working her every other day on the flat below
the barn, trotting her half a mile, then galloping her half a mile
farther, always quitting when she was fresh. Gradually, as she
legged up, he worked with her every day. If she showed resent-
ment, which was unusual, he gave her the day off. That way the
workouts would continue to be fun. Instead of starting her with
a western saddle as he had the rambunctious Land Rush, he
used an exercise saddle, figuring the less you had between you
and her, the more you knew what she might do.

Next, he hitched the horse trailer to the pickup and vanned
her to the short track on Cal Tyler's place and schooled her in
the gates. Head straight. Feet solid. Sometimes walking her
through. Sometimes making her stand. Sometimes starting her
against other horses to provide her with the feel of competition.
At this point a further lesson: teaching her to run flat out from
the break, because a quarter horse runs short, whereas a Thoroughbred, going the longer routes, can't expend all its speed
early in a race if there is to be enough left at the finish.

Cindy took a cold in February and missed a week's training.
Early in March, when she was well legged up, Lee hauled her to
Wildhorse Downs, in the oil fields near the little town of Lind-
say. She was running against Smoky Osgood's three-year-old
Badger Bee stud, Buzz Boy, and Cal's eight-year-old gelding,
Whipstock, who could still bend the breeze. It was Saturday and
a small crowd had turned out.

"You boys like to make up a little pot?" Smoky ventured, that
look in his eyes.

"Listen to the gambling man," Lee said, smiling. "Suits me. How much?"

"How about ten bucks apiece?" Cal suggested, and winked at Lee. "However, we'd better take into consideration that Buzz Boy skunked the field in his last out at Stroud."

"Shall we draw for post positions?" Smoky asked. "Don't make any difference to me."

"Me neither," Cal said. "Why don't we put Cindy in the middle? She'll be away from the rail and she needs the experience of having horses on both sides of her. Too, Buzz Boy and Whipstock both break pretty straight."

Agreed.

Lee, riding a borrowed pony horse, led Cindy out on the track, Doug Adams in the saddle, Lee keeping between her and the rail.

Strange sounds rode the wind, the labored pulse of oil wells pumping, and the air smelled of sulphur. Cindy danced nervously. Her eyes rolled. She was sweating heavily. Lee held her head high. He took her past the watchers at a walk. Freeing the lead shank, he told Doug, "Trot her to the end of the straightaway. Gallop her back if you like. She's tighter than a fiddle string."

While Doug warmed her up, Lee noticed that she kept turning her head, as if trying to locate the source of the guttural oil field voices.

"She's scared and trembling," Doug reported, bringing her back. "It's those pumpers."

"She has to learn," Lee said.

She stood quietly enough as the horses loaded for the start and the handlers steadied them in the gates. Too quietly, Lee thought. Buzz Boy was full of stud eagerness, while the veteran Whipstock looked indifferent.

When the gates clanged open, the stud and the gelding broke together. Cindy stood frozen till Doug tapped her. She was already out of it when she took off, but she appeared to run with heart. Doug didn't tap her again. He wisely let her run her race, find herself.

Suddenly the sprint was over, Buzz Boy by a length over Whipstock, Cindy three behind the gelding.

Lee was waiting when Doug brought her back and dismounted. "She was too scared to break," Doug said, shaking his head. "But once she got going, she took hold of the track real good. Was making up ground at the end. It was those damn pumpers."

"She'll have to get used to a lot more noise than that," Lee said, hiding his disappointment. "She's just awful green. Glad you let her go on her own, Doug. Good ride."

Lee unsaddled her and led her around. After she was cooled down and watered out, he ran his hands over her front legs. They felt cool and firm. No fever or puffiness. Good! The front legs bear almost two thirds of a horse's weight and straight bones can stand more strain than crooked ones. Cindy's legs were straight. Starting just below her knees, he rubbed with the hair, down the cannon bones to below the ankles. After that, he put her in the trailer and sought his friends and paid Smoky his bet.

"She failed to fire," Lee said.

"Well, she was sure enough firing at the finish," Smoky said. "She closed fast and she ran straight."

"More gate work will take care of that," Cal said. "Give her some time and let her run some more. She was like a little kid on her first day at school. Everything was new and strange. She learned a lesson."

Riding home with Doug in the pickup, Lee commented, "We still don't know if she can run."

"I believe she can if she will. I felt like I had plenty of horse under me."

"I like for a horse to run low to the ground. She seemed too high to me."

"Wouldn't trade her off, would you?"

"Not yet," Lee said, laughing.

At six o'clock on Saturday, Lee walked Cindy for twenty minutes, then fed her a breakfast of oats—no alfalfa hay on race day and not much water. Alfalfa made a horse sweat and water could bloat. When Doug arrived, they took off on the seventy-mile trip to Midway Downs at Stroud.

Cal was waiting along the shed row when they drove up.

"You must of got up with the chickens," Lee said, pleased to see him.

"When a man wakes up at five every morning, he might as well go somewhere. I want to see Miss Cindy break her maiden today."

"We're in the third go," Lee said. "Number five hole. Three hundred and thirty yards. Ten horses. Wished it was earlier. By post time she'll be as nervous as a country girl at her first pie supper."

He went to the racing office, got a stall assignment, sprayed the stall with disinfectant, and led his horse in.

He stopped her when she nosed the straw on the floor, and when she sniffed the empty water bucket brought from home, he said, "You can have a sip or two at noon—that's all." Aside to Cal, "Never fails. Take a kid to a strange place and the first thing they want is something to eat and a big drink of water."

A man came over. "Need a pony rider?"

"Sure do," Lee said, and introduced himself, Cal and Doug. "We're in the third race."

"I'll be here. Glad to meet you fellas."

The three of them took seats outside the stall on bales of hay. Cindy hung her head over the door, curiously watching the arrival of more horse trailers, and horses being unloaded. Whenever the filly showed nervousness, Lee or Doug would get up and talk to her or rub on her. "She just does that so she'll get some pettin'," Doug said. "She loves company. She's a people's horse."

After a while, Doug trailed off to the jockeys' room. When he returned, Lee and Cal walked across to the track. There was the constant stir of spectators filing into the grandstand. The day, which had dawned bright and cool, was turning humid.

"Be over a thousand people here by post time," Cal predicted. "It's like a family outing. Children enjoy it, too. Some of these

folks bet, sure, but most come to watch the horses run or they
know somebody who's got a horse or maybe they got a horse
that can run a little. You don't see any rough stuff. No drunks.
Boy, I'd like to have the contract for the concessions."

Not far from the grandstand a knot of horseplayers, mostly
men, clutching race programs and pens, huddled around a pot-
bellied man in pink sports shirt, Levi's, sunglasses, cowboy hat
and cowboy boots.

"Right there is Oklahoma's poor-boy pari-mutuel betting system at work," Cal said, shaking his head. "And the state's not
getting a dime out of it. Even Arkansas is ahead of us. Last year
they say Hot Springs paid the state over five million. We had
that, it could go for teachers' salaries, or crippled kids, unless the
politicians got it first. We'd have pari-mutuel betting now if so
many folks weren't scared of the preachers."

"What people don't realize is how many jobs these quarter
horses provide," Lee said. "Racing is not just a pastime anymore,
it's a big business."

Cal peered at the bookie. "Say, believe I know that ol' boy.
Runs a little ranch south of Sapulpa. I'll go over there and see
what the odds are on the third race."

Lee gazed about, enjoying the scene. Over by the jockeys'
room teen-aged girls in tight jeans and tighter sweaters traded
quips with the young jocks. In the parking lot, pickups outnum-
bered passenger cars. He thought: Rural folks and folks from the
small towns and big towns. Come to watch quarter horses run.
The people's horse. Had been since colonial days. The short
horse. The all-purpose western horse of Grandfather Banner's
time. Pull a plow with him. Pull a buggy. Put the kids on him.
Work cattle on him in the morning. Run him that afternoon—
maybe twice. Running longer distances now. His short muscles
refined by Thoroughbred blood.

Cal came back grinning. "They've got Cindy at ten to one. I
just took me some of that. Put it on her nose to win."

"Guess you know that's illegal." Lee grinned. "Who's favored?"

Cal eyed his program. "The number one horse—that's Little

Go Go. And the four horse—that's Early Delivery. Both colts. You gonna bet a little?"

Lee shook his head. "The only time I ever bet on one of my horses was at Columbus, and you know what happened."

They drifted back to the barns.

"She's been walking her stall," Doug told them, swinging an arm for emphasis. "Just like her daddy. Back and forth. Back and forth."

"Guess I'll have to get her a dog or a goat mascot," Lee said. "I'd hate to haul a goat around, though. Ever smell one on a hot summer day?"

Doug, a conspirator's gleam in his eyes, took his transistor radio from the pickup. "Let's try this. See if she likes country western music." He turned to a station and a man's voice sounded, heavy and low and tuneless, backed by a listless guitar, moaning about a woman who didn't love him "no more."

"Can't stand that," Doug said, and switched stations. Now another male singer. More lost-woman troubles. Doug tried another station. This time a sweet, feminine voice. In a short time Cindy stuck her head over the stall door, ears perked toward the radio.

"She likes it!" Doug cried. "Don't tell me a horse doesn't know good music. That's Tammy Wynette—three-time winner of the top female country vocalist award." He turned up the volume and swayed to the music, while the filly continued to listen.

As post time neared, the parking lot filled to overflowing and racegoers seemed to be coming from everywhere.

"There's fifteen hundred folks here today if there's one," Cal beamed. "Day's gonna come when a man can bet and not sneak around."

Over the PA system the announcer was calling horses to the saddling paddock for the first race, a 400-yard quarter horse allowance for three-year-olds and up. In minutes the starting bell clanged and the gates banged open and hooves pounded, rolling closer and closer. Cindy perked that way, ears flicking. Lee rubbed her nose and talked to her. She wasn't jumpy yet, but she would be soon. The crowd was roaring at the finish.

When the call came for the third race, Lee bridled her and cleaned her hooves with a brush.

"She's in the lucky hole," the pony man said. "Number five horses won it all so far."

Lee didn't comment, thinking three times straight would be mighty lucky, contrary to the law of averages.

Taken to the five saddling stall, Cindy fidgeted at the commotion of horses and the chattering paddock watchers crowding the fence. To calm her, Lee led her around the paddock, pushing against her shoulder when she stepped too fast, sometimes forced to dig his bootheels into the soft earth to hold her back.

"She's all right," Cal said, brushing her. "She's not sweating much."

Doug, in green silks, stepped quickly from the jockeys' room with his tack. Lee was deliberate about saddling her, not wanting to get ahead of the others, for then she would stand idle and fret.

Shortly, Lee gave Doug a leg up and said, "Let her run as she will, but tap her if you think she needs reminding." Watching them go, Lee thought it was like seeing a child off to romp with the big kids for the first time.

As the pony riders led their charges to the track, Lee and Cal headed for the grandstand to be near the finish line. Now and then, during the post parade, Cindy turned her head toward the buzzing crowd.

"She's looking for you," Cal laughed.

"She's probably scared. I just hope she gets off this time."

The crowd grew quiet as the horses, finishing warm-up trots and short gallops, reached the rear of the starting gate. The first four runners were led in. As she had at Wildhorse Downs, Cindy loaded like a lady. The six horse refused, then behaved. The last horses moved in. But the four horse was acting up, delaying the start. At last he steadied.

The bell sounded, the gates opened.

"She took the break!" Cal yelled. "She's comin'!"

Indeed, she'd won the break, Lee saw, and she had the announcer's first call. She was on the lead, running straight and free. No bumping, though the six horse was bearing in on her hip.

Lee froze, afraid for her, but saw her pull away from trouble just as the six horse, suddenly veering out of control, wiped out the four horse. Lee was shouting and punching the air. Mercy, mercy, she was opening daylight on the field.

And then it happened about halfway. He saw her check and turn her head a little, as if looking back for the pack. Lee groaned and put his hands to his face. When he looked again, the field minus two horses, was catching up, then sweeping past her. When Doug tapped her twice, she started making up ground, passing horse after horse.

By that time her bid was too late.

"Where did we finish?" Lee asked, looking away.

"Fifth, I think. But she was on the fly. Another fifty yards, she'd caught that one horse."

Lee worked through the crowd to the track.

"She broke like a shot," Doug said, biting his lip, "and I thought we had it won. About then she eased up, like she was waitin' for the other horses to catch up. Sorry, Lee."

Lee slapped him on the shoulder. "One thing for sure, you broke her clean. She's over that."

He cooled her out, washed her down with a hose, then rubbed her with alcohol and soybean oil. Except for a slight cut on her left hind fetlock, she had come out of the race without hurt.

"Guess she's just too sociable," he said, frustrated. "I saw her look back and check. Maybe she was thinking of her old brood-mare band back home? Maybe she needs blinkers?"

"Give her time," Cal cautioned. "Before you start foolin' with blinkers, send her to school some more. This filly's a runnin' horse."

Doug said, "I should've tapped her when she first let up. Next time I'll be ready."

"You can bet we're gonna work on that hesitation waltz of hers," Lee said firmly.

"You know," Cal said, "the way she winds up and comes on at the finish, she could be a natural quarter-mile horse or longer."

Lee frowned. "When she's older, maybe. She's too young and green now to go longer than she ran today. Another thing: She still runs with her head too high to suit me. Landy did that too at first. Cured him with a shadow roll. Funny, how that little roll of sheepskin over the noseband tends to make a horse keep his head down so he can see over it." He knelt to check her front legs again, nodding to himself. "We'll go again in a few weeks or so. I don't want to hurry her."

Bound for Garfield Downs at Enid, they toiled along on the busy interstate at an unsteady fifty miles an hour, bucking the wind, cars and trucks whipping past them disdainfully, ignoring the fifty-five-miles-per-hour speed limit; frequently, Lee felt the tug of the loaded horse trailer. On this last Sunday in March the open land, rolling and green, treeless except for stubby cedars lining the draws and dotting the slopes, suggested early spring, though you could never tell about Oklahoma's weather.

"Daddy," Nancy announced, "you're going to have to get another pickup. Old Faithful has just about had it. That's all there is to it!"

"Doug has promised me a valve job when we get back," Lee said, watching their speed drop to forty going upgrade. "That should stand up for another hundred thousand miles. Besides, I've got my eye on a used two-door for you."

"I'd rather you put the money in on a good pickup. At least a low-mileage job that can get up a hill!"

At times his daughter seemed to speak mostly in exclamations. Lee attributed that to her age, her impatience with her erring elders, who, in her eyes, would smarten up as they grew older, and to her youthful faith that all things were possible if you just did them.

"Sis," he teased, "look back and see if we've run off and left Cal and Doug."

"Are you kidding? You know they're following in case we break down." She looked out the window and waved.

He sniffed. "This cab hasn't smelled this good since we all

used to haul Landy around." He glanced at Serena, sitting next to him, wearing a plaid skirt and a navy-blue jacket.

"So you've finally noticed," she said. "Yes, I'm wearing my old good-luck outfit. Had to shorten the skirt."

"Still looks nice. We'll need luck today. Be some fast horses in from Kansas."

"You sound skeptical," Nancy said. "You know Cindy can run."

"Question is with a young horse like her, will she, and when will she? She's mighty green yet."

"If she wins today, will you run her again soon?"

"Whether she wins or loses, I won't put her on the track for several weeks. We're racing these horses too young. Almost all horsemen are. That's why I turned her out to rest and had her x-rayed again, after she ran at Stroud. She checked out sound or we wouldn't be hauling her today." He drove on a way, thinking. "If she was the fastest horse in the world, and I had plenty of money, I wouldn't of nominated her for the three big futurities at Ruidoso."

"Why?"

"Because she'd likely shinbuck or break down before she got to the All-American trials. That's asking too much of a two-year-old. Too hard on their front wheels. I'd skip the early-season futurities, the Kansas and the Rainbow, and point her just for the All-American. Furthermore, if I had my say, I'd turn the All-American into a three-year-old race, and I'd run the derbies at four. Save a lot of horses that way."

"Do you think they'll ever do that?"

"Not a chance. These two-year-old stakes purses are too tempting. Getting bigger every year."

"I take it you're opposed to yearling futurities?"

He almost snarled. "Opposed? I'd outlaw 'em. They're ruination. That's putting babies on the track with their knees wide open."

"I hope Cindy runs up to her potential today."

"Whatever that is, Sis. Right now we're a long way from water and she'll need luck along the way."

"If she does well today, will you pay the late penalty and enter her in the All-American? I mean, will you consider it?"

Lee laughed. "You sure are asking a lot of questions today. You'd better ask your mama and J.B."

Serena merely smiled.

Before noon they were at the track and unloaded. Coming back from the track office, Lee sprayed the stall as usual.

"I'd forgotten you always do this," Nancy said approvingly.

"I'm afraid of viruses. You never know what a horse might pick up." He took folding chairs from the pickup and set them around. Serena had packed a big picnic lunch and a gallon of coffee.

"We're in the first race today," Lee worried. "Number eight hole. Glad we're on the outside."

"Daddy always worries," Nancy said.

"I'd worry if this was a milk-cow race."

"Sometimes you draw some extra wild ones in these maiden races," Doug agreed, and turned to Nancy. "Take a horse that likes to run next to the rail. If he draws an outside position, he'll still want to get to the rail. Then look out!"

After lunch, Cal went to the grandstand for a race program. He wore a dubious look when he came back. "I see the number seven horse, a four-year-old gelding called Chain Link, is listed as a first-time starter," he said, passing the program to Lee, who read the lineup and remarked, "I'll bet he's been out on the bush tracks somewhere. That's an old wrinkle."

"The bookie's got him bet down three to one."

"Could be the horse to beat. Where does he have us?"

"Eight to one. I didn't bet today, as much as I believe in her."

"Not gettin' superstitious, are you?"

"Ever see a horseman that wasn't?" Cal took a hitch at his belt. "Believe I'll scout around a little and keep my ear to the ground."

An hour before post time, Nancy braided colored ribbons in Cindy's black mane, while the filly listened to music on the radio.

"She looks more ready for Sunday School than a race," Serena said. "I only hope she'll do more than look pretty."

Nancy stood back to admire her handiwork. "Sometimes I think perhaps I should change my major to veterinary medicine . . . go to Oklahoma State and be an Aggie."

"Pampering," her father lectured, "is not part of the course, and if a certain young lady changes her major again . . . she could find herself in the ranks of the unemployed."

Cal did not show up until the announcer was calling horses for the first race. "Got news for you, Lee. Just talked to an ol' boy who thinks that seven horse is a hard-knocker from up around Eureka. Won a bunch of races under another name. Something like Dusty Bob. That means there's two sets of papers on him. Can you beat that?"

"Guess the track has to trust somebody. I don't mind if she is up against an older horse. Be a good test for her."

"That's not all. That seven horse is also a bad actor in the gate."

"In that case, we'll have to hope he breaks to the inside. Well, here's our pony rider."

Once in the saddling paddock, Lee could hardly keep Cindy's head turned away from the noisy crowd as he led her around.

Chain Link, alias Dusty Bob, was late arriving, and when he did, Lee's interest sharpened. The chestnut gelding was big of bone and heavy of muscle and high-strung. Led into his stall, he made a sudden lunge that cleared the area of all handlers but the man hanging on to the bridle. Of the remaining horses, Lee remembered from the program, four were three-year-olds, the others two, like Cindy. He liked the balanced looks of the one horse, a sorrel two-year-old listed as Billy Bam, with speed stamped all over him. Cindy had her work cut out for her today.

Lee saddled, checked bridle and girth and overgirth, decided to tighten the overgirth, and boosted Doug up with these words, "Tap her early if you think she's about to loaf again," and joined the family and Cal to go to the grandstand.

After the parade to post, Lee watched the first six horses load in calm order. Now the seven horse. Cindy, led in, was looking around. *Get her head straight, Doug. Quick—that's good!*

Just when all seemed about ready, the one horse decided to act up. His actions set off a chain reaction of restless thousand-pound bodies that rattled the gates. Suddenly the seven horse humped up, forcing his jockey to dismount. At the starter's shouted instructions, the gatemen backed the gelding out and led him around. His saddle was askew. While he was being resaddled and his rider mounted again, the whole field was unloaded and walked around.

"You don't see that very often," Lee said.

They loaded once more, smoothly this time, and just as all heads settled straight, the starting bell clanged. Lee stiffened as the veteran seven horse, matching Cindy's getaway, broke to the outside, crowding her.

Nancy gasped.

For an instant the horses brushed, then bumped, the gelding striding ahead powerfully. The collision knocked Cindy off stride. She was dead last.

"Chain Link's out in front!" came the PA announcer's authoritative voice. "Billy Bam second! Rocket Doll third! Moon Dancer fourth! Flying Dan fifth!"

Cindy was all but out of it, Lee saw, though Doug had her back on stride. There just wasn't much time. At 330 yards she could hardly recover from that bad-luck start.

About a third of the way Doug still hadn't tapped her. He was hand-riding her, settling her down, and she was running lower, beginning to dig in. He had her running straight, conserving ground. Along the rail the one horse was moving like a storm. The seven horse, while still on the lead, was bearing out despite his jockey's tuggings.

Cindy caught up with the field. She passed the five horse. Doug took her around the six horse, which had drifted out slightly, and thereby lost some precious ground. Fifty yards more and she was in the thick of it. Still, Lee knew, she was fast running out of track.

Suddenly, with a rush, Lee saw Cindy closing on the leader,

her ears laid back. She continued her charge and abruptly was lapped on the gelding.

It came at that instant. The 7 horse, running wider, started to carry her to the outside.

Lee swore to himself. *Now, Doug. Now. Tap her.*

Doug's arm cut a downward arc with the long stick.

Serena and Nancy were screaming and jumping up and down as Cindy poked her nose in front, her head, her neck. At the same time Chain Link's jockey got his mount straightened for the run to the wire. And then all Lee could see was dust and horses bunched in a blanket finish. He couldn't tell for certain, because Billy Bam had closed like a shot in those final jumps. Some moments passed, then Lee heard the announcer's voice:

"It was Cindy by a neck. Billy Bam second. Chain Link third. Rocket Doll fourth. Winning time: 17.41."

Lee whooped and bear-hugged his girls and stood numbed, so damn proud for his horse he could pop. He looked down and rubbed at something in the corner of his eye.

"Well, Daddy, don't just stand there!" Nancy yelled him out of his trance. "Let's all go down to the winner's circle!"

Lee turned, not forgetting. "Come on, Cal. We sure want you in this, too."

They wound down through the crowd to the track.

"She just couldn't stand to have those horses get ahead of her," a jubilant Doug sang out as he dismounted. "I felt a runner under me today, the way she came on."

"Believe her jockey had something to do with it," Lee said, taking Doug's hand.

They gathered on the happy ground of the winner's circle, while the track's photographer took their picture. In addition, there would be a photo of Cindy's come-from-behind finish.

At wonderful peaks like this, anything seemed possible. Thus, while holding Cindy's bridle, Lee could not but envisage the long road to Ruidoso and all that lay between. All the inevitable ups and downs that befell every horseman along the way. Did he dare dream again?

Chapter 6

The telephone started ringing in the motel room as Melvin "Boom Boom" Chumley was hanging up his suit pack. He rubbed a hand across his queasy stomach and moved on heavy feet to the table between the two beds, picking up the receiver on the fourth ring. Before he could speak, a voice impatient and resonant greeted him. "Welcome to Big D, Chumley. Have a smooth flight in?"

"Mighty smooth, Mr. Trent."

"How's everything?"

"On the lead." You might as well say so, even if things were not.

"Meet me in the club in a few minutes. We've got a lot to go over."

"Okay. Fine."

"I'll be looking for you."

Chumley searched his dop kit for the bottle of white pills, took one, chewed it to powder and washed it down with a swallow of tepid water. He dreaded this head-to-head meeting with Hack Trent, whom he knew only by reputation: a self-made millionaire, an aggressive s.o.b., harder to satisfy than a West Texas banker in a lean year. But money talked when you were down and out after that long suspension by the New Mexico Racing Commission, and you were here at Trent's invitation and expense. Chumley removed his dark glasses, which he wore outdoors and in, and took a last appraisal in the mirror of his heather-colored western suit, his flowered shirt and brown kerchief knotted at the neck, and his fawn-brown hat with the rodeo-rider crease. He saw sad, dark eyes, pouches underneath, framed in a long face that at thirty-eight was picking up too much loose flesh along the jaws. Worry, worry—that was the life of a racehorse trainer. He smiled then, a white, even smile of reassurance that offset his customary moroseness, and centered the horse-head bronze belt buckle restraining his growing paunch, dusted off his python-vamp boots and headed for the club.

The chunky man advancing to meet Chumley had the chest of a circus wrestler, the forearms of an old-time blacksmith, and the aggressive jaw and direct eyes of a doer. His apparel was a clash of colors: blue-and-white striped sports shirt and red-and-yellow plaid slacks. His shock of thick black hair, cut short and high above the ears, was combed straight back and unparted, in defiance, it might seem, of the hirsute styling of the day; unfortunately, combined with his sloping forehead, it tended to create a bullet-shaped look. He seemed to move with the clomping step of a man once accustomed to walking over plowed ground.

Chumley all but flinched at his crushing grip, and a picture flew into his mind: a man who never wept and who went straight at his objective.

"I'm Hack Trent."

"Glad to meet you, Mr. Trent."

"If we're gonna get along, you'll have to call me Hack." He led the way to a table. Swiftly, a short-skirted waitress materialized, smiling down at Trent. "Let's have a drink," Trent said. "What'll you have?"

"Make mine one jigger of scotch in a glass of milk," Chumley said, somewhat apologetic about it.

"No Bourbon?" Trent responded, surprised.

"Scotch likes me better."

"I'll have the usual," Trent said, turning to the young woman. "You know what that is, don't you, doll?"

"Think I'd forget, Mr. Trent?" she smiled back, and swiveled away.

"Just look at all that class stuff goin' to waste, would you," Trent said, watching her co-ordinated walk to the bar. Within a very short time she returned with the drinks, and as she set them down, Trent said, "You're a real doll," and reached for her hand.

Surely yet tactfully withdrawing her hand, she retreated behind her public smile.

Trent took a long swallow and said, "I didn't go into details over the phone, Chumley, but I'm looking for a trainer who can produce."

"I thought Si Queen was handling your string?"

"*Was*. Till I pulled my horses last week. In a big business if the earnings are low, what do you do? You fire the president. In horse racing it's the trainer. His job is to produce or get off the pot."

At that, Chumley recalled, Queen had lasted longer than most of Trent's trainers.

"I'm looking for a class trainer—somebody who'll do more than lead my horses to the saddling paddock and collect their daily training fee." Trent's big right hand enveloped the glass, dwarfing it, and clapped it down on the table for emphasis. His square-rigged face tightened until the cheekbones stood out like knobs. He leaned right at Chumley as he spoke. "I'm gonna tell you how I look at things. My philosophy. . . . Nothing comes easy in this old world. I grew up on an East Texas red-dirt farm. There were ten of us kids. I got as far as the eighth grade. I've gone hungry. I've picked cotton for a dollar a day—and glad to get it. I've roughnecked in the oil fields from Texas and Oklahoma to Illinois. I've been a pipeliner. I've fought carnival fighters for five bucks, won the fight, then had to whip both the guy again and his manager to get my money—but I got it. So there's a price for everything in this old world, Chumley. Tell me if I'm wrong."

Any man who said that wasn't expecting contradiction. Chumley sipped his milk and scotch in silence.

"And you don't get anywhere if you don't take a chance sometimes." Trent was clearly enjoying his recital of self-accomplishment before so attentive a listener. He said, "One day I bought an oil lease cheap on borrowed money . . . hit it lucky. There was enough oil under that cotton patch to run Chicago for ten years, day and night. Since then I've branched out. I've gone into construction. Built dams and stretches of interstate highways. I've built pipelines all over the world. I've got Cadillac agencies in two states. I've got a ranch in West Texas. I own this motel and others. I bought real estate in Houston at the right time." This last told with a broad wink. "Now I'm into the fast-food business. Guess you've seen my franchises? That big T that flashes? Trent's T-Burgers. Burgers and fries. . . . A man can get rich if he knows the shortcuts and how to run a business enterprise. A young fella can make it big if he rides with me . . . is a member of the team. Keeps his fingers out of the till and learns how to manage. If he can't, out he goes. That's only fair. Tell me if I'm wrong."

Chumley had another sip.

"Although I tell you all this," Trent said, his face changing and smoothing, "I'm really just an ol' country boy."

Uh-huh, Chumley thought, with a mind as deadly as a bear trap.

"Wise management. Following rudimentary business practices. Selecting personnel not afraid of work. Working toward a common goal. Teamwork. Marketing simple products. A racehorse is no more than a simple product to be marketed where profits have the greatest potential. Tell me if I'm wrong."

Chumley took a breath and said, "I can't quite agree with you there, Hack. There are too many unpredictable factors in a horse race."

"Like what?" Trent gruffed.

"Like how a horse feels the day he runs. Like the condition of the track. Maybe the track is muddy, as it often is at Ruidoso, and maybe our horse is no mudder. Maybe the horse steps in a hole and breaks a leg and has to be put down. Maybe, if he's lucky, he just breaks his stride and cuts himself. Maybe the track is hard and hurts his feet and he won't run his best." Chumley had a sip. "Like how the horse gets off. If he gets bumped. And there's the jock. Like maybe he makes a wrong move. In a quarter horse race there's seldom time to recover from a mistake. Too, these two-year-olds are hardly more than babies. Their bones aren't completely formed. Sometimes they break down. Or they can be kickin' up their heels one day and the next be too sick to outrun a fat man. You bring a young horse in from Texas or Oklahoma to Ruidoso and one of the first things that happens is he comes down with a cold. That costs a week or so of training. Then a youngster can set the fastest time in the qualifying trials and still run last in the big one." He sipped again. "Racing is a nervous business. Owners get nervous. Trainers are always nervous, like me. Horses are nervous and jocks are bundles of nerves. You can have the fastest horse and the best rider and still run out of the money. It's a gamble, Hack."

"I still say racing can be conducted like a business," Trent insisted stubbornly.

"A stud farm, yes. At the track it's a different ball game. There another element figures in."

"What's that?"

"Luck. Horseman's luck—good or bad."

The waitress swished up to the table. "There's a phone call for you, Mr. Trent. You can take it at the end of the bar."

"Thanks, doll."

Without excusing himself, Trent clomped to the bar. He felt like ducking the instant he heard the clear, feminine voice, "Hi there, honey. This is Connie. How are you?"

"What's the idea of calling me here?"

"Where else would I find you but at the bar?"

"I'm in a business conference."

"I have some business with you, too."

A sudden suspicion exploded through him. "Say, are you on long distance or are you . . . ?"

"Honey chile," she finished for him, "I'm right here in Big D. In the same motel you are."

"What! God damn it, you're not to come to Dallas, ever, remember? You know—" Realizing finally that his voice had risen above the murmur in the club, he turned to see the bartender and the waitress, both watching him, hurriedly avert their eyes. He gave them his back and lowered his voice. "Listen, Connie. I told you a long time ago . . ."

"You listen to me, Hack Trent. We've got to come to some kind of understanding. I won't go on any longer like this. Understand?"

He was silent. He could never quite handle women. They were too clever for him. Too emotional. They drove him to distraction at times, and they always expected too much.

She said, "Happy hour starts most places at five o'clock. Mine starts at four. I'm in room two-fifteen. On your way, fetch me a bottle Chivas Regal."

"All right."

His expression inscrutable, he ignored the two at the bar and rejoined Chumley. "You talk about luck," he picked up. "Can't say I've had any with trainers. Hell, I could've grabbed some bird off the street and done as well."

"How did you get into racing?" Chumley asked curiously. Of all the owners he'd seen, Trent struck him as the least likely to have a fondness for horses. The new wave of owners, the rich lawyers, the contractors, the doctors, the oilmen, the real estate developers, generally came in because they had always dreamed of owning a fast racehorse. Sometimes the memory of a gentle childhood pony illogically led them into the risky world of racing, often to their disappointment and financial loss. Then, again, a newcomer's two-year-old would jump up and win a rich futurity. One was enough to fuel the dreams of others. And, of course, there were those who used racing as a tax write-off for more profitable ventures.

"Some years back," Trent said, "an oil friend asked me to go in with him on some quarter horse yearlings. When he lost interest, and that didn't take long, I ended up with the whole shebang. Since that time, guess I've paid up some twenty-five horses into the All-American and the best we ever did was run fifth. As a businessman, I believe when an owner sends a trainer a stable of class horses, he ought to produce some winners now and then. That's why I got in touch with you, Chumley."

"Why me?"

"I notice you've consistently been listed among the five leading trainers at Sunland and Ruidoso. You're an expert."

Chumley had to chuckle. "There's an old saying in the horse business that an expert is anybody who's been right once."

"That's more than I can say for the dudes I've had to contend with."

"Maybe you don't know I'm just coming off a year's suspension by the New Mexico Racing Commission?"

"I know. I've checked you out. Care to tell me about it?"

"Don't mind. It was big in the papers. A Thoroughbred filly I was training for an El Paso doctor showed a positive test for Ritalin. She was a long shot and won the Pan Zareta Stakes."

"Ritalin?"

"Yes. It's a stimulant. I asked for a hearing before the Commission and they gave me one, all right." Chumley's face was wry. "I told 'em I didn't know how Ritalin got into that filly's urine. Well, they laid it on me good. What it was was a frame by another trainer. He knew I had the best horse. He was jealous of my record. Somebody got to the filly the night before the race, but I couldn't prove it. Under New Mexico rules a trainer is responsible for any drugs found in any of his horses."

"I seem to remember," Trent said, cocking a cynical eye, "that the papers reported urine samples from the ten winning horses that day were stolen while awaiting shipment by bus to the state racing chemist at Albuquerque. However, the state vet at the track had kept enough of the samples for a second test."

"Oh, they accused me of that, too," Chumley said with a shrug. "How could I prove I didn't, anymore than I could prove I didn't shoot up the horse? By the way, that suspension applied not only to New Mexico, but on all recognized tracks. They took away my living for a year."

"Were you ever suspended before that?"

"Just once. It was another frame."

"I see. Do you use Bute?"

"I do in New Mexico. It's legal there, illegal in Arizona."

"I see there's a big controversy about that now."

"I'll tell you this. People complain. But there are lots of crip- ples at the smaller tracks where the money handle and the purses aren't much. Just chicken feed. If those cripples weren't out there running, they'd be in a can of Alpo. Which is more humane? Keep 'em on the track through medication or send 'em to the canner?"

Trent signaled for another round and said, "A trainer pulled this one on me. I had a sorrel roan colt by Go Man Go, no less, out of a class speed mare. The trainer kept tellin' me he was ready to run. But he never won. Finally, I sold him to the trainer. Next thing I knew the horse started winning. One day I happened to run across the jockey and when I asked him why the horse didn't win when I owned him, the boy said, 'Why, old so-and-so had me pull that horse every time, so you'd think he was no good.' I've smartened up since then. Now, you wouldn't pull that on me, would you, Chumley?"

"What do you think?" Chumley replied, meeting Trent's eyes.

"Would you shoot up a horse if you thought you could get by with it?"

Chumley's answer was an enigmatic shrug. What was this, anyway, a confession?

"Tell you what I want, Chumley. I want to win the All- American. I won't be satisfied with anything less."

Chumley's eyebrows flew up. "That's a mighty big order. Some men would sell their souls in hell to win it."

"I want it for a number of reasons. One . . . I want to show up that uppity bunch that bellies around the Jockey Club in Ruidoso Downs. You oughta hear 'em blow about their horses and put on airs. I want to show 'em that an ol' country boy from East Texas has just as much class as they claim and more. Espe- cially them born with silver spoons. I've worked for mine." He waved an appropriating arm. "Take this motel. I stopped here one time when I'd left my credit cards someplace and was short of cash. Nobody knew me. They wouldn't let me in. I stayed at a friend's house that night. Two days later I came back and bought the place. First thing I did was fire the son of a bitch that turned me down. You bet I did, and you can bet they all know me now."

Chumley drawled, "I think you'd better get another trainer," and pushed back from the table and reached for his hat. "I can't promise you we'd win even one race." He could read Trent like an open primer. The man was uncouth. Coming from the wrong side of the tracks, so to speak, he longed for prestige and social acceptance. That was it. He didn't care about the horses. Horses were no more than playthings to feed his ego.

"Hold on, Chumley. Don't get your bristles up. All I want you to do is train exclusively for me." Trent was sneering. "I've seen them big-time trainers with thirty-head stables or so. Too busy to give individual attention to every horse. That was one of Queen's faults. He couldn't manage."

Chumley put down his hat. "How many two-year-olds you got?"

"Fifteen were nominated for the All-American. Eight are still in."

"A trainer can't make a living off eight head unless some noses are going across that finish line on the lead."

"You can with mine. Win or lose, I'll put you on a monthly retainer that'll make that twenty bucks a day you guys charge for training and keep look like peanuts. Your usual ten per cent of the purse money will be in addition—all red-eye gravy. Of course, I'll expect you to produce."

The man, Chumley sensed, would be constantly on his back. But money talked. It always had, always would. And that regular check sounded like sweet music. He could put up with Trent till he got back on his feet. Still, Chumley was cautious. He said, "You left out the vet bills and shoeing. That runs—"

"I know," Trent interrupted impatiently. "The owner pays that."

"What about the Kansas and Rainbow futurities?"

"We're paid into both. All eight head."

"You're pumping money in with both fists," Chumley said, visibly impressed.

"You're damn right I am. Hoping a horse of mine goes into the All-American with a chance to be the first Triple Crown winner in quarter horse history."

"You're talking now about a Cinderella horse. A one-in-a-million shot. A horse like Tiny's Gay, that almost pulled it off. Guess you know what happened?"

"Easy Date beat him by a nose in the All-American."

"I mean the bad luck. Tiny's Gay broke a bone in his foot forty yards from the finish line. That probably cost him the Triple Crown. His only loss was his last race. But who can say? Easy Date was coming up fast."

"You're a pessimist, Chumley."

"I'm a realist."

"Well, is it a deal? Are we on the same team?"

"Is . . . maybe . . ." said Chumley, playing his covering smile, "when you get down to some exact figures."

Trent's reply was to scribble large numbers on a napkin, which he slid across to Chumley with, "Tell me if I'm wrong."

Chumley eyed the figures, continued to do so to conceal his pleased surprise. But again a warning ticked. Trent wasn't used to being talked back to—that was evident. Standing up to him was likely the one way to get his respect at the start and to hold it. Masking his face of any anticipation, Chumley said, "I would want it understood how I operate. I'd call you when your horses did well, I'd call you when they didn't, and I'd call you if there'd been an accident, if any. You wouldn't hear it from the grapevine, or from some two-bit trainer trying to get my string of horses. That's the only way, Hack. And when I'd call you, I'd expect you to talk to me. I don't like to be ignored."

"No problem there. I'll talk to you anytime, and you'll find me calling you when you least expect it. I'll give you a list of numbers where I can be reached most times. Well, what do you say?"

"It's a deal," Chumley said, and felt his stomach knot as he spoke.

They shook hands. Hack Trent signaled the bar.

He remembered to fetch the bottle of Chivas Regal, and when he knocked on the door at 215, he found that his annoyance with her had left him and that he was thinking of more intimate things.

"Hello, doll," he greeted the blue-eyed woman when she opened the door.

"The same old salutation," she said wearily, and gave him a peck on the cheek. "It never changes, does it?"

He pulled her to him. "That's not much of a reception for ol' Hack."

"You don't deserve that after all your excuses," she said, freeing herself.

"Ain't you been gettin' your checks regular?"

"I have . . . but there's always something missing when they come."

"What's that?"

"Hack Trent is what."

"I'm a busy man. You know that, Connie. Last week I was in Alaska. Week before that in Oklahoma." He made a show of setting the bottle on the dresser table and reached for her again. She stepped away. Of a sudden she seemed to see him fully for the first time. "Look how you're dressed! That god-awful striped shirt with those horrible plaid trousers. Once out of my sight, you start looking like a circus clown."

"This was the handiest to put on when I got up."

"I believe it. How many times have I told you when you want to wear a striped shirt, put on plain trousers. When you wear plaid trousers, put on a plain shirt. And the colors should blend, not clash." She shook her head in despair. "And your hair is cut too high above the ears. Your scalp shows. Like something out of World War I, when the boys came back from Over There. Next time you go to that sheep shearer, tell him to leave it full on the sides and let it fall over your ears a little. It would look a lot nicer that way." She smiled at him, just a little, as she might after admonishing a small boy.

That broke the tension between them. But when Trent sought to kiss her, she pulled away, resenting his rough manner. He looked at her, puzzled and alarmed.

Connie Eaton was fifteen years his junior. Today she wore a silky-looking pink dress, her favorite color. Although she wasn't as pretty as the little cocktail waitress, she was neat and clean and attractive. Her face was full, too full for beauty, but her skin was fair and smooth and she had a full, passionate mouth and the clearest of blue eyes. She had just come from the beauty parlor, judging by the perfection of her amber hair, worn shoulder length and set off with pearl earrings. Connie, a legal secretary when he first met her, could put a man down like no other woman he knew, including his wife, Myrna. Except Connie did it without humbling a man, without wrecking his confidence, like Myrna tried. Connie always built you up after she had her say, always gave you a smile. Long ago he had discovered that she was a giving woman—giving was her weakness. She was still young, only thirty-three. Came from a nice southern family. She had class. That and her availability were the reasons why he held on to her.

He filled two glasses with ice, opened the scotch, poured two stiff drinks at random, his nose wrinkling distaste at the peaty smell. Why the hell didn't more women drink Bourbon? Handing her a glass, he asked lightly, "Now, what's this all about?"

She took a chair by the window and sipped her drink, as if gathering her thoughts, while Trent maintained a discreet silence.

"Hack," she said finally, "I've waited as long as I'm going to."

"You're forgetting the good times we've had together."

"Your times mainly—at your convenience and bidding."

"You forget I'm a busy man."

"Doesn't matter. I've waited too long."

"Now, hold on. You don't understand."

"I understand that I've waited three long years for you to do something. Also, that I haven't seen you or had a call from you in four months. Not since you came through Little Rock on your way to Houston."

"Which proves I'm on the go all the time."

"That's no longer the excuse it used to be. A man in your position can be anywhere he wants to be for as long as he wants to be."

"Doll, you simply don't understand."

"Hack," she said, her soft southern voice rising sharply, her blue eyes glinting, "can't you drop that doll stuff? It's so common. So meaningless."

He looked down for her benefit. "Habit, I reckon."

"Then break it."

"I'll try," he said, ostensibly accepting the rebuke, knowing that if he appeared to, she would soften. They had finished their drinks. He refilled the glasses, giving her a double when she wasn't looking, and sat across from her, on his good behavior, showing her an attitude of penance.

"I didn't like the way you talked to me over the phone," she said. "I don't like to be cursed. I wasn't brought up that way."

"I'm very sorry," he said, keeping his voice low and humble.

She looked at him with a directness that turned him uneasy. "When I first met you," she said, "you told me you were unhappy and about to get a divorce. I was unhappy, too, and lonely, after losing Dick. We needed each other—or so I thought at the time. You said you loved me. You asked me to wait for you till you were free. I said I would. I have—but I can't wait forever. I'm still unhappy and lonely. I feel I've made a mistake by waiting this long. I can always go back to work."

"I've got troubles, Connie."

"You," she threw back at him. "What troubles could Hack Trent have?"

"Reason I talked to you like that at the bar is Myrna. She's looking for cause. She's got a detective on my trail."

"Why don't you just give her a divorce and get it over with? I mean, if you don't love her."

"Because Myrna has threatened to take me to the cleaners—and she would. Man, how she would."

"Couldn't you afford a generous settlement?"

"I could—but not what she would want. Everything."

"Oh, come on, Hack. You can hire attorneys. Good ones." A look of troubled conscience rose to her face. "I never wanted you to get a divorce unless you didn't love your wife. Do you or not?" He shrugged and she said, "How are your children?"

"They're fine. Both in college. Grown up. Gone from home."

"If you don't love Myrna, then it comes down to me. What about me? I've tried to be like a wife to you. I've dated no one else."

"Aw, you know how I feel about you, doll." Damn, he'd let that slip out at the wrong time.

She flushed angrily. "I know. I'm good to sleep with whenever you're in town. You'd rather keep things just as they are. Your official family in Dallas, me far away in Little Rock, or flying to meet you in some motel you own whenever you snap your fingers. You gone the next morning. I won't have it, Hack. Not anymore." She was weeping quietly, which worried him, for he had never seen her so upset and determined. She went on, "You don't love Myrna. You don't love me, you don't love anybody but Hack Trent. Women are just so much property to you. Like a burger stand. Or an oil well or one of your poor, sore-legged quarter horses, which you run when you shouldn't sometimes for your own self-glorification . . . so people will look up and say, 'There goes Hack Trent, the big-time horseman.'"

She meant it. He saw that. She had touched on sensitive areas, and she was making him mad as hell. But he held himself in check, knowing that once she had spent her feelings she would come around as she always had. Rising, he went over and held out a conciliatory hand. She brushed it away.

"Listen," he said, "I promise I'll have things settled."

"You've promised before."

"Be different this time. I'll push harder."

"When?" she choked. By now she was clutching at anything.

He groped for an answer and took the farthest date he could think of that she might accept. "By the end of summer. When I go to the All-American trials . . . late August."

"That's a long time."

"Sorry. That's the way things shape up right now."

"Can't I go along, too? Can't we have some time together out there?"

"Won't work. Myrna will be there. She never misses the races."

"There's always something, isn't there?" she said bitterly, turning away.

"Aw, now." He circled his arms around her. She was always vulnerable at a time like this, after they'd had a spat and she'd lost, realizing she had but the one course. He kissed the back of her neck, worked around to her cheek, turned her and found her mouth, forcing his tongue to hers, feeling her reluctantly giving to the increasing pressure of his hard body, feeling her lonely dearth. He ran his hands over her breasts.

"You're always so rough about it," she said, but she didn't push him away.

"You've got to admit that ol' Hank is a pretty good man in the hay." He released her gradually, watching the clash of emotions struggling in her tearful face. It was flushed, both bitter and in need.

Suddenly she took off her earrings and laid them on the dresser and began fumbling with the snaps on her dress. "Let's get it over wich," she said, and as suddenly she was weeping again. "That's all you want, isn't it? That's all it's ever going to be for me, isn't it?"

"Aw, you know better'n that, doll." He was already out of his shirt. "And maybe we can work out a way you can go to Ruidoso."

Chapter 7

At times the old pain and anger took possession of Lee Banner, burning no less than in the beginning. It returned again as he parked in the bank's lot and went across to the courthouse and up to the sheriff's office. Undersheriff Caldwell was his usual sympathetic self; however, he said, there were no new leads of any significance.

"But the NINA people—that's the Narcotics Information Network of Arizona—and agencies in the Quad State Program—that's Arizona, Utah, Colorado and New Mexico—think Green and Dolan are operating in and out of southern New Mexico and possibly southern Arizona."

"How do they figure that?" Lee asked.

"Because of the number of planes stolen within the last several months from the Las Cruces Airport—five, in fact. Drug smugglers simply hopscotch the border in these light planes and touch down at some remote strip, in the mountains or out on the desert, unload and take off. That's Green's *modus operandi*. He's been busted under other aliases, but Green is what he goes by most times."

"Have they said they ever heard of a drug trafficker called Bruno?"

"Bruno?"

"That name sorta slipped out during one of the bribe offers over the phone. I take it that Bruno is a bigwig trafficker, that Green and Dolan fly for him."

"The name hasn't come up," Caldwell said, showing a lively interest. "I'll check it out. You bet." He made a notation on a yellow pad.

Lee stood. "I know this case is a long shot, Bob. All I ask is that you fellows keep at it."

"We are, Lee."

Discouraged, he walked through early April sunshine to the bank, entered and stood a moment in the refrigerated coolness. Seeing that J. B. Foster was on the phone, he took a seat and waited. Presently, Foster waved him over. "What's on your mind, Lee?"

"A little money."

"I believe we still have some left back there."

Foster was a rolly, fidgety bear of a bachelor in a rumpled dark suit, wrinkled white shirt and loose tie who constantly complained of his weight and liked to refer to himself as "just a country-boy banker that learned to figure before he could whittle."

"How's the family?" he asked.

"Fine. Except Serena's peeved at you. She wants to know why you didn't come out for dinner last Sunday like you promised."

Foster looked pained. "I was called out of town. But it's just as well. I'm on a weight-watcher's diet, which means everybody is watching me to see that I don't break over. I tell you, it's living hell for a fat man brought up on country cookin'. I've started smoking again to dull my appetite." He spread his big hands appealingly. "So what do you gain?"

"The invitation is still open for next Sunday."

As if he hadn't heard, Foster leaned back and cradled the back of his head in both hands. "I hear you have a promising filly."

"I believe she is—so far. As of now she's enrolled in the school of hard knocks. Broke her maiden at Enid. Got in trouble at the start, but came on to win it. I'm proud of the way she ran."

"Glad to hear it, particularly after the terrible thing that happened at your place. What do you need, Lee?"

"Five hundred on an open note. I don't owe you anything."

"Okay." Foster filled out a note on a portable typewriter and handed Lee a pen. "Guess feed's getting higher."

"Is . . . but it's not for feed. It's entry money for a winner-take-all race at Anadarko next Saturday. Four hundred yards. Each owner puts up five hundred."

"Has she gone that far?"

"Not yet. But she's well rested now and I want to see what she can do at that distance against older horses. It's an open race."

"At the Anadarko Fair Grounds?"

Lee grinned. "It'll be a real bush track set-to."

"Older horses? On a bush track? Winner takes all? Sounds like she'll be up against some seasoned campaigners. Aren't you placing her at a disadvantage?"

"A horse learns through competition. First time we ran her, she froze in the gates. We cured that. Next time she took the break at Stroud, got out ahead and eased up, lookin' for company. I hope we've cured that, too. Last time, at Enid, she got bumped and still won, which convinced me she can run a little. I'd like to see her run just once with nothing happening."

"I'll get your money," Foster said.

What Lee hadn't told him was that he was down to his last fifty dollars. Cindy had won a few hundred at Enid, her purse going for feed. Neither did Lee want Serena to know that he had reached the bottom of his part of the ranch budget.

After counting out the greenbacks, Foster paused, a guarded hopefulness in his manner. "Serena wouldn't be baking a cherry cobbler on Sunday, would she?"

"She will be, same as last Sunday, if you're coming out. And she said something about having ham hock and pinto beans, cornbread and—"

"Get out of here! Tell Serena I'll be there. Meanwhile, I'll deny myself as usual."

Only Cal and Doug made the haul to Anadarko with Lee and Cindy. They reached the Fair Grounds around noon and Lee's first concern was the condition of the track. He scowled as he walked over the course from the grandstand to the head of the straightaway. Though it showed evidence of having been dragged recently, it looked rough and hard, overladen with large clods, and the inside lane was cupped. His doubts gathered. This was what a man ran into. To meet your needs, sometimes you had to take chances with your horse. He could still scratch, he told himself. But wasn't every race a gamble, on a supervised track or out in the bushes? It was. And what if you needed the money to carry on your racing program? He did.

"How does it look?" Cal asked him.

"Rough as a cob, but we'll run it."

They drove around below the track, past some weathered barns, and parked on a grassy stretch near other trailers, backed Cindy out and walked her around some minutes, then tied her to the trailer. "We'll stay out here," Lee said, viewing the run-down stall area. "She might catch something in there."

A smiling man hustled over from the barns, where a group squatted in the shade of the overhang. "I'm Jack Hemp," he said, shaking hands. "You could be Lee Banner?"

"I am. What's the field, Mr. Hemp?"

Hemp's manner was quick and obliging, on his pink face a perspiring sincerity. Lee had talked to him over the phone.

"Five horses have showed up so far, counting your filly," Hemp said. "Horses from Elk City and Apache. One from the Panhandle and one from the Lone Butte Ranch out in western Oklahoma. Was expecting an eight-horse field, but that five hundred is a mite steep for some of these boys. I'll hold things open a bit longer in case some more come in. We'll race about two o'clock. You want to put in now?"

Lee nodded and paid in, thinking, A five-horse field instead of eight. Four horses to beat, fewer horses to cause trouble.

"Gosh, I hate to have her stand out here in the sun so long," Doug worried. He brushed her mane and rubbed on her.

"Won't bother her," Lee said. "She's been out all her life. I've never stalled her unless the weather got real bad. Wanted her to grow up hardy. You might give her a few sips of water, though."

Lee studied two horses tied to trailers. An Indian man and a boy stayed close to a smooth sorrel mare, and two white men watched a smallish brown gelding. Their pickup bore an Elk City feed store sign on the driver's side.

A man left the shade of the barns and ambled toward the trailers. He nodded to the Elk City pair and eyeballed their horse, passed on to the Indians, where he did likewise, his attention more than casual. Approaching the Banner trailer, he gave a neighborly nod and glanced at Cindy. His hooded eyes became fixed on her, lingering, assessing; nodding once more, he ambled back to the barns.

"He paid us a longer size-up than he did the others," Cal said. "If he figures we've got the horse to beat, he's right."

At one-thirty Hemp called the horsemen together for the draw. He wrote numbers on small squares of cardboard and shook them in his big straw hat. "Who's first?"

One of the Elk City horsemen, peering through thick glasses, stepped forward, drew and looked down. "Number two hole," he said, and held up the square for the rest to see.

Hemp shook the hat again. Lee took the next draw. "Number three," he called, and showed it, glad that he hadn't pulled the cupped inside lane.

The Indian followed. "Number one," he said, and frowned at his luck.

A burly man of medium height came forward. "Number five hole," he said, showing, and Hemp echoed him, "Number five position for the Lone Butte Ranch."

That left the stroller, an angular individual, his hooded eyes a dull gray, with scar tissue around his chin.

"Panhandle," Hemp said genially, "that puts your horse in the number four gate, but draw anyway for the record."

Grinning, Panhandle did so, and displayed the square.

"Be three judges," Hemp explained. "I'm one of 'em. There'll also be a timer. Remember, it's winner take all. Now, you gents saddle up and take your horses to the gates. Luck to you all."

Lee saddled, handed Doug up and they walked to the track.

No pony horse today for Cindy. Surprisingly, to Lee, several hundred persons had collected in the stands.

"Let's hold up and look over the field," he said. "I'm a little curious about the Panhandle horse and the Lone Butte horse. They kept 'em back in the barns."

The Indian mare, with the boy in the irons, stepped nicely, eager to run. The Elk City gelding appeared almost undersized, but he had speed lines. The man called Panhandle was ponying a gray gelding of large bone and long muscle. A bush track campaigner, Lee judged, if he had ever seen one. An older horse. Cindy would break between the gray and the Elk City entry. The Lone Butte runner, a dark brown gelding, was a roughlooker of exceptional muscle up front and behind. Not balanced, but powerful. A crablike man was in the saddle.

"You can't always go by looks," Lee said after the horses had passed. "But that gray gelding could be the scorpion in the bunch. Or that Indian mare." He slapped Doug on the leg, raising his voice, "Just turn 'er loose," and stationed himself behind the fence near the finish, inwardly concerned over his judgment in coming here.

"Believe I'll shake the bushes, see if somebody wants to wager a dollar or two," Cal said.

Lee watched while Doug walked Cindy to the homestretch turn, on halfway down the backstretch; from there alternately walking and trotting for the gates.

By that time Cal was back. "They're bettin' the bush track gray and the Indian mare," he said. "I took some of each."

"Any book on the gray?"

"He's outrun everything in western Oklahoma. That Indian mare has cleaned out everything from here to Red River."

"Oh, boy," Lee groaned. "I bit off a big 'un, didn't I?"

The last runner trotted around to the gates, which would bang open when the starter jerked a release rope. Lee saw the Indian mare go into the 1 gate and stand like stone. The little Elk City gelding stopped short, until a headman pulled on his bridle and two men got behind. Cindy obligingly entered the 3 hole. In, she turned her head from side to side, seeming more curious than nervous. *Keep her headed straight, Doug. That's better.*

His eyes were still on the filly, standing ready, when the dark brown shape of the Lone Butte gelding suddenly looming up in the 4 gate on Cindy's right seized his attention. As quickly, the gray moved into the 5 position.

A warning whipped through Lee as he caught the switch. He could do no more than shout at the judges and point, his words lost as the gates clashed and they were off. In the same slice of time he saw the Lone Butte horse slam into Cindy and knock her off her feet, narrowly missing the fast-breaking Elk City gelding. Two racers flashed out front, the Panhandle gray breaking from the outside five gate and the Indian mare on the inside.

Lee hollered at Cal, "They switched on us—the four horse and the five horse. Five's a put-in, knock-down horse!"

Cindy was running last.

In pain, Lee saw her level out as Doug asked her to run, shaking his stick a little. She picked up and began to settle into her long stride. So late, so late, Lee saw. Lone Butte was trailing in fourth.

All at once she began closing on him. She took him. Hell's fire, that horse couldn't run. That put-in, knock-down horse.

Elk City was struggling third. Midway, she came up, lapped on him, now running head to head with him. He faded, hanging gamely.

She had open track now. The Indian mare rushing along the rail, the gray on the outside. It was Enid all over again as Doug, coming from behind, sent her down the middle, hand-riding her, low on her.

Cal whooped. "She's comin', Lee! Lordy, she is!"

But could she hold it? She'd never run this far.

At about three hundred yards Doug tapped her twice on the right, quickly, calling for more run. She took on the leaders, still strong, still determined.

The gray's jock stole a startled glance over his left shoulder and began sticking his mount every jump, angling toward the inside to shut her off.

But abruptly, very abruptly, she moved up before he could. As if pulled on strings, Cindy and the gray, going stride for stride, drew away from the mare.

Lee bit his lip. If she could just hold her surge. Fifty yards to go.

They flashed across the finish. In the final strides, Lee saw her get there, but you never knew about bush-track judges.

"She won it!" Cal shouted, shaking his fist.

"Be hell to pay if they say she didn't," Lee swore, and charged out to the judges, huddled by the finish pole. They were still conferring as the tail-end runners passed. Hemp jogged his head and the other two nodded assent.

"Well—?" Lee broke in, cocked for trouble.

Hemp turned. "Your filly won it. It was close, between a head and a neck win. Here's your money."

"That Lone Butte gelding interfered with us at the break. You saw the jock turn his horse into my filly, knock her off her feet. He was put in so the Panhandle horse could win."

"That's how it looked, all right. Haven't seen that mossy stunt pulled since I was a boy. We'd had us a real ruckus if Panhandle had won."

"You can say that again."

Shouts from the crowd pulled Lee's attention downtrack. Doug, still mounted, was arguing with the Lone Butte jockey. Doug let go a wild swing that missed. Cindy shied sideways.

Lee ran and grabbed the filly's bridle. When he did, Doug jumped down and yanked the Lone Butte rider from the saddle. Instantly fists started flying. The crowd poured from the grandstand.

Lee said, "Hold 'er, Cal," and shouldered through to separate the two, the judges close behind him.

"That was deliberate," Doug accused the other jockey. "Dirtiest thing I ever saw." He kept struggling to get at the older man.

Lee flung an arm around Doug and led him away, saying low, "Let it go. Let it go."

Hemp followed, his voice apologetic. "I'm sorry about this. I never saw those birds before today. They sized up the field and figured your filly was the horse they had to beat. They got lucky on the draw, side by side, or they couldn't have pulled the switch. What they overlooked was I wouldn't have paid Panhandle after they changed gates."

A man clutching a stopwatch caught up with them. "In case you're interested," he panted at Lee, "your filly ran that in twenty flat."

Lee gave a pleased whistle.

"Been under that but for the knockdown," Hemp said, interested. He tipped back his hat, a considering expression wreathing his round-cheeked face. "Would you . . . would you like to sell that filly? Money on the barrelhead?"

"Don't believe so today."

"She's as well-balanced an individual as I've ever seen, and she's got that good shoulder and that long stride. Have you ever measured it?"

"No, I haven't."

"You ought to. I'll bet every jump she covers twenty-five feet." Hemp dug the toe of one boot into the turf and looked up, canting an eye at Lee. "I'll give you five thousand for her . . . maybe more."

"That would be like selling one of my own family," Lee said, shaking his head. "Thanks just the same."

On the eve of the two-day elimination trials of the $500,000 Kansas Futurity at Ruidoso Downs, Boom Boom Chumley, on his fourth try, reached Hack Trent at his Houston motel.

"I've been calling you since early morning," the trainer said, unable to screen out a note of impatience from his voice.

"I got in an hour ago and that stupid jackass on the desk didn't tell me, else I'd called you. What's up?"

"The Kansas trials start tomorrow and continue through Friday," Chumley said, searching for the trainer-to-owner tone he liked to convey, neither discouraging nor effusively optimistic. His stomach was acting up again and he felt wretched.

"I know that," Trent said bluntly.

Boy, what a stud-horse disposition, Chumley thought. Managing a forced conversational ease, he said, "I think we're all set except for Gem Three and Reb's Rocket. Right now The Gem is hurting. He's got both legs packed in ice and he's hanging his head. He's had his Bute, so he feels a little better than he did this morning when we walked him around. He was stiff and swollen. He'll get Bute again tomorrow to reduce the inflammation. . . . He runs Friday in the second heat and it's been raining. If the swelling won't go down, I'll have the vet drain off the fluid. If The Gem comes around, we'll send him to the track. If not, I think we ought to scratch him."

"That would be a big personal disappointment to me, Chumley. You know what I paid for that colt at the All-American Yearling Sale—thirty thousand dollars."

"I understand. But, Hack, we have to keep in mind that we're pointing The Gem for the All-American. He's your best two-year-old, the most consistent runner you have, after the way he looked losing the Sun Country Futurity by a nose to Easy Injun. Hula Moon's in Friday, too. Ninth heat. Regardless of how The Gem feels tomorrow, it might pay to rest him at least till the Rainbow."

"I'll have to think about that. What about the others?"

"High Cloud, Hey Now, and Going Thing all run tomorrow. Friday, it's Bunny Barbara and On Time."

"You didn't say what's wrong with Reb's Rocket."

"I was coming to that. Reb is definitely out. Same old problem —bone chips. That colt should never have been run in those yearling futurities. But he only hurts when he runs," Chumley said, trying for the light touch. "In my judgment, we need to ship him to Texas A and M . . . put him under the knife. He might come back. He's well bred."

Trent groaned. "I'd hate to figure up how much I've got tied up in my racing operations. Close to half a million, anyhow. Too damn many leg problems. That reminds me, Chumley. I don't want any trouble at the test barn. Are you registering all medication with the track vet?"

Chumley's stomach seemed to twist. He wasn't about to chase

the vet down every time he wanted to give a horse some Bute when it was legal. He said, "After what I'm just coming off of with the Commission? You bet I am." It was time to change the subject. "We're getting a break in the trials. Everybody is. New system this year. Be fifteen trials each day. They'll take the top five qualifiers by time each day, instead of as they did last year, putting the twenty-five fastest each day into a second set of trials."

"What are our chances?"

"As good as anybody's—no better, no worse. You have to keep in mind that a total of three hundred horses will be going after those ten spots in the finale."

"You don't have to remind me," Trent said sourly. "You just get us in there."

Chumley felt like laughing. He was on to Trent by now. Pressure, pressure. Push a man, keep pushing. Never let up on the poor bastard. "Why, Hack," he said, and it wasn't every day that you could call a millionaire by his first name, "as unpredictable as horses are, looking great one minute, hurt or sick the next, I wouldn't promise you we'd even make the post parade."

"I expect you to do a damn sight better than Si Queen did. Another thing. I happen to know that post position is everything at Ruidoso when the track is sloppy. What did The Gem draw?"

"The seven hole."

"And Hula Moon?"

"Eight hole."

"Godamighty, Chumley, don't you realize the advantage the outside gives us—one length over the inside horses in them deep lanes? You said it's been raining out there."

"You mean *if* The Gem is right," Chumley corrected, "and *if* Hula Moon doesn't throw a fit in the gate. She's a bad gate horse, Hack. I've worked and worked with her. If she ever learns to behave herself, she could be a runner. If not, she's a canner."

"All right, all right. If she keeps on that way, maybe we can still breed a profit out of her. What did the rest draw?"

"Not so good. Hey Now—the two hole. High Cloud—the rail. No chance there. Going Thing—same position. Bunny Barbara and On Time drew into the same heat on Friday. She's in the four hole, he's in three. If she can get outside a little bit, she could do something, way she's been working. She's on the improve and she's got a lot of will to run. I like that filly. On Time? Well, he needs to mature. Enough said."

"You make it sound tough."

"It is. I don't like it that the Sun Country and the Kansas trials come so close together, with the futurity only a little more than two weeks after the trials on June fourth. The Gem needs the rest. But that's the way it is." Chumley wanted to say, "That's the way it is because that's the way you planned it—run, run, run, and by God, you wouldn't change it if they all broke down."

"That twenty-three grand The Gem took home in the Sun Country was a mighty pleasing tune to this ol' country boy. Don't forget that."

More of that country-boy crap, Chumley thought. "Yeah," he said, "money talks."

"What horses we got to worry about, mainly?"

"Rest of the field."

"Damn it, be specific. I've been on the go. I can't keep up with every broomtail in the Southwest. I want the rundown."

They were on the brink of shouting at each other. Chumley sensed that and didn't care. Then, calming himself, he said, "I'll bet a hundred to one right now that a horse we never heard of sets the fastest qualifying time. As for the known runners, ones I know can knock a hole in the wind . . . there's that Easy Injun colt. We know about him, plenty. He's already got a money line that would choke a Missouri mule. . . . There's that filly Dial Me, who topped the All-American Sale. She's got a money line of forty thousand after winning the West Texas Futurity. . . . There's See You Soon—a gelding—six wins so far in six starts. Took the Rocky Mountain Futurity. There's . . ."

"All right. Now, about The Gem. Here's what I want you to do. If his legs come down, run 'im. Tell me if I'm wrong."

"It depends on what's more important to you, the Kansas Futurity or the All-American. Gem Three needs rest."

"Just remember we're not running a riding academy for the public. This is a competitive business."

Chumley didn't argue, weary of the circling talk, wishing now that he hadn't made the call, instead had waited until after the trials.

"You hear me, Chumley? Speak up!"

Chumley had heard every word, but he said, "This connection's not very good. What did you say?"

"I said we're not running a riding academy—that this is a competitive business. And something more. It would be nice to win the first leg of the Triple Crown for two-year-olds. With The Gem in that good outside lane, he'll qualify all right. He's a class colt. You know he can run with the best."

"That's the trouble, Hack. He's been run too much and too early."

A knocking on the motel door interrupted. Trent said, "Hold on, Chumley," and clomped across. A boy waited with a bucket of ice. "Over there," Trent said, motioning. Back to the phone, he was about to answer when he saw the boy tarrying for his tip. Trent started to ignore him, thought better of it, and digging for change, flipped a coin at him. The boy, making a deft catch on the wing, glanced down in disbelief at the dime and made a display of his disgust as he sulked out.

Trent said, "Do you read me straight, Chumley? Do you? If the swelling comes down, The Gem runs. Tell me if I'm wrong."

"I've already told you what I think, but he's your colt. I'll call you Friday evening. Where'll you be?"

"Right here," Trent said, and hung up, rather pleased with the way he had handled Chumley, who talked back more than Si Queen ever had. Chumley was also a superior trainer, more experienced. Knew how to point a horse for the big stakes races. They had come within a nose in the Sun Country, bad knees and all. The horse business was no different from any other. You either booted some butts and made your people get out there and compete, or they sat back and profits failed to accrue.

Trent glanced at his watch, thinking, She oughta be here by now.

He was taking a bottle of ten-year-old Bourbon, 100 proof, from his suitcase when he heard a light rap at the door. He fairly bounced over there. Grinning, he opened the door and saw a shapely woman clad in matching yellow halter top and shorts. He sized her up and down without speaking, liking her class. She still looked like the attractive, middle-class housewife she used to be.

"I thought maybe you'd forgotten me," she said, a teasing in her purring voice. Her green eyes behind the huge sunglasses were wide and lustrous.

"You don't know ol' Hank. Come in, doll."

Leaving the phone booth, Chumley walked to his pickup and sat in moody silence, his mind juggling Trent's orders against his own professional judgment. Gem Three was in no condition to run—that was certain. The chestnut colt wouldn't be, even after the vet drew off the fluid, which would have to be done. The Gem needed rest, lots of rest. Rest meant time and time was a luxury. Bute helped, but it wasn't a cure. It could make a horse feel better than he was; by the same token, it could make a horse overextend himself, unaware of his injuries, causing him to put too much pressure on a bad ankle or knee—in short, to break down. Ice packs tightened muscles and tendons and eased pain, but that practice also made fragile bones dangerously brittle. Racing came down to a brutal crush of economics: training, feeding, stabling, doctoring, often long-distance hauling—and luck. You had to win to stay in it, and even millionaires didn't like to go on losing money indefinitely.

There was another aspect to running in the Kansas trials. The Gem, as Chumley liked to refer to the colt, was the best juvenile he had ever trained. Maybe the best he would ever have in his stable. Had the greatest potential as a stakes horse. Consistently ran the quarter in twenty-two seconds and very small change, as the saying went, and he could gun it under twenty-two seconds— when he wasn't hurting and resentful. A do-everything horse. Good in the gates. Shotgun getaway. Plenty of early lick. A driving finisher. Good mudder. But only one man could train a race-horse. What if The Gem broke down in the trials?

Chumley turned that over in his mind. He was still in debt after that long suspension, another factor to take into consideration. If The Gem broke down, that would be the end of the season so far as big stakes money was concerned, because the other youngsters, with the possible exception of the promising Bunny Barbara and the unpredictable Hula Moon, likely wouldn't do much. Why not bring The Gem along carefully and shoot for the All-American—the world's richest horse race—$1 million plus—every trainer's dream of winning? Let the Kansas and the Rainbow futurities go? These days the winning trainer took home some $33,000 or more. Equally important to a trainer was the cumulative effect. Horsemen coming to you with their fast futurity hopefuls, and their proven threes for shots at the bulging derby purses. Until you had thirty or forty head, all well bred; then narrowing and culling to a stable of consistent winners. He could see it all opening up if he won the All-American: Sunland, Ruidoso, Los Alamitos, Bay Meadows. Name it.

What was it Trent was continually blowing about, as if he had a corner on it? Class. Yeah, class. That's what the All-American was, the classiest race of all.

Chumley started the motor and drove toward town, thinking of an unhurried dinner, feeling better than he had in weeks.

Only one man could train a racehorse.

Chapter 8

Other than soring up, Cindy had come off the hard-knocking Anadarko sprint as sound as ever. By doing his own galloping, Lee was in position to judge her development and iron out little problems. The shadow roll, used for the first time at Anadarko, seemed to help. She was running lower, filling out, maturing fast, as fillies do, and, Lee thought, she's found out who she is and what she's supposed to do when the gate opens. She knows where the finish line is. She's learned that racing is more than a pasture game. Gone was the green, bewildered youngster at Wildhorse Downs, the hesitant filly at Stroud, as full of play as she was of run. Wisely, he felt, following Cal's experienced suggestion, he had not experimented with blinkers. Blinkers, Cal said, were for an erratic or nervous horse and, Cindy, being neither, had learned by now to concentrate straight ahead.

Lee was hopeful for her, but, superstitiously, did not say he was. Another outing would tell him more and advance her training. With Midway Downs booked full, he drew into a 350-yard allowance at Eureka, Kansas, the first week in May.

"I'd like to see her run one time without trouble," he mused, driving north with Cal and Doug in the pickup, Cal's veteran pony horse, Booger Red, in the trailer with Cindy. "She never causes it. Trouble seems to come to her."

"I'd like to see you make her a late entry in the All-American," Doug said. "What is it they call that?"

"Supplemental nominee. Means the same." He added ruefully, "Also the same big hunk of money."

Doug's voice took on a dreamy tone. "World's richest horse race—richer than the Kentucky Derby, the Preakness, and the Belmont—the world's fastest quarter horses going four hundred and forty yards. Be a thrill to ride in that."

"I don't dare think about Ruidoso yet," Lee said, quite serious. "Main reason, we don't know how fast she can run that distance. To stand a chance in the All-American, she'd have to cut it around twenty-two flat or less. Winning time last year was 21.75. You have to run close to twenty-two flat even to get into the final go. I'm talking about on a dry track. And she's never run in the mud, which you often have to do at Ruidoso. We don't know how she'd do on a heavy track."

"Well, she ran herself one hell of a four hundred yards at Anadarko," Cal put in. "She finished strong. She can go that four-forty and plenty more, I tell you. Right now she's a twenty-second horse at four hundred. She's a runnin' horse, Lee."

"You make me feel optimistic, and you make me pull up when I think about how much heavy cash it would take. It's still too early, Cal."

"Why wait? That June supplemental payment is less than half what it takes on August fifteenth. And you may never have another filly like her."

Lee withheld a reply. After what had happened to Landy, he guessed he was still afraid for her, still uncertain. In addition, thinking of the size of the supplemental money flat scared him.

Turning east from El Dorado for Eureka, Lee saw the sky, overcast since they had crossed the Kansas line, changing to a darker hue. A line of inkish clouds lay across their path. The wind, just a whisper until now, was rising to gusts. The worn pickup labored every time the trailer jerked.

Lee flipped on the radio. As the half-hour news summary

ended, the crisp voice added, "Now for the weather. Scattered thunderstorms are predicted for central and eastern Kansas during the afternoon, with the possibility of hail and high winds. Highs will be in the upper nineties. Stay tuned for later details."

"Miss Cindy could get her first lesson in the mud," Lee said. He hadn't thought about that day in Columbus in a long time. Now it reappeared, heavy, portentous, and he decided that horsemen were too superstitious for their own good.

Pulling two horses instead of one and bucking the wind, they reached Eureka only half an hour before post time. While Lee checked in at the racing office, Doug led the filly around to relax her after the long haul that had begun in early morning darkness.

"I don't like this," Lee said, eyes on the darkening southwestern sky while they waited for the second race.

Thunder was rumbling and a light rain falling when the announcer called horses to the paddock for the allowance race. Donning Cal's slicker, Lee mounted Booger Red and led Cindy to the saddling paddock. They were hardly ready when Lee heard the voice on the loudspeaker: "Attention—horsemen in the second race. . . . Make the parade to post as brief as possible. . . . Go immediately to the gates, so we can hurry along. Thank you."

Before many moments the rain, slanting in from the southwest, became a wind-whipped drumming. By the time Lee was hurrying with the others for the gates, it changed to buckshot rain against a background of constant thunder. Circling in behind the gates, he jerked at a flash of jagged lightning off west. He thought, Lightning and metal gates. A bad combination. Eight uneasy horses.

The assistant starters hastened the loading. The 1 horse obliged. But the 2 and 3 horses were jumpy. That cost moments. Cindy, in number 4, caused no trouble, but she was trembling and taut. Five stepped in, as eager as its handlers. The 6 horse balked. They loaded him quickly, forcibly, two husky gatemen armlocked behind him, one at his head. Seven, a good-looking buckskin colt, entered nervously. He kept arching his back, wanting to buck. Rear hooves chattering now against the steel braking block at the rear of each gate. Number 8's handlers no more than had him pointed straight when the gates flew open.

Cindy and the next three horses on her right broke on top, off cleanly and quickly, heading into the gray teeth of the whipping downpour. Lee's tension eased. She looked in favorable position, running straight, showing no dislike for the wet track. Four horses charging head to head.

It happened without warning about one third of the way. A crackle of lightning. Very close, behind the stands, nerve-shattering, and the 7 horse, terrified, spooking away from it. Careening wildly, 7 slammed into the 6 horse, and the 6 horse into the 5 horse, and the 5 horse into Cindy, the horse on her left somehow untouched and squeezing by.

Lee swore. My God, was she going down?

Not yet. But Doug was pulling her up, knowing that she was out of the race. And, mercy, if she wasn't limping.

Six was down, its jockey flung overhead, and 5 was buckjumping all over the track. Seven didn't slow till he hit the rail. The colt bounced back, lost his rider. The colt broke down.

Paralyzed for an awful moment, Lee clapped heels to Booger Red and tore around the gates.

The 6 jockey was on his feet, dazed, his face a smear of mud. He groped toward his horse, which was struggling to rise and could not, one foreleg flopping like a rag doll's arm. Lee swore as he raced downtrack.

Doug was out of the saddle, holding the filly up close while she hobbled about.

"She got knocked around and stepped on," Doug called. "I tried to pull her up, but she kept wanting to run."

"It's all right, Doug. It's all right," Lee said, coming down from the saddle. "You okay?"

Doug could only nod miserably. "It's her. She's hurt. She's hurt bad."

Lee looked at her, sick at heart. Cindy's eyes were wild and baffled, as if she didn't understand what had happened. Lee took her bridle.

They started through the confusion toward the barns. An ambulance was coming, a low white blur against slanting gray rain. Horsemen, their voices high, were swarming onto the track. The 7 horse's jockey was up, staring helplessly at his mount, down and kicking. There wasn't a sound from the shocked stands.

As Lee led Cindy off the track, a big-eyed girl dressed like a barrel rider ran up and stopped by the outside rail and looked across, hands pressed to her mouth. Suddenly her face crumpled and she burst into tears. The buckskin, Lee guessed, sorry for her.

Cal was there when they hobbled to the barns. Lee unsaddled and took her inside the stall, and in dread crouched down to check her front legs. Rubbing with the hair below the left knee, he worked down beneath the ankle and found no heat or swelling. Turning to her right leg, he leaned in suddenly. "Part of her foot's broken off. Look!"

"It will grow back," said Cal, the calmest of the three. "Check that ankle, Lee."

Lee did that. "It's puffy and hot, and so is her cannon bone."

"Now the knee. Both the knees."

Lee examined the right knee, his hands gentle, there and above, along the heavily muscled forearm, on to the point of the shoulder, and the same on the upper left leg. "I think she's all right in that department," he said.

"I tried to ease her up after we got hit," Doug said, blaming himself. "Tried to keep her straight. Maybe I should have taken her to the left."

"You did exactly right," Lee assured him. "As it was, the inside horse just missed you. Two of those horses will have to be put down. That good-looking buckskin colt that started the trouble—the seven hole horse—and that six horse." As he shook his head, the impact of everything got to him and he stared long at his horse, his lips compressed. "It's hard to believe this could happen twice, just when you think you might have a real stakes runner."

"That's when it happens," Cal said, somber of face.

Lee looked at him, remembering the promising Bug colt that

Cal had lost as a two-year-old on the eve of the Kansas Futurity, and, in flashback, seeing the distraught girl weeping at the sight of her crippled horse. Purposefully, then, he set about examining Cindy's hind legs from hooves up through the gaskin area. Her legs felt cool. "She'll be sore for a while all along her right side," he said, running his hand over her stifle, thigh and hip, "but she seems sound back here."

"Would some leg brace help on that right foreleg?" Doug asked hopefully.

"There's an old saying about doctoring horses. 'Never put hot on hot.'" And Cal nodded. "First, we have to take the heat out. If we don't, the leg will blister. Let's take her outside and start cooling that leg. Doug, get a bucket of water and we'll soak bandages and wrap her leg and keep pouring water on it so the fever will go down."

Later, while they watched the tag ends of the fast-moving storm rumble on to the east, Lee said again, "I still can't believe this could happen twice."

"There's a difference," Cal insisted. "Her knees are okay. The hoof will heal and grow back. Take her home, pull her plates and turn her out. Give her some time. She's a runnin' horse."

Chumley reached Trent on the first call to Houston. He opened with, "Got some good news for you, Hack. We qualified two into the big finale and one in the first consolation. Hula Moon and Bunny Barbara made the main go. Hey Now, the first consolation."

Trent virtually exploded. "What happened to Gem Three?"

"Had to scratch him."

"What the hell you tellin' me?"

"That's right," Chumley said, holding his ground, while careful to sound disappointed. "The Gem's legs didn't come down from the swelling like I expected. Was afraid they wouldn't when I told you. I sure hated to scratch that colt, I tell you."

"That's one helluva note, Chumley."

"He'll shape up in time." It was never wise, when dealing with owners, to stay on bad news any longer than it took to tell it.

"Wish you could have seen Hula Moon. A different filly. For once, she behaved in the gate and got off without running over everybody. Won by daylight. Posted the fourth fastest time— 18.24. She'd been under that, easy, but for a head wind. . . . Bunny Barbara got outside like I hoped she would. Finished like she was shot out of a gun. Fifth fastest time. . . . Hey Now is on the improve. Missed the top ten by just three one-hundredths. I hope you're satisfied."

"I'm never satisfied. But I got to say I'm pleased, except for Gem Three."

"Will you be here for the futurity?"

"I'll be in western Oklahoma. Got some deep gas tests goin' out there."

"Where can I reach you?" Now, why hadn't Trent said?

"Elk City. Pioneer Motel."

"I'll call you as soon as I can after the race. Keep your fingers crossed."

"You keep yours," Trent said.

Chumley hung up on him, swearing silently. You ungrateful s.o.b., you non-person, and turned to meet the upraised eyes of Dr. Victor Witt, the Ruidoso Downs track veterinarian. Witt said, "Did I hear you say Gem Three's legs did not respond to treatment? That's why you scratched him?"

"You heard right. But if you ever tell Hack Trent otherwise, I'll swear you're lying. You know the colt needs rest."

"A great many of them do, but they still run. They're professional athletes—and athletes learn to compete with pain. If we kept every horse off the track that hurt, there wouldn't be any races. Moreover, one of my jobs is to hold a race together after it's filled. We owe the public something."

"Now, Vic," Chumley said, spreading his hands, "would I call from your office if I wanted to hide something?"

"Just curious, is all." Doc Witt reminded Chumley of an ascetic in monk's robes. Slim-bodied. Slim-featured. Studious, serious brown eyes. Receding gray-streaked hair. A thin mouth pressed into a line. Thick glasses. Behind that disciplined front, however, lay the experienced eyes of a keen observer, an amused mocking of human nature and its many frailties, and where could you find a more evident gamut of hopes and failures, of gambling short cuts and, once in a while, phenomenal payoffs, than at Ruidoso Downs? The sardonic lips stirred again. "Could be I'm looking at the new Boom Boom Chumley, interested in preservation of *Equus caballus.*"

"Don't get me confused with some bleeding heart from the animal shelter."

"I doubt that any of us could rate that."

"Especially somebody accused of stealing test samples at Sunland?"

Witt tendered him an askance look. "Your candor is disarming, Mel. You've never been one to hide your head when trouble hits. You meet it straightaway and let the world be the judge."

"Why not? Everybody thought I shot up the horse and stole the evidence, didn't they?"

"Eh, now. I do believe you're feeling sorry for yourself."

"Me?" Chumley flared. "I don't give a damn what people think."

Witt took out a sack of Bull Durham and rolled a cigarette. For a precise man, he wasn't expert at it, spilling a good portion of the loose tobacco. He said, "Of course you care, or you wouldn't say that," and thumbnailed a match and touched fire, inhaled and let smoke funnel from aquiline nostrils. "What the fellow who stole the shipment didn't know was that urine specimens are always split at the test barn. Just a mere precaution, you know. Each sterilized sack is sealed and tagged with an identifying number. The sacks are then frozen to keep the contents unchanged. One of the samples is shipped to the State Racing Chemist's lab in Albuquerque. The other is kept at the test barn. The procedure isn't generally known, I guess."

"But it is. I've known about it for years. It's in the American Quarter Horse Association Regulations."

"Not about the split specimens. The regulations, in general, just say there shall be cooling and freezing of all urine specimens, and the track shall make provisions for them to be shipped to the lab packed in dry ice in locked and sealed cases."

Chumley shrugged. "A trainer knowing that would be a fool to steal the shipment, wouldn't he?"

"He would."

"That points to a frame. Somebody trying to discredit another trainer."

"Obviously. Though I wonder about the motivation."

"I can name you plenty. Jealousy. Wanting the other man's string. Trouble over a woman. Somebody outslicked in a horse deal. A disgruntled groom or jock. Who knows? I was framed. At the time, you may remember, I was leading trainer at Sunland."

"Know who did it?"

"I think so, but I can't be positive. If I told you, I might be smearing another man's name."

"You're more considerate than I would be." Witt's expression was not disbelieving, only dry and wondering. He reflected a moment. "We may have to come to a receiving-barn operation, such as they have in California, where all horses entered in a race are secluded in the barn twenty-four hours before they run. Only the trainers are allowed inside."

"Sounds expensive."

"It is. But it would protect the trainers. Protect everybody. It also would pinpoint the problem, put it squarely on the trainer's back, if a horse showed up wrong."

"Somebody would still try to slip in and fix a horse."

"But the barn makes it a lot tougher. It's bettors who talk the most about a race being fixed. They mean the order of finish. They complain in that vein after losing everything but their jock shorts at the track, or blaming what they call a sorry horse or rider. You know and I know it would be impossible to get ten trainers and ten riders to agree on a fix. It's impossible to get that many people to agree on the time of day."

"Amen, Doc."

"On the other hand," Witt continued, waving a lumpy cigarette, "the outcome of a race can be greatly influenced through drugs. Ritalin is an example. It can stimulate a horse to rip right through a field."

"Such as in the Pan Zareta Stakes?"

"You're interrupting my lecture." He smiled with tolerance. "Or a trainer can tell a jock to pull a horse so he'll look slow, which creates a higher betting price later when the horse runs up to his true speed index and wins."

"Believe I've heard tell of that," Chumley said, grinning lop-sidedly.

"It's the bettors who disgust me. I mean the ones who care lit-tle about the horses. They come just to bet, hoping they get rich. I have no respect for those people, even though they help make racing possible. They ought to go to Las Vegas."

"Then why do you stay in this?"

"I know nothing else. I've always been around horses. My fa-ther was a vet in Missouri—and a darned good one, too. His fa-ther was a trottin' horse man . . . owned and trained a gutty old horse called Red Cloud. Perhaps I ought to say the Witts don't know any better. It's in us. Part of our vulnerability. . . . See this left jaw of mine, how it's out of line? A stud did that when I turned my back on him. No warning. Tried to kill me. Knocked me down. Pawed me. Fractured my skull. Broke an arm and a leg. Though I was lucky at that. . . . Horses fascinate me, chal-lenge me. I don't love horses, yet they fascinate me. Their beauty. Their structure, their fragility. Thousand-pound-plus bodies making pistons of legs built to carry half that. It's a chal-lenge to me to bring an ailing horse back so he can run. This morning I fired a Thoroughbred . . . not so much to correct an injury, but to get the horse off the track for a spell because the trainer wouldn't rest him. That horse will run again. Give him three weeks, he'll be back." Witt's reasoning voice returned to his usual professional matter-of-factness. "I've watched Gem Three closely. He's a runner when he feels good. Frankly, I'm glad you scratched him for the Kansas. He could throw a leg off."

"Glad you agree. To tell you the truth, I doubt that he will even be ready for the Rainbow trials."

"Not afraid of Easy Injun, are you?"

"Hell, they all scare me."

"You wouldn't be the first trainer that saved his powder for one shot at that big pile of sugar on Labor Day."

"Isn't that what it's all about?" Chumley said, on a drift toward the door.

"Oh, by the way," Witt said, as if an afterthought had occurred to him, "everybody around the track ought to see that new lab of the State Racing Chemist's. It's really something. Very sophisticated. Computerized and everything. There's no way an illegal drug can be missed up there. No way."

Briefly, Chumley was resentful of the implication, then, grinning, he fed Witt some of his own mockery. "That's a great idea, Vic. Why don't you take us all on a tour up there as a sort of community deterrent to skulduggery?" he said, and went out, his concentration shifting back to Trent. The guy was impossible. Any other owner would be proud to have two horses in the Kansas finale, glad to know that you were extra careful with his top stakes horse. Anybody else. The s.o.b.

Only one man could train a racehorse.

Chapter 9

The blacktop highway narrowly flanking the winding Río Ruidoso still held puddles from a late afternoon shower, and the air
of the Sacramento Mountains swam with pungent odors. Catching his first heady scent of the pines, Todd Lawson could feel
the swell of anticipation. He inhaled to the bottom of his lungs,
savoring, remembering, and slowed the pickup. An impatient
honking sounded behind him and a Cadillac sedan barreled by
showing a Texas license. The broad-hatted driver waved. Todd
waved back. An Oklahoma car passed next. Texans and Okies,
he thought. Ruidoso is their playground and their racetrack. If
you don't believe that, mister, just stroll through the parking lots
at the Downs and count the cars and motor homes. And in the
cool of the early evening, like about now, see them sitting in
front of their motels, enjoying their Bourbon and scotch, the dry-
county Texans in particular. If you still don't believe me, mister,
just go to the fifty-dollar-win window any afternoon, or down to
the barns and see the well-bred quarter horses they've hauled in.

Nothing has changed much, he mused. Only Todd Lawson has
changed. Todd Lawson, whose mounts had won over three quarters of a million dollars that one big, wild, unbelievable, disas-
trous year on the tracks from New Mexico to California, now

with seventy-five dollars and a used pickup-camper to his name. But I've never felt freer, he thought. Once you've hit the bottom, the only way back is that lonely road you must travel on your own. He drove on, alternately retreating into the past, then projecting into the future. Nothing has changed, he decided wryly, except Todd Lawson and the size of the purses.

Passing through the village of Ruidoso Downs, the river on his right now, he began to notice more houses than he remembered. He passed the track, becalmed at this hour, soon passed the Y where Highway 70 from Alamogordo came in, and drove up-canyon for Ruidoso itself, past a new shopping center and supermarket, a clutter of small shops, filling stations, drive-in burger stops, and real estate offices. Traffic thickened. A busy restaurant caught his eye: Babe's Place, Mexican Food Our Speciality. It looked inviting. Already crowded. He overcame his hunger and drove on. Later, he thought. I've got to see the whole layout first.

One feature hadn't changed: Ruidoso's one traffic light on the main pathway, called Sudderth Drive. He stopped, waited for the light to change, and turned right, going down and up, and was soon climbing toward Alto, seeing more cottages, A-frame cabins, lodges and motels, more town houses in the distance. When the highway broadened, he turned around and stopped. Lights were blinking on below. A valley of lights. Lights along the mountain sides, lights downcanyon as far as he could see.

The Ruidoso he remembered, named for the lovely little mountain stream the Spaniards called Noisy Water, had grown from a village into a town. No, it hadn't grown, it had exploded. He continued to watch, enjoying the scented coolness, hearing the muted growl of traffic from below, content within himself. Peace of mind, he thought. Nothing equals it. Nothing is as needed. The shoulder harness he wore beneath his shirt was itching his chest and he scrubbed vigorously under the awkward apparatus.

After several minutes, he turned on the pickup's lights and drove down the mountain to Babe's Place, wedging in between a green Lincoln Continental and a bevy of motorcycles with loaded luggage racks. Entering, he found an opening at the counter, took off his cowboy hat and started reading the menu.

"Be with you in a minute," a hurrying waitress said.

"I'm in no rush," he said, and glanced around.

Babe's Place wasn't large as restaurants went in Ruidoso, some remindful of dining halls, needed to serve the thousands of race-goers flocking in on the big race weekends. But informal and clean, the decorations in harmony with the cuisine. An adobe fireplace on the west side. Painted gourds hanging by the windows. A colorful bullfighting oil on the north wall. Here and there framed black-and-white photos of racehorses. One of a bald-faced horse drew his eyes a second time. Parking his hat on the stool, he crossed over and looked. It was Kiowa Bar in the winner's circle. Old Man Henderson at the bridle. Kiowa Bar. A grandson of the great Three Bars. A real running machine. Guts galore. Todd gazed wistfully at the horse and hardly recognized the jockey's exuberant face, he looked so young.

Unexpectedly warmed, he returned to the counter and resumed his idle looking. No jocks in here that he recognized. About this time they would be hanging out at the Villa Cantina. This evening's customers were mostly middle-aged tourists or older. Overweight, gray-haired men and their overweight wives in comfortable sportswear. A few younger couples and their children, the kids' voices clear and pleasant to the ear. Four young men he took for bikers occupied one table. They ate voraciously. Shaggy young men in the uniform of their cult, denim jackets and jeans.

Thinking again of the bald-faced horse, he remembered when he would come in—or was it saunter, then?—come into places like this or bigger with Eve on his arm, every man's eyes trailing her, and people would wave and call out and men would come over and shake your hand and slap you on the back and say sure glad to see you, Todd, and that was a great ride today, Todd, and I sure bet the jockey today, Todd. Texans and Okies flashing belt buckles as big as headlights, some of solid turquoise ringed in silver. Their well-dressed women smiling at you, looking bent over under the weight of squash-blossom necklaces.

Reaching back, he discovered no bitterness. He was a different person then as he was a different person now.

"I can take your order," a woman's voice brought him back.

He turned and scanned the menu again. "I'll have the beef *burritos*, with salad and coffee, please."

"I'm sorry. We're out. Seems everybody is eating *burritos* tonight. I can recommend the *chiles rellenos*." She was looking directly at him, somewhat curiously, he thought.

"Sounds good. I'll have *rellenos*, with an order of pinto beans."

"And salad and coffee?"

He nodded, aware that her eyes were big and brown, wide set in a fine-boned face that a man would look at again and again. She went quickly away and his attention followed her. Gold-colored hair knotted tightly behind her neck. She was trim and small, yet not slight, her short, tight skirt revealing smooth hips and shapely legs and neat ankles. As a veteran horseman might judge, Good balance. Good conformation. She wasn't young in years, as he was no longer young, but that body and clean look would keep her young long after prettier women had grown lumpish and old. A nice woman. You could tell.

He saw her pause before a table near the kitchen, her hands busy, and glance back at him. That curious look.

Caught, he turned his head away. He guessed she was used to stares. A nice, attractive woman like her.

She served him a bowl of *salsa* and a basket of *tortillas* cut in triangular shapes. He dipped into the red sauce and got an instant sensation of hot, red hot, New Mexico hot, and nodded. Just right.

And the cheese-stuffed chiles, covered with a crispy egg batter, served with lively tomato sauce, were also just right. Likewise, the beans, with a further seasoning of red chiles. He dug in hungrily, his first meal since morning, conscious of a steady coming and going. The woman seemed everywhere: at the cash register, speaking to some customers by name, at the kitchen window giving orders, or directing the two girl waitresses, one Anglo, one Mexican, or the long-haired busboy clearing tables. Throughout the comfortable disorder, which seemed almost organized, she remained unruffled, at the right place when needed.

For dessert, she served him a basket of *sopaipillas* and a plastic squeeze bottle of honey, which he spread on the still-warm fried biscuit puffs. Finished, he dawdled over another cup of black coffee and considered where he might park the pickup for sleeping.

Paying his check, he noticed a hand-printed sign over a little box that read: Babe's Tips $1. The box was empty. Suddenly he remembered. He'd forgotten the tipsters' sheets. Used to be half a dozen or more. You'd see them all over town.

"Give my respects to your chef," he said to the woman. "The *chiles rellenos* were great."

She smiled. "Estela will be pleased to hear that. She's proud of her cooking." Her eyes on him were curious again. "Did you see the Kansas Futurity today?" she asked, her tone saying she knew that he had.

"I just got in. Who won?"

She was about to answer when Todd heard chairs scraping loudly behind him and saw her gaze lift questioningly toward the doorway. Her mouth fell open, then firmed. The brown eyes flashed. "Excuse me," she said, and moved quickly along the counter. Turning, Todd saw her striding to intercept the four bikers.

They saw her but did not pause. She reached the door first. "I don't believe you gentlemen have paid your checks," she said distinctly, facing them.

They pretended utter astonishment and stared wonderingly at one another. One snickered. They all snickered.

"I said you haven't paid your checks." She was icy calm.

"It's on the house," one replied, baring a curling grin. He loomed over her, a bulky, loose-lipped man in his middle twenties.

"You know better than that," she told him.

"We always eat on the house."

"You don't here. You either pay or I'll call the police." She folded her arms.

The busy room stilled.

As if highly entertained, the four slouched nearer the door.

She held her ground, blocking their exit. "You're not getting out of here without paying," she said, growing very pale.

They shuffled to a halt, their grins fading. The spokesman looked down at her, his manner and size intimidating. "Get out of the way," he said.

She didn't move.

The spokesman laid a hand on her shoulder. Furiously, she dashed it off. He grabbed to shove her aside. At once they were struggling.

Todd didn't remember getting up. But suddenly he was over there. He yanked on the man's jacket and spun him backward, at the same time seeing the other three bikers closing on him. The woman screamed in warning. Todd threw a left-hand punch. It took the lead man fully on the jaw. His eyes flew wide with surprise as he reeled backward. But there were still three of them and the spokesman came bulling back. Todd punched the man's middle, felt his fist sink into squashy softness, saw the man recoil in pain. The others rushed Todd. One slipped to his right. Instinctively protecting his right shoulder, Todd wheeled to meet that threat and threw his left again, knowing that he was leaving himself open.

His fist struck a face. Blood spattered like Ruidoso Downs mud. At that instant Todd's head seemed to burst with blinding lights and he felt himself crashing down, down, taking blow after blow. Dimly, he could hear the woman screaming at them and feet scrambling around him. Her outraged voice was the last sound he heard.

Boom Boom Chumley's efficiency apartment was near the Y, therefore providing handy access to the track, and therefore expensive. He particularly appreciated its proximity this very minute, spent after the strain of yesterday's consolation and today's running of the Kansas Futurity. For the first time in a long time he could afford to relax and think about the future. Counting yesterday and today, his trainer's 10 per cent of the winnings amounted to slightly more than $6,700, every cent of which he had more than earned, putting up with Trent, and which he could now afford to bank, all of it. More and more these recent weeks, he had found himself thinking of the little horse ranch coming up for sale on the other side of the mountains near Carrizozo. It was like a dream, a refuge. If a man could make a sizable downpayment, maybe the bank . . .

The phone shrilled as he was unlocking the apartment door. Sensing who it was, he didn't hurry.

"I couldn't wait," Hack Trent all but shouted, as if that would make the scratchy-sounding connection clearer. "I'm in Oklahoma City. Been stuck way out in western Oklahoma in the boondocks. How'd we come out, Chumley?"

"We won a hunk of money. We ran second. Bunny Barbara ran a real gutty race. Won herself a cool fifty thousand. I'm proud of that little filly. She's gonna be super as a three-year-old. I was just getting ready to put in a call. Just now came in."

"Why didn't you call from the track?" Trent asked, as if what's a mere fifty grand, Chumley?

"In that mob? Besides, you told me you'd be in Elk City. Wait a minute, Hack." He laid down the receiver, paced to the dresser, shook out a couple of the white pills from a bottle, which unfortunately he had forgotten to take to the track, and chewed them bit by bit. Let the old boy wait. Trent's aggressive voice was plainly audible as he continued to talk. Laughable, Chumley thought. As if anybody—*anybody*—would tell Hack Trent to wait a minute. Feeling better, he lagged back to the phone. "Had to take some pills," he said. "Your horses are wrecking my health, Hack."

"Who won the race?" Trent demanded, as if never mind your health, Chumley.

Chumley cleared his throat, tense despite his self-coaching. "Easy Injun. A neck win. Another jump our filly'd tied it to him. She was gaining every stride when they crossed the wire, believe you me."

"What did Hula Moon do?" As if never mind that Bunny Barbara had run a close second, Chumley.

"Messed up in the gate. Same old habit. Coming out, she

junked her jock and ran off. If a filly ever needed to grow up, she does. I'm disgusted with her. We oughta take her out of training till next year or send her to the Alpo factory. She's tearing me up." What Trent didn't know was that when Hula Moon was finely tuned and behaving herself, she could outrun both Bunny Barbara and Hey Now, everything in the stable with the exception of The Gem. At this stage she wasn't earning her keep, of which Trent was well aware. Why not stress that to Trent, then at the end of the season buy her off him for a song? If brought along carefully, she could develop into a hot derby contender. A likely stakes star in the Chumley Stables. The thought passed through his mind as he switched to a positive note. "You haven't heard all the good news. Hey Now ran himself a real sizzler yesterday. Won the first consolation by daylight. That's worth seventeen thousand. How's that for two days at the track?"

"Not bad."

Not bad. Any other owner would be overjoyed. If there was any genuine pride and thanks in the oilman's gravelly voice, Chumley couldn't detect it. The s.o.b.! He wanted the winner. Place money wasn't enough, and first consolation wasn't enough. And he wanted his pride in there, Gem Three. Getting a hold on himself, he said, "I'm hoping Bunny Barbara and Hey Now can qualify for the Rainbow."

There was no reply. Chumley spoke again. Trent wasn't on the line. Was that a woman's voice in the background? Well, it wouldn't be the first time. The old boy was quite a swinger for his age. Almost inaudibly, Chumley heard Trent say, "Put it over there, Connie." Chumley strained for more, but heard no more. Connie? That was the Little Rock woman Trent had mentioned at Dallas in an unguarded moment. Said she was bugging him. Chumley couldn't blame her. He could sympathize with her. He pitied her. He wondered what she was like. What she looked like. In a way, they were both in the same boat, vainly trying to satisfy the ego of a rich man from the wrong side of the tracks, no pun intended.

"What was that now?" Trent came on.

"I said I hope Bunny Barbara and Hey Now can qualify for the Rainbow."

"Sure, sure. Say, what was Easy Injun's time?"

"Let's see . . . uh. It was 18.41."

"Godamighty, Chumley, Gem Three can run that fast backwards in the mud."

"The Injun was bucking a head wind and the track was slow. That's fast time for three-fifty under those conditions."

"All right. Now what I want to know is will Gem Three be ready for the Rainbow trials early in July?"

"I can't promise you he will. He'll have to show me more than he did this morning. We worked him lightly. He's still hurting."

"I want him in the trials if at all possible. Understand?"

"Do you have to remind me? Remember, I can't put The Gem on a hydraulic lift and run a new set of front wheels under him." The colt was improving, but why tell Trent? "The track vet says The Gem's pathology is enough to make you want to get religion. Did you know the sesamoids in his right front ankle have a big buildup of calcium?"

"How would I know?" Trent replied crossly.

"Didn't Si Queen tell you?"

"Si Queen was always crying hard luck, but he never told me that."

"Well, the vet says The Gem's got the sesamoids of an eight-year-old claimer." Sometimes it was wise to exaggerate a horse's ailments. Helped keep an overambitious owner in line, besides providing you with an alibi if the horse failed to light up the board. "He says we've got to be real careful—and lucky—if we bring The Gem back to his peak. He says the colt shouldn't be pressured between now and the All-American trials."

"You sound like a funeral director."

"Just telling you how it is, Hack. No more, no less."

"Let me tell you something, Chumley. In any business, it pays to take a positive attitude. Talk negative, you get negative results." They could be back in Big D, Trent in his corporate, statistical voice. *Burgers and fries.*

"I can't be any more positive than bone and muscle will allow."

"A horse can be trained to the utmost of his ability."

"A horse is not a product. He's a pure gamble out there. A thousand-pound missile on pipestem legs."

"If a horse has the breeding, he should produce."

"What do you call sixty-seven thousand in purse money? Those young horses ran their guts out for you." Chumley was breathing fast, his insides were bouncing and his self-control was ebbing fast. *Burgers and fries! Oil wells and Cadillacs!* Aggrieved, he burst out, "If you don't like the way I train your horses, get another man!"

"Take it easy, Chumley. I didn't say you haven't produced—you have. My one disappointment is Gem Three." A pat on the head now, Chumley. Good little boy. Press the flesh. Pressure, pressure, then let up, after show and tell at the staff meeting for the new breed of entrepreneur trying to cut a swath in the quarter racing world. And have a good day.

Chumley bit back further hot words.

Trent said, "I guess we've gone over about everything. Tell me if I'm wrong."

"I've told you all I know tonight," Chumley said wearily. "I'll be in touch."

"That was a good report, Chumley. We're both on the same team. Good night."

Chumley could picture Trent by the phone, a drink clutched in one big, hairy hand, the other around the woman. Chumley pitied her anew. *Good luck, Connie. You're gonna need it.*

Todd Lawson opened his eyes on an expanse of white. Sky, he supposed. No, not sky. Not really. Needed some blue up there. It didn't matter. He hurt too much to care. Every time he breathed he hurt. Thinking was an effort. He was, he discovered by slow degrees, flat on his back, staring up at white ceiling . . . that's what it was. Smells registered in a shock wave: all too familiar hospital smells, which jarred him alert.

"You're feeling better." A woman's pleasant voice.

He turned his head, even that slight movement bringing a rush of pain, and saw her sitting by a window, hands clasped in her lap. The gold-haired woman of the restaurant.

He mumbled, "I feel like a punching bag," his voice sounding dim and strange, unlike his own.

"You have a concussion, several cracked ribs and multiple bruises. You will be all right, but you must stay quiet."

Concussion? Cracked ribs? He'd heard that before. His head throbbed like a drum. He felt his face; it was swollen and hurt at his touch. His left eye was partially closed. He was a solid ache through his neck and back and left shoulder and down his left arm and tightly taped rib cage. After a bad spill, the licks you had taken always hurt more the second day. Fortunately, he had shielded his right shoulder; it alone felt normal, thanks to the harness. Little by little, his mind backtracked to the Mexican restaurant, replaying bits of scenes like slides on a projector: the informal atmosphere, the busy woman here and there, the horse photos, the satisfying dinner, and then . . .

"Oh, yes," he said, "the bikers."

"You tried to stop them. They got away. They beat you dreadfully. They knocked you out. I'm so sorry."

"Where am I?"

"The Hondo Valley Hospital in Ruidoso."

That gave him a start. "Since when?"

"Yesterday evening."

"I've been out that long?"

"You've been under sedation. The doctor says you must rest."

"How long?"

"He didn't say." She smiled. "But you needn't look so restless. And it's time we got acquainted. I'm Babe Younger. I run the restaurant."

"Glad to know you, Babe . . . and thanks. However, I don't need all this attention." For some reason he withheld his name.

"You do need it. And you . . . you're Todd Lawson."

That seemed of no importance whatever at the moment, yet he was vaguely pleased. "So what's new?"

"The police looked in your billfold for identification, but I already knew or thought I did."

He sat up a notch, found that too much, and sank back as her face blurred before his eyes. "How's that?" he asked, feeling drowsy.

"I remembered you. I saw you ride Kiowa Bar when he won the Rainbow Futurity. Quite a race. He drew the number two hole on a heavy track and you took him between two horses to the outside. He was going away at the finish." Her eyes shone. "That was some ride."

His face cracked into a grin that pained the muscles on the left side. "The jock always looks good when he's on a fast horse that runs when you ask him to. Glad you have Kiowa's picture up, so people won't forget. He was the first quarter horse to come close to winning the Triple Crown. Tiny's Gay was the last. Kiowa was coming into his own as a three-year-old when a virus got him. . . . I thought a lot of that horse. He always ran his best." Despite wishing to listen to her, he was drifting off to sleep.

She left the chair to stand by his bed. "I'm letting you talk too much. When you wake up this afternoon, I'll take you home to rest."

"Home?"

"My home. There's plenty of room. I owe you that, at least."

Her insistence alarmed him. "No—" he protested. "You don't owe me anything. No— I have to get out of here now." Determined, he raised up and clutched the side of the bed, jaws set against the pain, only to drop back as a wave of blackness rolled over him. "No—" he repeated.

"Yes," Babe Younger said emphatically, smiling.

That afternoon when she came in, there was a genial Mexican teen-ager with her whom she introduced as Johnny Chavez. The youngster, who helped Todd dress, had the smile of a television weatherman and chatter to match. He and Babe Younger assisted the bent-over Todd into a station wagon. Riding up-canyon through the pine-scented coolness of an afternoon shower, he took stock of his situation. His incapacity would set him back ten days or two weeks, just when the racing season was well under way, and when he should be establishing himself again with trainers and agents. But cussing your luck didn't help. Jockeys knew all about hospitals. You took your spills, toughed through to a state of recovery so you could ride again, whether the doctor agreed or not, thankful that you hadn't a broken neck or back.

When Babe Younger drove around behind the restaurant, Todd saw his old pickup-camper parked under stately ponderosa pines. The ride, energizing to him at first, had tired him by the time they stopped. Once more to his annoyance, which he did not hide, he had to have assistance. They took him to a bedroom, and she turned down the bed; sliding between cool sheets, he sank gratefully into sleep.

He woke to the smell of Mexican food coming from the front of the building, and saw her standing at the foot of the bed. "Tonight," she said, "you'll get the beef *burritos* you didn't get the other night."

He thanked her with his eyes, though not really caring, and sat up, aware of an increasing discomfort. He said, "I want to ask you about my hospital bill."

"It's covered."

"I won't have you paying it."

"Everything is covered by insurance. You know . . . the kind where if any person sustains bodily injury while on the premises."

"I'll still pay it."

"You're very independent," she said, close to exasperation.

"I pay my own way."

"You paid yours and then some the other night," she said, dismissing the subject.

"And if my old pickup is in the way," he pursued, his voice stubborn, "just park it anywhere."

"There's enough room back there to park ten pickups. Now, is there anything else that's bothering you, Mr. Lawson?" She was teasing him.

"There is." He was embarrassed and about to panic. "I'm

gonna wet this bed if somebody doesn't help me to the bathroom mighty fast. Where's Johnny?"

"Johnny's out on an errand," she said, eyes crinkling. "He'll be back in an hour or so. Maybe not that soon." She was working on him again.

"Then get somebody else—quick!"

She seemed in no hurry whatever. "There is somebody else. It will have to be me."

"If you can help me in there, I guarantee I can make it back on my own."

"I wouldn't be so certain of that if I were you."

Teeth set, he swung his legs over the side of the bed. She was vexingly slow reaching him. She said, "I'll put my arm around your right side and you lean on me."

When she hesitated, as if she might hurt him, he hacked, "Hurry!"

They hurried, Todd hobbling, unable to straighten himself. There was a delightful fragrance about her, and he liked leaning against her, his left arm around her slim waist. To compound his helplessness, he discovered that his badly bruised left thigh couldn't fully support him.

Babe Younger got him there on time.

Could he make it back on his own? To his chagrin, he could not. Downing his pride once again, he leaned across and opened the bathroom door and called for her and, as if he were no more than a child, she assisted him back to bed. As he lay down and looked up at her, he saw that her eyes were a soft brown, not as dark as he had first thought that evening in the restaurant, and that her brows were a darker brown.

"Tomorrow," he swore, "I'll make it on my own if I have to crawl."

"That brace on your shoulder?" she asked with concern. "Do you have to wear it all the time?"

"Even in bed," he said, and flushed. "I mean most times. A precaution to keep my shoulder from popping out. I had it made to order. An old fellow in a saddle shop did it. Webbing and leather. Somehow it works." He made a regretful face. "There's one drawback. I can't fight much with it on."

"Have you considered an operation?"

He shrugged. Why tell her he'd had it fixed twice and twice afterward had it knocked out in spills?

"They kicked you, too, when you were down," she said, still furious. "Do you remember anything at all after you went down?"

He could grin about it a little now. "All I remember is that it was like your horse clipped the heels of another horse and went down, and you felt yourself going into the rail."

"This is the first time I've had any trouble with bikers. They're not all like that. Generally, they hang out at the lounges, mainly the Buckaroo. They wrecked it once. The week of the All-American Futurity is when it really gets rough around here. Then the bikers come in droves and the local folks take to cover. Winter brings a wave of skiers, but nothing like the summer."

She chatted on at random about Ruidoso, how it had grown as the quarter horse racing program attracted more horsemen and the stakes purses climbed each year. How the citizens were alarmed as the town mushroomed, threatening the environment. How their newest worry was the water supply, if more real estate developments were approved. Listening, he was lulled, and he wished she would talk more about herself and her background. She did not. The name Younger plucked at his memory, but he couldn't place it.

He dozed. When he roused up, she was gone.

Rested, he noticed the room in detail for the first time. Neat, austere, cheerful. Bright drapes drawn back at the windows. A dresser and a hanging mirror. An old-fashioned, ornate wardrobe. A drop-leaf writing desk on which sat a portable typewriter, and a four-drawer steel filing cabinet occupied one corner.

When someone rapped at the door, he said, "Come in," and Johnny Chavez bobbed inside. "How you feelin', Mr. Lawson?" he asked, flashing that smile.

"I only hurt when I breathe. Otherwise, I'm on the improve. I could use a shave."

"No problem, Mr. Lawson. I'll bring you a pan of water."

"Fine. And everything that goes with it. I'm beginning to smell like a horse. My shaving stuff is out in the pickup."

"All your things are here," the boy said, opening the wardrobe, and Todd saw his clothing hanging there, scant enough to be embarrassing: jacket, some shirts, a few slacks and jeans. Cowboy boots below. Cowboy hat on the shelf above. The worst of his belongings, including his tack, they had prudently left in the pickup. "You travel light," Johnny said. He brought a pan of warm water, soap, washcloth and towel, from the dresser, Todd's shaving kit, and helped him snake out of his pajama top and the shoulder harness.

"You're black and blue all over," Johnny exclaimed. He stared at Todd's shoulder and the harness without asking the obvious. "Bet those bikers are hurting today, too, the way Babe kicked and fought them. The girls said she grabbed a catsup bottle and hit one guy as he ran out. Wish I'd been there with a big club."

Todd decided to rib him gently. "Thought you worked here?"

"I do. Part-time. My mom cooks here."

"Where were you?"

"I had a date," was the sheepish reply.

"Did Babe get hit?"

"Not slugged, like you. But they roughed her up, shoved her around."

"Yeah, Johnny, I wish you'd been there, on my right side. Did anybody try to help her?"

"It happened so fast there wasn't time. The girls said when some men got up to help, those bikers broke out of there fast. Those guys aren't brave at all. They have to go in bunches."

Johnny lounged in a chair while Todd washed and shaved. "Babe says you've been leading rider here and at other tracks. Few years ago you rode winners in the Kansas and Rainbow futurities. Ran second twice in the All-American Futurity."

"That was more than a few years ago," Todd said. He did not elaborate, to Johnny's disappointment.

"Boy, that All-American—that's something. I never miss it."

"It's the ultimate," Todd said flatly. "The big buckle of all the quarter horse stakes. The glamour race. A jockey's dream. Win that, you're up in the world, Johnny."

"Babe says she saw you win some big ones."

"Years ago."

"You been riding lately at Sunland, maybe?"

"Some."

"I been rubbing horses this summer and cleaning out stalls," Johnny said importantly, leaning back and gazing at the ceiling. "I think I'll be a jockey. But Babe wants me to finish high school and go on to college."

"You better do that."

"What's wrong with being a jockey?"

"Nothing wrong with it. It's just a hard way to make a living. Hard to get started. Get an education. College is a better track to run on."

"Why?"

"You're gonna get hurt sooner or later, I don't care how good a rider you are, how much experience you've had. It's a very risky profession. A horse snaps a leg, down you go. A lot of jocks get hurt in the gates. Your main fear is you'll be crippled for life —maybe paralyzed. It happens to the best."

Todd studied him. Johnny Chavez was a good-looking kid. Blue-black hair worn semi-long. Clean-cut. Personable. Well brought up. Idealistic. That great sweeping smile. He wasn't too heavy—yet. But he could get that way if he wasn't careful. Todd concluded to let the matter go by, neither to encourage the boy nor to put him down.

Johnny persisted. "How did you get started? Tell me?"

"I grew up on a ranch in Texas. We didn't own it. My father ran it for an oilman. I was like you. Not very big. I tried the rodeo circuit. Rode bulls and buckin' horses. But I kept coming back to running horses—quarter horses. I rode a lot of match races. That's how I got started, on Texas bush tracks."

"What do you have to do to get started, really?"

"What you're doing. Rubbin' horses. Muckin' out stalls. Handyman work. And learn to be responsible. When the trainer expects you to be there at five in the morning, be there. Make a good stable hand. Meanwhile, observe, listen and don't talk. Eventually you'll get to be an exercise rider. One day you'll get a mount and you'll be so cotton-pickin' excited, and scared, it's all you can do to hang on."

Johnny pulled his chair closer, his dark eyes as bright as black buttons. "When did you become a first-line rider?"

Todd evaded with a simulated yawn. "That's a long story, Johnny. We'll talk about it some other time. Afraid I'm getting a little tired." He yawned again.

"Oh, sure, Mr. Lawson," Johnny said in apology, rising.

He was at the door when Todd, out of understanding, could not resist adding, "There's something more you can do now. Most jocks stop riding because they can't make weight. When you're young it's easy, but the older you get the harder it is to keep down. So learn to push back from the table." He followed that with a condoning grin. "Not too many double helpings of Mexican dinners like your mom fixes."

"Thanks, Mr. Lawson. I'll remember that." He went out on airy feet, his face wreathed in hope.

Babe Younger brought his dinner shortly before dark: the anticipated beef *burritos*, and Mexican tomato-pepper cream soup, and Mexican kidney bean salad, and Mexican pudding and coffee.

Todd switched on the bed lamp to stare at the laden tray. "I don't remember seeing all this on the menu."

"It isn't. Something Estela fixed special for you."

"That's nice. It's sure not a jock's diet."

"It will get you out of that bed so you can get back to being a jock again," she said, positive about it. "You're tall for a jockey, but you look awfully thin to me. I'll send Johnny for your tray."

Every dish on the tray was super. He gorged. Afterward, he literally crawled to the bathroom and back, a feat that left him trembling, hurting, sweating, and elated.

Johnny came for his tray. Did Mr. Lawson want to go to the bathroom?

"I've already been, and you can drop the Mr. Lawson title."

"Hey! Babe says you're not to get out of bed on your own."

"Don't tell on me."

The boy dallied, obviously wishing to talk about riding. Todd, pretending weariness, said, "Tell Estela the dinner was great," and the boy, disappointed, went away.

Soon he heard the onrush of the dinner crowd arriving. The din continued on and on. After a long interval, he heard the cars and pickups leaving, and little by little the clatter and drone of voices in the restaurant changed to cleaning-up sounds. The roar of traffic along Sudderth Drive, although never ceasing, dropped to a slower pulse. He kept the bed lamp on and realized that he was waiting, hoping she might come by.

Ten-thirty had passed before he heard her approaching step and her light tapping at the door. She entered hesitantly, a newspaper in hand. By some feminine alchemy she still looked morning-fresh.

"I saw your light," she said. "I'm surprised you're still up."

"Slept most of the day."

"You made the paper. Care to see it?"

"Might as well, I guess."

"On the sports page," she said, handing it to him.

As his eyes followed the print, it was as if he were reading about another person:

RUIDOSO—Todd Lawson, one-time leading jockey at Ruidoso Downs, was injured here late Sunday when he attempted to break up an altercation at a restaurant.

Police said Lawson, rushed unconscious to Hondo Valley Hospital, went to the aid of restaurant owner Ms. Babe Younger when four bikers refused to pay their bill and walked out. The veteran jockey suffered a concussion and multiple bruises, hospital attendants said.

Lawson has not ridden on major quarter horse tracks in recent years. Following a spectacular 1971 season, when he piloted

Kiowa Bar to come-from-behind wins in the Kansas and Rainbow futurities and missed capturing the All-American by a neck, he rode in California, then disappeared from the racing scene. His whereabouts has not been known for several years.

"Very mysterious," he said, and shrugged.

"I thought you ought to see it, even though I don't like the story. I think it's unfair."

"I guess it's news in a way." He forced a dim smile. "Has-Been Jockey Returns to Ruidoso."

"You don't mind, then?"

"It's accurate enough. It doesn't bother me."

Questions were building behind the soft brown eyes, and also concern. Instead of prying, she said, "Maybe you can have a tub bath tomorrow."

"That would be a welcome shock."

"I'll have Johnny help you . . . unless you'd rather have me?"

Their eyes met and held and it was he, flushing, who looked away, which kindled her merriment—which, he knew by this time, was always near the surface of her generous nature. On that note, she said good night and he turned off the bed lamp and stretched out while his mind rushed here and there. Babe Younger made him wonder about man–woman things. It was impossible not to. Old emotions and hopes, long buried and once true, spread through him, and the strain that had been upon him for so long seemed to lift a little, and somehow the road back seemed more clearly defined before him and more attainable.

Chapter 10

Lee Banner stopped at the house for a drink of water before driving on to the barn to unload the feed sacks from the pickup. You saved twenty-five dollars when you hauled your own, and consequently you didn't count your labor. If you dared do that, he thought dryly, figuring time spent against the income the little horse operation had brought in, which was down to rock bottom now with Landy gone and Cindy too hurt to run, it wouldn't even tally up to the minimum wage. He and Serena were facing a big change. He had been giving that a great deal of thought on the way home. Before long he might have to sell some horses, and the very thought depressed him. But the feed bill had to be cut. Either sell some horses or find a steady job. There was one hitch to the last option: there were no jobs in sight. He had spent most of the morning looking in town. Neither, he knew, was there anything at the small neighboring ranches. His friends, like him, did the bulk of their own work. If he found something in Oklahoma City, there was the immediate problem of transportation. Could the old pickup take the daily going and coming? He doubted it.

Burdened, he cut the motor and got out.

As he walked around the pickup, Serena came out of the

house and stood on the steps, her movements more deliberate than casual. He thought nothing unusual until he saw her half smile. He knew what that meant. She was harboring something that particularly pleased or amused her.

"Feed is up again," he said. "I've never seen anything like it." She still hadn't spoken and she still wore that feline smile, that provocative I-know-something-you-don't. "What's up?" he asked.

She could hold back no longer. She said quickly, "I wished you'd been here. You missed the show."

"The show?"

"Cindy's show. She's been galloping and running and kicking up her heels ever since you left this morning."

His silence spoke for him. She couldn't be sound, the way things had been going.

"Lee, I think you'd better take a look at her. A good look. You know we haven't paid much attention to her lately. Just left her alone."

In a noncommittal manner, he took a lead rope from the pickup's cab and started walking, Serena beside him, both silent for fear hopeful words might prove groundless.

The blood-bay filly was at the lower end of the pasture, tail-switching flies as she grazed. They studied her in worried silence from the gate, while Lee tried to hold down his longing. The healing feel of a sandy pasture, plenty of good grass and time. What better medicine could they have given her? Her broken hoof had grown back the last time he looked at her. He hadn't bothered to check her legs, figuring that she was through running as a two-year-old. Neither had he noticed her cutting up much. In his disappointment, he guessed he had pretty much ignored her. This was the middle of July. Going on three months now since she was hurt. He had pulled her plates and turned her out, wanting her to make it back on her own. No medication.

Still, he hesitated.

"Aren't you going to look at her?" Serena said, facing him.

"I am. Guess I'm almost afraid to find out." He turned and whistled shrilly.

Cindy did not look up. Had she forgotten the game they used to play?

He whistled again.

She raised her head, glanced their way, then resumed grazing.

"The little devil," Lee said with a tense laugh. "She's playing hard to get. Let's go in."

"Shall I get some feed?"

"Not yet. Let's see how she runs, if she will."

He opened the gate and they went inside. Lee whistled again, a longer whistle.

Cindy looked up as if curious. That was all.

Lee's hopes sank. Was she sored up after all that morning running? He shrilled another whistle and clapped his hands and angled away from her, walking fast, now jogging to draw her after him, and clapped his hands and whistled once more.

All at once she trotted after him, her head held high. He ran faster. She broke into a gallop, mane flying. Watching her closely over his shoulder, he stumbled over a clump of grass, damned his awkwardness and kept on going.

She was coming faster now, caught up in the game. She romped past him, kicking and bucking, and Lee shouted back to Serena, "Look at Miss Feisty Britches, would you!" And when Cindy slowed and turned, he whistled at her again and hollered encouragement and clapped his hands and wheeled the other way.

She took off running.

Lee slowed to sight back at her. She was running true. If she hurt, she didn't show it. She was running naturally. Striding, not favoring herself. A piece of silk again. She sprinted past him like a shot. Fifty yards on she turned, ready for another dash.

To hold her up, Lee drifted casually toward her, saying, "That's enough, that's enough," hiding the rope behind him.

She was restless, still keyed up, still wanting to run. Going up to her, he slipped the short rope around her neck and led her back to Serena. While Serena held the rope, he began to examine her forelegs, starting just below the knee, rubbing, sensing. He broke into a sweat. To be certain, he checked the right leg a second time. It felt cool and firm. He felt like whooping.

Looking up at Serena, he said, "I do believe she's sound again."

His wife's eyes were glistening and so were Lee Banner's.

Cindy pricked up her ears at the throaty coughing of pumps from the oil wells as Lee backed her out of the horse trailer. Head high, eyes alert, she whirled to ascertain the strange, unbroken sounds.

"She's curious, but she's sure not trembling like she was the first time," Doug Adams said. The assurance of his voice did not equal the worry of his eyes. "She looks great."

"As long as she don't break out in a cold sweat, she's all right," Cal Tyler said. "That's when a horse is plumb scared in the paddock, when they lose strength. I'll tell you one thing. This filly's filled out since that first race back in March. She's grown up. She's a young lady."

"You two windies keep on like that and she'll mess up for sure," Lee growled.

Across the way Smoky Osgood was unloading his three-year-old sorrel stud, Buzz Boy, who was developing into a hard-knocking winner on Oklahoma bush tracks. Lee would have run her against time today, but Smoky said his colt needed a tune-up for the upcoming derby at Raton's La Mesa Park. So much the better, against a good horse. Lee had tried to bring her along carefully these past few weeks. She had trained like a sound horse. Doc Drake said she was sound. But would she come back and run with heart? There was only one shot left in the barrel for her as a two-year-old. Today would tell whether to take her on from here, because time was short. Today was August 7.

Smoky joined them as the Wildhorse Downs starter ambled over, followed by a straggle of helpers and railbirds. "Good thing you boys got here early," he said, shaking hands. "It's gonna be a ring-tailed scorcher today. We'll be ready whenever you are. How far you goin'?"

"One quarter mile," Lee said. "Cal, here, will time it. My

filly's never gone that distance. I want to see what she can do. How's the track?"

"Fast—but not hard. We dragged it smooth this morning. Tell you what, though. If it's all right with you boys, I'll start you from the five and six holes. Those inside lanes could be just a little heavy after that shower we had yesterday. That way no advantage to either horse. Okay?"

"Is with me," Lee agreed, and looked at Smoky, who nodded and said, "Pick your hole, Lee."

Lee shrugged. "Five."

As the track crew left, Smoky added slyly, "Like to put a little on the line?"

"Why not?" Lee said, smiling. "Maybe I can win back that ten bucks you took off of me in March."

They saddled and mounted and Smoky and Lee ponied their runners past the crowd and back up the straightaway to the gates. The filly appeared to have forgotten the noisy pumpers.

The horses loaded. The strong-willed Buzz Boy wanted to run *now*. The headman settled him, pointed him straight. Cindy seemed lackadaisical, she stood so quietly.

Lee was tense, his gaze riveted on her. Her whole season had come down to this one race on a remote Oklahoma bush track. Her whole future, maybe. What if she failed to fire? Was the heart gone out of her after the battering she had taken? Doubt beat through him.

The starter yanked the rope and the gates slammed open and the horses broke almost as one, the stud slightly ahead. Lee, relieved, saw them hit their strides after a few jumps. Running straight. Running hard. Running fast. Both horses. . . . No change the first hundred yards or so. Cindy sticking with the speedy sorrel. Buzz Boy surged out a bit. Maybe a neck. Doug hadn't touched her yet. *Don't wait too long, Doug. Make her run. Make her run. Tap her. Remind her.*

Some 300 yards down there, Lee saw Doug's arm blur up and down several times. At that she seemed to shift gears, seemed to run lower. She began to make up ground, she was running flat out. All she had in her. At last she was coming on the way she was meant to run, the way she was bred to run. Buzz Boy wouldn't quit. It was a horse race.

They charged past the finish line, where Cal stood, his stopwatch clutched in front of him.

Neither man spoke for a space, their eyes still on the horses. Finally, Smoky shifted about and said, "I believe your filly won it, Lee. Either that or they dead-heated."

"Too close to tell from here. They both ran like the heel flies were after 'em, didn't they?"

They rode to the line, where Cal awaited them among some railbirds.

Cal, who wore an expression of controlled excitement, had put on his glasses. He studied his stopwatch with the intent of a man making certain. Not until then did he glance up at them. A broad smile, widening by the moment, cracked across his leathery face. "Lee, you and Smoky may not believe this. I couldn't myself when I first looked at my stopwatch, though I knew the race was fast. Cindy won it by about a neck. She broke twenty-two seconds. So did Buzz Boy."

"Broke twenty-two?" Lee repeated. The time seemed unreal after the tough luck she had endured.

Cal checked the stopwatch again. "To be exact, she ran it in twenty-one and four fifths seconds. She won it in the last forty yards. Put on that finish. Buzz Boy's head was right at her shoulder when they crossed the line. Never saw a prettier race. Never saw horses run any straighter. They didn't veer once. Arrow straight. Didn't waste a foot of ground, which helps explain the time."

"Twenty-one and change," Smoky chortled, and slapped his leg. "That's stake-race time, Lee. Look out, Raton!"

The horses were coming back, and Doug sang out, "She was kinda unsure of herself in the early going. Like she wanted to keep company with Buzz Boy. When I tapped her a couple of times, she got down to business."

Lee turned as a hand was thrust before him, in it a ten-dollar bill. He took it with a shake of his head.

"What do you figure you'll do now?" Smoky asked seriously. "It's mighty late."

"I think," Lee said after a pause, "I think I'll go talk to my banker."

Waving a wedgelike hand, J. B. Foster gestured to the straight-backed chair facing his desk that he laughingly called the "hot seat," leaned back, folded his arms, on his face that preliminary banker's expression, that middle-of-the-road look somewhere between yes and no, and spoke the familiar greeting, "What's on your mind, Lee?"

Lee hesitated. He and Serena had gone over it so many times, assessing it from every possible angle, trying to be practical, until they had virtually exhausted themselves. How could you be practical when racing was always a gamble? Yet why build dreams around a promising horse, possibly a once-in-a-lifetime horse, then back off when decision time came? Lee was torn, never doubting his judgment more than now, while at the same moment believing in it. Last night Serena had said it in her level-headed way: "We knew Landy could run. We thought we'd never have another runner like him, even close to him. We overlooked Cindy till she showed us. What she really represents, Lee, is a second chance. Now, you do what you think best."

Lee said, "I sure need to talk to you, J.B."

"Fire away."

Lee cleared his throat. "I want to borrow some money, and not just a little bit."

"About how much do you have in mind?" Foster pulled at his loose tie.

"Fifteen thousand."

"Ummph." Foster's Adam's apple bobbed.

"I want to enter Cindy in the All-American Futurity Trials at Ruidoso. She ran the quarter mile in twenty-one and change day before yesterday at Wildhorse Downs. To be exact, she ran it in twenty-one and four fifths seconds. That's hand-timed. Could be off a shade, one way or the other. She beat Smoky Osgood's stud. Anytime you beat Buzz Boy, you've got a horse."

"That's a lot of money, Lee."

"I know. I know. It scares me."

Foster made a half turn in his swivel chair, looking off across the lobby, and turned back. "Now, Cindy is the filly that looked so sharp early in the year and got hurt?"

Lee nodded. "She's sound now. To be certain, I had Doc Drake check her out before we took her to Wildhorse Downs, and again after she ran . . . x-rays, tests . . . everything he could think of. That filly's been rubbed on and prodded and eyeballed so much she ducks when she sees me comin'."

"I see. Glad to hear it, Lee. How does this entry procedure work?"

"The deadline is August fifteenth. She'd go in as a supplemental or late nominee with a payment of fourteen thousand, two hundred and fifty dollars, plus another seven hundred and fifty put down for the trial entry fee. The race is Labor Day."

"When are the trials?"

"August twenty-fifth."

"The ten fastest horses go into the big race, don't they? And all the trials for the All-American are run on the same day?"

Lee nodded. J. B. Foster had done his homework.

Foster swiveled again in his chair. "Twenty-one and a little piece of change. I like that expression. And that's fast."

"If she can run close to that in her trial, she can make it into the big one."

"If she doesn't?"

"She's got a shot at the three consolations."

Foster's thick fingers drummed the desk. "How does that break down?"

"The first consolation pays from about twenty thousand dollars for a win, down to around nine thousand or so for the tenth horse. In the second consolation last year, I recollect the winner took home around eight thousand and the tail-end horse, four thousand or thereabouts. You get down to the nubbins in the third consolation. Winner about four thousand, the last horse about two."

Foster's dispassionate tone seemed more so as he asked, "How many horses are generally in the trials?"

"I'd say around two-fifty. You need some luck to make it into the runoff."

"If you did make it and ran tenth, what would be the payoff?"

"Last year . . . it was around twenty-seven thousand."

"Hmmnn. Pay the entry fee and then some. And the winner's take?"

"Just three hundred and thirty thousand last year. They say it'll be bigger this year."

"Bigger!" Foster roared, laughing. "I think I'll give up banking and go in for racing."

"Don't," Lee said, holding up a warning hand. "You don't need luck on this track."

"You just think you don't. I could tell you . . ." He let it drop and laid his arms across his lap, his eyes fixed on the desk calendar. When a bespectacled young woman deposited a mound of official-looking papers on his desk, he didn't seem to notice. "Fifteen thousand," he mulled. "Twenty-one and change. Hmmnn."

Lee said, "I've always leveled with you, J.B. All we have to put up for security is our place, which is clear, and hope in our filly. I believe in her. I know she can run and I know she'll run with heart. She gets that from both sides. That's all there is. That's what it all comes down to."

"What does Serena say?"

"She says it's up to me"—his mouth curled in a faint grin—"and J. B. Foster."

"It's a lot of money, Lee. I don't know what the board would say . . . let alone the auditors." He stood up. "I'll call you sometime tomorrow."

"Thanks, J.B."

They shook hands.

He hung around the house throughout the morning and nothing happened. Meantime, he brooded. He wanted the loan for Cindy; he didn't want the loan because he was afraid something might happen and he couldn't repay it . . . still . . . Noon passed without a call. Same until past three o'clock, when, giving up, he decided to vent his unrest on the north fence.

He had no more than stepped outside when the phone rang. He stopped in mid-step, prepared for a turndown at this late hour. A moment and Serena called from the kitchen door, "It's for you. It's J.B."

Lee walked painfully back inside. J.B. had said no word to her either way, he could tell by her face. He picked up the phone. "Howdy, J.B."

"Lee," Foster began, his tone as neighborly as if they were sitting across from each other at the bank and talking a little feed money, "back in the Dirty Thirties, when the dust blew just about every day, an ol' country boy would venture into town needing a hundred bucks to make a crop and buy the kids some shoes and more times than not all he could get at the bank would be twenty-five. Maybe not that."

"I remember hearing my father tell how hard money was to come by, I sure do." J.B., an old friend, was trying to let him down easy. Well, he didn't blame him. Fifteen thousand was a pile of money, even in these inflated times.

"Point was," Foster said, "that ol' country boy was no better off with the twenty-five than he was without it. Because it wasn't enough to do anything with. You can see that."

"Reckon I can," Lee agreed.

Serena stood near Lee, her hands knotted together, her face strained. Unable to stand the suspense any longer, she suddenly paced to the kitchen, her head down.

"Well," Foster rambled on, "I learned something back then. . . . Me, I was just a kid bank clerk and scared to death every morning when I went to work that I'd get fired. . . . Like I said, I learned something. You see, I learned to figure before I could whittle. Maybe you've heard me say that?"

"Believe I have." Lee laughed. J.B. was a kind man. He could say "no" and you'd still feel good, knowing he really wanted you to have the money.

"Lee, I know the cost of living is high in Ruidoso and feed is always higher than a cat's back around a big racetrack. So you're going to need some additional money for expenses."

"You . . . you mean," Lee said, swallowing, "we get the loan?"

"That's what I mean, Lee—you're covered all the way. We'll put it on an open note and—"

Lee Banner couldn't wait. He whooped, bringing Serena out of the kitchen on the run, and then he was shouting at her, "We're going! We're going!"

Chapter 11

On Tuesday, when Babe Younger checked on him, Todd Lawson was sitting up in bed, gingerly flexing arms and legs, face squinched against the soreness.

"You're doing much better," she said, pleased.

"Credit Babe's Health Spa and Estela's cooking."

"Would it bother you if I work on my tip sheet here? I keep all my records here."

He had forgotten about *Babe's Tips*. "Glad to have company. Didn't know you were a handicapper."

"It's really just a fun thing," she said, going to the desk. "I start putting it together on Tuesday in preparation for the racing weekend. I get the *Daily Racing Form* and go over that. And I have to consider the conditions of the race. And the altitude is a factor for horses fresh on the scene. They don't all run well up here at sixty-eight hundred feet."

"Guess you figure in the jockey, too?"

She pursed her full lips, affecting exaggerated seriousness. "Above all. Though I've yet to see a jock get off and push a horse over the finish line."

"I've felt like doing it many times."

"And I try to interpret workouts for a major race. Sometimes I hear scuttlebutt from the barns. That can be both reliable and unreliable. Sometimes Johnny gets a hot line on a horse. Guess he told you he helps out there. Sometimes a favorite gets sick—a cold, maybe. That sets training back a week or two, and if the race is near, you know a horse may not run up to its peak. These two-year-olds are just babies away from home, shipped in here from far away, vulnerable to a variety of ills."

"You keep a batting average?"

She reflected a moment. "So far this season it's about thirty per cent winners and fifty per cent picks that finished in the money."

"That's extra good. Guess you bet some?"

"I'm conservative by nature. I break about even by the end of the season. Last year I was a little ahead. It all comes down to guesswork. I have a tendency to favor the outside horses on a muddy track in the quarter horse races."

His smile was teasing. "What if the fastest horses have the middle or inside holes?"

"Then sometimes I'm in trouble.

"Yet, on a rainy day, say after eight or ten races have chewed up the track, those inside post positions get heavy and slow. And there's the hump, that doggoned hump, where the homestretch turn comes in on the straightaway. If a horse stumbles going down it . . ." He shook his head at the memory.

"And then," she recited, "after I've taken my final look into the crystal ball, I cut the stencil and have it run off on a mimeograph. Johnny and I do the folding and stuffing of the envelopes and he drops them off at places around town." She regarded him instructively, as if he were a tourist. "Tip sheets are part of the local color. Merchants display them in their windows and on their counters. You have to give the customer something for his money. He'll buy a tip sheet once just for the novelty. If he wins a few, he'll buy again. If he gets wiped out, he'll never buy you again. At the end of the season we generally show a small profit for having had the fun of doing them. It's a great thrill when you pick the winner of a major race." She seemed to catch herself. "Here I am, telling you about things you've known for years."

"I've never been a 'capper. Sounds interesting."

She settled herself at the desk and worked steadily without looking up, writing on a long, ruled yellow sheet, while Todd reread yesterday's newspaper.

"Would you like some coffee?" she asked after a while. He nodded agreeably, welcoming that as another way to keep her here longer. As they drank the coffee, she became thoughtful. "I started the tip sheet after my husband died, because I still wanted to stay close to racing. He was a jockey, too . . . Don Younger. Did you happen to know him?"

"I've been trying to place the name at Ruidoso. Yes, I believe I met your husband one time."

"We came out here from western Oklahoma the year you won those futurities. I thought Kiowa Bar was the greatest horse I'd ever seen. I fell in love with the area. I wanted to put down roots. Don didn't. He was always footloose. Always wanted to go somewhere else, thought it would be better. Wouldn't take care of himself. He was killed in a car crash between here and Tularosa four years ago."

Todd groaned in sympathy. "Oh, Lordy."

"My folks wanted me to come back to Oklahoma. I almost did. But something held me here." She was smiling inwardly, more to herself than to him. "It was New Mexico and its people. They make me happy. I like the Mexicans. They're strong family people. They love their children. They respect their elders. They're loyal friends. They laugh a good deal. I couldn't run this place without them. It's said if you stay here just a little while you'll never want to leave. I believe that. So I took the plunge . . . invested my savings and opened this small restaurant. Something I'd always wanted to do."

"You picked a winner."

"I didn't mean to burden you," she said, her voice apologetic.

"You didn't. It's good to have somebody to talk to. Not everybody has." He regretted the last the instant he spoke it, because he had sounded bitter, and he wasn't bitter any longer. He had purged himself of self-pity when he took the first halting step on the long, narrow road that wound back to the top of the mountain.

Her big eyes widened on him and remained there. He could see concern and understanding for himself, restrained by her unwillingness to pry. A further moment and she turned back to the desk.

He was silent, content to gaze at the curve of her pretty neck as she concentrated on her racing picks. After some time, when she turned to him again, it seemed the most natural of responses for him to say, "I might tell you my story now."

"You don't have to because I told you mine."

"It's not a pretty story. I've never told it to anyone."

"Whatever you like," she said, and crossed her hands in her lap, waiting.

"Maybe I shouldn't."

"We're being very formal, aren't we?" Her laugh dispelled any doubts. "I don't mind and I'm a good listener."

The beginning was easier than he had thought. Step by step, he described his biggest year: winning the two quarter horse futurities leading up to the All-American, the victory he sought most and lost. Leading rider that year on pari-mutuel tracks with 232 wins, some 200 seconds and close to 200 thirds from a total of 1,400 mounts. Throwing money around like chicken feed. Flying his own plane. And then what happened to him gradually: boozing and partying and riding, making no excuses for himself, his weight ballooning to 120 pounds, and how he had gone into steam baths to get down, and taking pills when that failed.

He paused. "There came a time when I wasn't riding winners except now and then, even on good mounts. I would come to the track and I'd be floating around, like a man in another world. I couldn't concentrate. I lost my feel. The good mounts became fewer. My agent did all he could, but the trainers started to shun me. I didn't blame them."

"Were you an alcoholic?" she asked.

"No."

"Don said that, too, but he was."

"I wasn't. You'll have to take my word for that. However, the combination of alcohol and pills was killing me. My reflexes were gone. For the first time in my life I lost my desire to ride. I got hurt . . . that was at Bay Meadows. A colt went into the rail. When I woke up in the hospital, I was numb all over. I couldn't move. I thought I was paralyzed from the neck down. A young doctor said it was broken. But when an older doctor reread the x-rays, a doc who'd put a lot of jocks back together, he said it wasn't. Just a pinched nerve. . . . I wound up with a broken leg, a collapsed kidney, a punctured lung, a busted hip and this shoulder. They put in a bunch of pins. I was lucky at that, because I wasn't paralyzed or crippled. I was out for a year. . . . When the money stopped coming in and the party was over, my wife, Eve, left me. I didn't blame her. It was time to go."

"What happened to her?" she asked softly.

"I don't know. I heard she was somewhere in the Southwest."

"Were you bitter?"

"I was at first, but I got over it. Oh, I was running over with self-pity for a while."

"Do you miss her?"

He said, "We were ready to split the blanket before I got hurt," and his voice trailed off. His breathing became heavier, his voice less emphatic when he went on. "About that time something happened that I don't understand to this day. My best friend, a jockey named Web Parker, a boy from back home, was found dead by asphyxiation—a suicide. He was having problems making weight, too, but I thought he had himself under control. Maybe that was it, but somehow I don't think so. It puzzled me then, it puzzles me now. Web was easygoing. Never the kind to worry. It was hard to take. He was like a brother. In some ways, we were closer than brothers. With that and everything else, I hit bottom." He smiled, still thinking back. "Web liked to go first-class. Good cars, good food, good clothes, good liquor, good-looking women. Was a great guy for turquoise—rings, bolos, chokers, bracelets—particularly Navajo work. Didn't give a hang for diamonds. He was a pilot, too. A good one."

He fell silent again, reliving the past. She waited for him to go on.

Presently, he said, "Getting hurt was a blessing in one way. I finally saw myself for what I was—a worthless wreck. No good to anybody. It gave me time to do a lot of thinking and reading. I read everything. My perspective began to change. It was like a dry spring filling up after a long drought. . . . I'd never finished high school. Was too busy riding match races. . . . Broke, I drifted back to Texas and found work on a horse ranch near Aledo. Just doing chores, helping wherever they needed a hand. Working with the young horses was the right medicine. They led me back. I stayed till I wanted to ride again. Starting over, I figured it would be wise to go where I wasn't known—back East, where quarter racing was catching on. The jocks there treated me all right, but I never felt at ease. I was an outsider in cowboy boots and hat, western shirt and pants. Texas, again. . . . I made the bush tracks for a couple of years—Graham, Ross Downs, Columbus, Goliad, Laredo, Lubbock, Del Rio. I started at the bottom. You name it . . . clean-up boy, groom, exercise rider. Sometimes I'd get a mount. I know now that I was testing myself . . . just to see if I could hack it. My rep didn't help. It was always there ahead of me: Has-Been Jockey. Who'd trust a high-priced runner in the hands of a thirty-seven-year-old ex-pill-and-booze hound?"

He was silent for so long, thinking of what had happened, that she asked quietly, "What then?"

"Sunland Park. If I was gonna make it, I had to get off the bush tracks. At Sunland I don't think I drew one good mount. Like being an apprentice again. Show money got to looking pretty big around mealtime. Ruidoso was ever on my mind." He raised his eyes. "Whatever happens here, I'll know I tried to make it back."

Her impulsive movement took him off guard, disconcerted him. For suddenly she was standing beside the bed, looking down at him, her face open and appealing, saying, "You've already made it, Todd. Don't you see? You have. All on your own."

"Not yet," he said, shaking his head.

"But you have." She reached out reassuringly and touched his shoulder.

Her proximity affected him. Before he quite realized what he was doing, he took her hand and gently kissed it, and afterward held it, surprised at himself, gazing up at her. Neither spoke, each confused, each ill at ease, each startled.

Her voice uneven, she said, "I think I'd better go now," and began to remove her hand.

"Thank you, Babe," he said, slowly releasing her.

She started toward the door. Some hurried steps and she turned, her eyes straight upon him.

He feared he had offended her. He said quickly, "Those were awful things for a man to admit about himself. I shouldn't have told you. I'm sorry. You'll think I'm nothing."

"No, Todd. They needed saying and you were man enough to say them."

"Not that. I said them because you listened. It was like a catharsis." He kept shaking his head. He looked away.

To his shock, she came swiftly back, bent down and kissed him on the cheek, then fled the room.

Babe Younger did not see Todd that afternoon or evening as was her custom, and in the following days when she did, her visits, though invariably cheerful, were brief and impersonal and matter-of-fact. How was he feeling today? Much better, thank you. Did he want anything? No, thank you. He thought of her constantly. Meantime, Todd's strength returned, the adhesive binding his ribs came off, and grimly, still hurting, he set about exercising in the room. And early of a morning, when coils of mist like spider webbing laced the piney canyon, before the restaurant crew arrived to make preparations for the busy day, he took long walks in the cool, bracing air. As he walked, he thought of the horses working at the track, and knew that he would be leaving soon.

That day came.

After Johnny took his breakfast tray away, he shaved, dressed, carefully made the bed, folded his clothes and took them out to the pickup. Putting his toilet articles into his kit, he wondered how to tell her. Why not leave a note and just fade out? But that seemed sneaky after all she had done for him. No, he decided, he would have to tell her in person and he didn't know how.

He smoothed the bed once more and tidied up the room, even to rearranging the neat pile of newspapers and magazines that Babe and Johnny had brought him. His eyes strayed over the sunny room, aware that he would miss its cheerfulness and his patroness. He tried to rationalize his situation. Wasn't this just another fork in the trail? Hadn't he come to many a one? Fidgeting, he went over the room again for any item he might have overlooked, and sat by the window, waiting for her morning visit.

Babe Younger was late.

It was after ten o'clock when he heard her light knock. He reached the door quickly, feeling a mixture of anticipation and growing regret.

"I expected to find you resting," she greeted him. Although she was smiling, he thought her eyes disclosed that she already sensed something. Leaving the door ajar, she came in and gazed about. "You certainly keep a neat place here," she said, forcing a light laugh. Instead of her usual plain, workaday dress of light blue, she wore a loose-fitting house dress of a floral pattern.

There was a heavy pause.

"Babe," he said at last, "it's time for me to take myself off your hands. I want to thank you for everything and I don't know how to say it. Because thank you isn't enough."

She moved to the window and looked out. "Thank me after I almost got you killed?"

"Same thing could have happened if I'd stopped for a beer at the Buckaroo. Except there'd been no Babe to take care of me."

"I know you feel you have to go," she said, still not looking at him. "I knew it was near, you've been so restless. Guess that's why I put off coming this morning. Then, when I came in and saw you'd pulled on your boots, I knew this was it." She turned listlessly. "So . . ."

"I'll go to the track first. I need to get acquainted again. Meet people. Some I'll know. Most I won't. There's a world of new people in quarter racing."

"Are you fit to ride?"

"I can gallop a horse. I've been exercising every day, and walking. My arms and legs feel much stronger."

"Where will you stay?"

"Around. Close to the track, I hope."

"You're very independent, Todd."

"No more than Babe Younger was when she opened her own restaurant. You have to be if you make it on your own."

It occurred to him that they were both intent on maintaining a scrupulous line of demarcation between them, and also they were back on that damn false formality again.

She stood quite still before she spoke. "You could stay here and go to the track every morning. Come and go whenever you pleased."

"Thank you. But how long have I been here? How many days?"

"I've never counted them."

"It's been a long time."

"Does it seem long?"

"You know better than that." He groped, floundered, blurted out, "It's been wonderful. Sometimes I have the feeling that I was guided here that night." He raised his hands, let them fall. "It's hard to explain."

Her widening eyes, those mirrors of her inner self, never left his face.

"What it comes down to is . . . I have to get back on my own. A man has to." He was stumbling over his words, unable to extricate himself, forgetting the succinct good-by that he had rehearsed over and over. "You know how that is?" he fumbled.

She didn't answer. He was doing all the talking and wishing he were not.

He flung up an inconclusive hand and suddenly his thoughts came in a rush. "I know you understand . . . well, because you're a wonderful person. . . . What I mean is, I love you." My God, it raced through his mind, I've said that!

Her eyes were brimming.

The last of his composure deserted him. He said, "Now I'd

better get the hell out of here," and turning to go, froze, aware
that the gap between them no longer existed. Their eyes locked.
Suddenly they threw arms around each other and clung together, staying like that until Babe lifted her face to kiss him.
When she looked up at him again, her eyes seemed to see beyond him and into the past.

"I didn't want to fall in love with another jockey. I've tried
hard not to, but I lost out at the wire."

He was too overcome to speak for a while. He could only hold
her in silence. "I still have to go," he said. "I can't lean on you
any longer."

"Even when you're welcome? And when it isn't leaning?"

He shook his head.

"You can stay just a little while longer." She became still again,
a stillness that seemed to deepen her eyes. Without another
word, she turned and drew the drapes closed and went to the
door and closed it and came back to him. His blood was pounding in his ears.

Her whole life seemed summed up in her face. He saw happi-
ness there, likewise a tinge of sadness.

She said, "You see, Todd, I was going to tell you I love you
even if you didn't tell me. There's so little time in life, really.
Life is so fragile. So many things can happen. A horse can go
down. . . . I want us to have what we can have together now."
She lifted her arms behind her neck. She gave a toss of her gold
head to free her hair and fumbled a moment. Todd heard faint
snaps. As she brought her hands down, her dress slid from her
body to the floor with a rustling sound. She stepped out of it and
stood naked before him. She was lovely, she was perfect. Her
eyes like great, warm pools. Her smooth skin almost transparent.
Her breasts like sculptured bells.

He smothered her in his arms.

Chapter 12

From mid-May through Labor Day, Ruidoso, New Mexico, is a horseman's town, as lively as a sale-ring filly, bright ribbons in her pretty mane. From a permanent head count of some 7,000 residents, it would bulge to 35,000 or more people as the season ended with the running of the "World's Richest Horse Race."

So Lee Banner knew from his one trip here as a spectator. Every horseman had to journey to Mecca once. He could not overcome a sense of awe, and unease, upon viewing the great sprawl of Ruidoso Downs—the cavernous stands, the maze of barns, the broad parking lots, the oval track and the long heartbreak straightway—and thinking of the fast quarter horses shipped in to run for the money.

He turned in at the Horsemen's Entrance, Doug Adams beside him, Cindy and Cal Tyler's pony horse, Booger Red, in the trailer, and Cal following in his pickup. Serena and Nancy would drive out in time for the All-American Trials, scheduled Friday, August 25. Thanks to Doug's valve job on Lee's pickup, they had made the tiresome haul from Oklahoma without incident, stopping frequently to check the trailer hitch and to look in on the horses.

Lee found the racing office and got an assignment for two stalls.

"I could put Booger in a corral somewhere," Cal offered. "Another stall is only an added expense."

Lee shook him off. "Wouldn't think of it. Booger goes first-class. He's back-home folks and company for Cindy."

"You should've bought that goat."

"Nope, I like horse smell better, and Booger will be right next door."

Lee's jaw sagged at sight of their stalls, ancient, run-down, unpainted, hardly bigger than milking sheds. The more modern stalls had been taken long ago; arriving late, you took what was left, for hundreds of horses were in residence. However, these stalls were at the end of a shed row and there was a wide overhang, shelter for lawn chairs and cots. Cindy would not be left alone, day or night. Not that you didn't trust people; it was that you didn't trust everybody, particularly if your horse became a contender, a precaution that hadn't changed since the early days of match racing.

While Doug and Cal saw to the horses, Lee fell to work cleaning out Cindy's quarters and spraying disinfectant. No telling what deadly viruses lurked within. On the floor he scattered a deep bed of wood shavings instead of straw, because a horse will nibble straw. Next, he took a hammer from the pickup and beat in any loose nails. Booger's stall, with Doug helping, got the same cleanout.

In the back of the pickup was a box of first-aid items that smelled like a vet's office: scissors, thermometer, eye medications, leg brace, Epsom salts, liniment, Flyshield, healing powder, Vaseline, turpentine, alcohol, iodine, Hooflex, bandages, cotton, gauze, tape, leg wraps, and bottles of Doc Drake's own colic remedy and cough medicine.

Concerned about the effects of the change in altitude and climate, Lee hoped that his timing was right. Cindy was ready to run now. Could he keep her at that peak, coming from Oklahoma's humid heat and 1,200-foot altitude to Ruidoso's 6,800, its hot afternoons, cool nights and brisk mornings? Veteran horsemen, Cal included, had cautioned him that some horses slumped, went off their feed and became lethargic after a while at the mountain track. But how soon? Condition was the main factor, they said. Well, Cindy was a healthy filly. There was an additional worry: New Mexico's rainy season started in July and continued into September. It was not unusual for a low-country runner to develop a cold shortly after arriving. Others simply could not adjust to the high country. Others developed breathing problems. Others didn't like to run in Ruidoso mud and rain.

Lee had decided to continue the simple training program he had followed in Oklahoma. No changes, no frills. Oats and alfalfa twice a day; some bran to keep a horse open. No pellets when running a horse; pellets had a tendency to compact. A running horse required plenty of roughage to stay healthy. Use only your own feed and water buckets. Gallop her every morning, now and then some gate work. A walk to cool her out after working, then wash her down with hydrant water to close the pores. Then a session on the electric-powered walker. A blanket on her at night. On Tuesday or Wednesday before Friday's trials, extend her in a tune-up over the distance she would run—and each day just hope your luck held.

The outfit soon settled into routine, Cal and Doug taking the early night watches on the cots, Lee the late hours. If a horse coughed at night and sounded uncomfortable, you got up and led it out and around. Often that brought relief; even more, it could very well be a matter of life or death for a sick youngster upset by being recently moved.

There was no lack of company. Horsemen dropped by. Drawling Oklahoma and Texas voices. Handshakes. Names. Coffee flowed like the Río Ruidoso. "That's a good-lookin' filly you got there." Inquiries followed as to Cindy's breeding and track performances. Lee carefully refrained from mentioning her "twenty-one and change" victory over the derby-bound Buzz Boy, but when a visitor learned that she was a late nominee, eyebrows shot up. "Then she can run more than just a little bit. My colt's been right sharp, too. He seldom makes a mistake and he loves to run. Likes this track. I've been waiting all my life for a stakes horse like him. Well, good luck to you boys."

"Good luck to you, and come back."

Without fail, talk would shift to pre-trial favorites for the All-American. Easy Injun, winner of the Kansas Futurity and second in the Rainbow Futurity, was the leading luminary. Another prospect was Sudden Deck, a hard-knocking California gelding. Held out of the Kansas go, he had taken the Rainbow by a neck from Easy Injun. Misty Maid, who had set the second fastest time in the Rainbow trials, then finished fifth in the finale after getting bumped down the stretch, was reportedly looking like greased lightning in workouts. Gem Three, runner-up in the Sun Country Futurity, was impressive. Another day, other horses would be named.

Lee worried, everybody worried, yet everybody had a shot—so everybody said.

Poor-boy horsemen with virtually unknown hopefuls had scored upsets in the All-American. One was Possumjet, the filly from Blanchard, Oklahoma. Overlooked when she qualified with the eighth fastest time, she took the 1972 classic by a nose. More recently, two Texas cotton farmers had hit the jackpot. Hot Idea, their twisted-knee filly, a mere $4,000 yearling in the All-American Sale, outran the 5–2 favorite by a length and a half.

In between workouts, chores and talking, the three-man outfit napped and swatted flies and read newspapers and magazines to pass the time until the trials. Lee bought Cindy a radio. She would seem to cant her head in a listening attitude whenever Tammy Wynette sang "Run, Angel, Run" or "Stand by Your Man." On the contrary, Booger Red seemed to perk up, ears flicking, only when Charlie Rich sang and played the piano, or when country music star Waylon Jennings sang "Mammas, Don't Let Your Babies Grow Up to Be Cowboys" and "Luckenbach, Texas."

"A Texan," Cal explained, straight-faced, "never gets over being born in Texas. Booger was bred and raised down there."

Lee and Cal were sitting in the shade by the stalls when a

short, round-faced, paunchy individual wearing a big hat waddled up the slope from the road.

"It's Smoky Osgood," Cal grunted. "Something's wrong."

Smoky waved and whooped and charged the hill on fast-closing bootsteps.

"Thought you and Buzz Boy were at La Mesa for the derby?" Lee said.

"Buzz Boy shinbucked and chipped a knee. But we'll get 'em next year." That was the irrepressible Smoky, always hopeful. A horseman had to be. He shook hands and Lee poured him some coffee. "I came down to help," Smoky said. "Figured you could use a stable boy with unlimited experience."

"I hate to hear that about Buzz Boy," Lee said. "What happened?"

"My own fault. After he set the fastest time in the trials, I got too smart. Cut it too thin. I worked Buzzer too hard, tuning him for the big run. Should've rested him more. Played radio music for him, like you're doin' for Cindy and Booger. Say, that Charlie Rich sure can tickle the ivories, can't he?" Smoky said, putting his bad luck behind him.

Lee was alone that afternoon when a stranger introduced himself. "I'm Todd Lawson. Wondered if you might need a gallop rider some morning?"

He was tall for a jockey, straight, clean-shaven and lean to gauntness, drawn down to bone and hard muscle. The black, friendly eyes in the roughly hewn face showed judgment and experience. His relaxed voice carried the soft accents of a Texan.

Lee looked at him for another moment before replying, thinking back. "Lawson . . . Todd Lawson?" He held out his hand.

"There's only one," the man said, grinning. "That's enough."

"I'm Lee Banner. I remember you. Believe you just about wore out the winner's circle around here."

"Been gone some years. Frankly, I'm trying to get back in the saddle."

"Glad to know you, Todd. I don't need a rider right now. I brought my jockey from Oklahoma and I have just this one filly. Like to look at her?"

"You bet."

Lee led her out and about, and Lawson, after a walk-around look, said, "She's a nice one, all right. Hope you have some luck. Guess she's in the All-American Trials."

"She is."

"I'd like to know her breeding."

"She's pure Oklahoma," Lee said, and recited her antecedents on both sides.

"I love those old quarter horses. They didn't get pampered the way they do today."

"Hope you're getting some mounts?"

Lawson smiled. He smiled easily. "I gallop a few head now and then. I'm not proud. I'll gallop anybody's horse, but I'm not begging. Same as starting over as an apprentice. Had some personal problems. Finally worked 'em out. It took time."

He wasn't complaining, he wasn't making excuses. Lee liked that in a man. He said, "You look good."

"Thanks. I am in shape. Believe it or not, I've gone in for this jogging craze. Keeps a man's weight down, and once in a while he can have a Mexican dinner. A jock's got to stay legged up same as a horse."

"Have you talked to an agent?"

"All of 'em. Here in New Mexico a hustler is limited to no more than two jocks at any given time. I checked in late, so—"

"Something will show up."

"I have to prove myself again. I realize that."

"You ride Thoroughbreds, too?" Something had happened to Todd Lawson years ago, but Lee couldn't remember what it was.

"My preference is quarter horses. I'm too impatient to ride Thoroughbreds. Least, I used to think I was." He smiled again. "Right now I'll ride anything with a saddle on it. In fact, I'm booked for my first mount Wednesday. A quarter horse allowance race. I got that on my own, when a jock got sick."

"I'd like to see you ride. What race is it?"

"The third."

"Tell you what, Todd. I'll try to be there. Like to see you win it."

Lawson looked down, surprised and gratified. "Thanks. You'll be my one fan." He took a spiral memo pad from his shirt pocket, scribbled, tore out the page and handed it to Lee. "Here's my landlady's phone number in case you need a rider. Glad to meet you, Lee."

Watching him stride down the slope to the road, Lee remembered how Todd Lawson had been up there with the best. He'd sure taken some fast horses down the track. Had his pick at one time. Lee wondered what had happened to cause him to drop out of sight so suddenly from the racing world.

Todd Lawson had known Art Yates, the Clerk of Scales at Ruidoso Downs, as a first-call rider until he broke his neck in two places and tore up his back, narrowly escaping paralysis from the waist down. Now portly, his hair iron-gray and thinning, Yates rode herd on the jockeys' room, keeping peace when tempers flared, affixing proper lead weights into saddle pockets, weighing riders, passing out riding silks, making certain the colors matched those on the program, and handling claim papers. Yates was the first familiar face Todd had found when he went to the track.

"You're early," Yates said when Todd checked in Wednesday afternoon.

"Thought I'd set an example," Todd said, tongue in cheek.

Yates took him aside. "They know who you are. Word's got around."

"The good or the bad?"

Yates chuckled. "You can blame me, partly, and some of the old jocks you used to know. I told some of the boys about those big stakes races you won. So you're liable to get ribbed today. Wednesday is a low-key day. Allowance races, maidens, claims. Everybody's relaxed and full of devilment. More bull going on than usual. More pranks. But just wait till the trials. This place will be like a pressure cooker."

"That's one thing that never changes."

"Our chief honcho is Flip Keller. He's pretty hot right now. Leading jockey. Making big money. Too bad he ain't learned how to wear it. Won the Rainbow aboard Sudden Deck. That did it. Thinks he's the world's greatest. Pretty obnoxious. Always looking for the edge. He's got most of the kids buffaloed."

"There's one at every track."

"I can't stand the conceited so-and-so. He's in the third race with you. On Smoke Screen, the seven horse, the favorite. I see you're on Speed Merchant in the eight hole. Keller will probably grind on you. Try to get his bluff in before the race."

"I can take care of myself."

"You sound like the old Todd."

"What do you know about the eight horse?"

"Two years ago Speed Merchant ran a close second in the World's Championship Classic here. Been up and down since. In my opinion there's been too many people foolin' with him. An idiot can ruin a good horse."

"Any bad habits?"

"Just two," Yates laughed. "Veers when the whip is used, and he drifts to the outside."

"Is that all?"

"He's still a good horse. Could be the horse to beat in this go with a good ride. Good luck, and don't say I didn't warn you. Take the locker over there. Hope you don't mind purple silks."

"I love purple," Todd said, and found his locker. Next to it an undershirted, towheaded youngster was hanging up his black-and-white blouse.

Todd sat awhile in front of his locker. By and by, he was invited to sit in on a game of racetrack rummy. As it progressed, the towhead strolled over and pulled up a chair close by Todd and leaned in and back, seemingly intent on how the newcomer played his hand. An instant after, something exploded under Todd's chair and he leaped high, thrown off guard, confused, until he realized it was a firecracker. Everybody cracked up with laughter, Todd included.

"This place hasn't changed a bit," he howled, holding his side. "You guys are all right." He went on laughing at himself, feeling younger for it. After all, when they pulled such a prank and you laughed, it was a form of acceptance. Still amused, he took his place again and played two hands. When he stood up, the tow-head filled his chair.

Todd eased over to the bench by the lockers and sat down. When the prankster wasn't looking, Todd quickly tied knots in the sleeves of the boy's riding blouse, then moved farther down the bench.

As the jocks played on, another drifted over to a locker, searched, fumbled, turned with an open letter and began reading, falsetto voice:

"'Dearest Danny: Just a line tonight, Sugar. How is my Honey Boy? Sure wish I could see my handsome rider for just one little minute. I would run up to Ruidoso, but my brother won't let me have his pickup anymore since I caved in the fender. Besides, I can't get away from my job here at the drive-in. You know how that is, Sugar. I cried all day after you left. I can still feel your strong arms around me and your lips on mine and—'"

A jockey threw down his cards and rushed over there, snatched free the letter, and the wrestling began.

"Break it up!" Yates shouted, charging across.

They quit just as he got there, the reader giggling, the other red-faced and furious. "Durn you, Steve!"

Todd took a chair apart, enjoying the atmosphere, the buzz of vibrant voices, the dressing-room compound of sweat, leather, tobacco. These shenanigans served as a needed safety valve, a release from the competitive spirit of slim-faced boys and wizened little men who simply liked to be around horses and responded to the thrill of hell-bent race riding.

He turned his mind to Speed Merchant, thinking of the times he would fly in, booked by his agent to ride a strange stakes horse. His knowledge limited to the trainer's brief instructions in the paddock and the feel of the horse gained during the parade to the post.

The towhead was changing for the first race. Suddenly he let out a yell, "Who tied my sleeves in knots?" and scanned the grinning faces. "Who did it, now?" They merely stared, relishing his bewilderment, all pretending cover-up guilt. "All right, now, you couldn't all have done it." His eyes switched to Todd and he pointed. "Hey—it was you—Lawson."

"Me?" Todd said, giving a shrug of innocence. "I just got here. But you might ask Art. Who else would pull such an old prank?"

Towhead advanced upon the clerk, simulating revenge.

"Enough!" the long-suffering Yates bellowed. "We've got horses to ride. This folderol is over."

And it was—for a while.

More riders were checking in, and when Flip Keller arrived, Todd knew immediately who it was, even before one of the very young riders called Keller's name and two more youngsters gathered around him, deferring to him. Keller drew only a scattering of nods from the older jocks. He had a swagger. A well-constructed man looking under thirty. Muscular. Big-jawed. Strong-featured. Wide through the shoulders, tapering down to a waist as slim as a girl's. His appearance definitely contemporary. His blond hair trendy. Color co-ordinates: casual tan suit, beige shirt open to the fourth button, revealing a hairy chest and a thick neck column, set off by a turquoise choker of deepest blue. Elevated loafers. His moody voice, replying to the boys' eager questions, combined with his droopy lower lip, suggested that possibly he had watched too many old Humphrey Bogart movies, and now sought to create an image of unbeatable toughness and cool. A summation came to Todd: *macho* rider. Not that Todd resented such. Riding in the thick of the charge to the wire required guts.

A boy whispered to Keller, pursing his lips in Todd's direction, and Keller turned his curly head.

After the second race was called, Todd dressed, weighed in and sat in front of his locker, feeling the return of pre-race nervousness, plus a stronger anticipation.

Keller changed into white knickers and boots; standing before a mirror, he combed his hair and flexed the muscular shoulders and arms. Then, dressed in orange silks, he ambled over to Todd.

"I'm Flip Keller," he said, his tone as much as saying that

Todd should know, and stuck out his hand for a perfunctory shake.

"Howdy. I'm Todd Lawson. Sit down."

"I've heard a lot about you," Keller said, sitting. "Understand you used to be the stud-duck jock around here."

"Oh, I wouldn't go so far as to say that," Todd drawled. "I won some, I lost some."

"I've seen you ride. As a matter of fact, I was an apprentice, just coming up in California, about the time you were—" He let the rest hang.

Todd said it for him, dry of humor, "—going down."

"Yyyyeah. Didn't mean to bring that up."

But you did, Todd thought, and said, "That's okay. I crossed that bridge a long time ago and it's way back there. Art tells me you're leading rider and won the Rainbow Futurity on Sudden Deck. Congratulations."

"Yyyyeah. I knew I had it won before Deck took a step."

"There's nothing like confidence," Todd deadpanned. "Of course, sometimes the unexpected happens. One time I had a colt, the favorite, too, refuse to leave the gate in a hundred-thousand-dollar stakes race. Very embarrassing."

"Yyyyeah," Keller said, "that would be." His eyes roved over Todd, as if gauging him.

There was a pause between them, and Todd, suspecting, said, "I see we're both in the third race . . . you on the seven horse, me on the eight horse."

"Yyyyeah. Thought I'd better tell you I like plenty of room at the break. Besides his other bad habits, Speed Merchant jumps to the inside sometimes."

"It occurs to me that neighborliness at the break is a two-way street. And who knows which way a horse will jump."

"Just thought I'd tell you."

"Wouldn't try to intimidate an old hard boot, would you?"

"I'd rather call it an understanding."

"That's a mighty fancy word for it." Todd's anger was simmering. In the old days, he'd have let fly and the two of them would be at it by now. In lieu, he said evenly, "Now, you stick this into your memory bank: Don't try to shut me off out there. If you do, I'll jam my horse through. And after the race, you and I will have us a toe-to-toe understanding. Get it, *Macho?*"

Keller blinked surprise and flushed. Quickly regaining his composure, he stood and said, "Okay, Pop, just so you know," and ambled away.

When riders were called for the third race, he was the last to go to the saddling paddock. He dashed out, flicking his whip, his appearance exciting applause among the racegoers crowding the paddock fence. He flashed them a white smile and swaggered to his horse, whip held high.

The 350-yard allowance race, for three-year-olds and up, and non-winners of $500 this year, had a field of nine going for the $2,600 purse. Tote-board odds on Smoke Screen, the favorite, showed 2–1, on Speed Merchant, 12–1. Hoping to bring Lawson some luck, Lee bought a six-dollar combination ticket on Speed Merchant and prepared to enjoy himself.

Watching through binoculars, he saw Lawson jump his horse away alertly with the 7 horse. They became the point of the pack as the 9 horse stumbled coming out of the gate and failed to get untracked, while the horses on Smoke Screen's left fell half a length off the pace.

The leaders were going head to head when Speed Merchant drifted toward the outside. Lawson, as if ready, corrected that immediately with a right-handed whip. The gelding then bore left. In one quick motion, Lawson switched the whip to his left hand and straightened his mount. But Smoke Screen had taken the lead.

Nearly a length back and still close to the outside rail, Lawson wisely settled his horse, let him collect himself. At the midway point, running free and easy under a hand ride, Speed Merchant appeared to find his stride. He closed, making up ground, just as the 5 horse challenged. Lawson had the gelding rolling, firing straight. He drove up abreast of Smoke Screen, and the race changed to a two-horse duel as they left the 5 horse struggling.

Some fifty yards from the wire, Lawson urged his horse into the lead. A head, a neck, half a length. When they crossed the finish line, Speed Merchant was drawing away, and Lee thought, A mighty nice ride by an old hand.

When the jockeys stood up, Lee saw Smoke Screen's rider shout something at Lawson and Lawson shout a repayment in kind and wave his whip.

Lee tarried awhile longer, enjoying having picked the winner, and glad for Lawson's comeback effort. He waited until Lawson rode to the winner's circle for the picture taking, then joined the throng streaming under the grandstand to cash tickets and crowd the refreshment stands.

Leaving the pay window, he reviewed Lawson's ride. Obviously, Speed Merchant didn't like the whip, resented it. Lawson had used it only to straighten the horse. Had he used it to call for more speed down the stretch during the two-horse duel, he'd have lost ground when the gelding veered from the stick, besides risking disqualification if his horse interfered with Smoke Screen. Instead, he had patiently let his mount right himself on his own. A less experienced rider might not have had that patience. In all, a heady ride.

A face broke Lee's preoccupation. A heavy-boned face beneath a gray western hat. Brown eyes. Bold eyes.

Lee stared, stopped. By the time recognition crashed through, recognition despite the full-faced dark beard, the man was lost in the churning, noisy crowd. Western hats everywhere.

Could it be Moss, who had come to the ranch preceding Landy's murder? Could it be, Lee demanded of himself after the shock of surprise? It was Moss. Hell, yes, it was. It was Moss behind that full beard.

Lee tore a path through the crush of bodies.

A sweet-faced elderly lady blocked his way, excited, confused, clutching a handful of tickets. "Sir," she shrilled at him, "can you tell me where the six-dollar combination pay window is? I can't seem to find it in this mob. You see, my little granddaughter is eight years old today, and on a hunch I picked the eight horse, and sure enough—"

"Over there," he said, pointing, and brushed past her, precious moments lost.

Breaking clear, Lee spied a counter where beer was sold in

paper cups. A heavyset man stood there, back turned. Gray western hat.

Lee grasped the man's arm to swing him about. The man turned, his beery voice genial. "Hello, podner. Have a beer with me."

Wrong man.

Lee wheeled and cut back into the mass, under his boots paper cups and crushed ice. Western hats everywhere. Gray hats, brown hats, straw hats. Looking, constantly turning, he zigzagged through the milling crowd, past the last pay window, to a sort of breezeway at the lower end of the grandstand, on his right, benches filled with resting racegoers, beyond them the saddling paddock; on his left a driveway leading to a giant parking lot for Jockey Club members and other VIPs.

A teen-aged attendant in green track uniform rested on a bench at the edge of the drive. Lee ran over to him. "Have you parked a green Mercedes sedan?"

The boy thought that over. "I've parked a few Mercedes and a whole slew of Cads and Lincolns."

"I said a green Mercedes sedan."

"Green? Not that I remember. I'll ask the other guys." He hollered at two buddies up the drive. They shook their heads no.

"If I'd parked a green Mercedes, I believe I'd remember it," said the first boy, and making certain Lee saw his indignation, added, "The owners are always so fussy, afraid we'll scratch a fender."

Painstakingly, Lee worked through the crowd again, on to the entrance under the stands, and back again to the benches, along them to the front of the grandstand, and along the track railing, and did not spot his man. From a public phone booth, twice going for change, he called every motel listed in the directory. No, sir, there is no Mr. Moss registered here.

Naturally, Moss wasn't his name, any more than he was from Tulsa. But the man was here, and the old nightmare, almost forgotten these hopeful days, rose darkly again.

Chapter 13

Hack Trent called Boom Boom Chumley from Houston.

"Want you to do me a favor," he said without preliminary, his tone assuming that Chumley would.

"Shoot."

"Er . . . uh . . . a friend of mine will be out there for the All-American Trials. She'll fly out tomorrow afternoon. I'm sending a company plane to pick her up in Little Rock. I want you to meet her at the Ruidoso airport. Her name is Connie Eaton."

"Okay," Chumley said, swallowing his dislike for the chore. He and Trent had not been on compatible terms since Bunny Barbara had run third in the Rainbow Futurity, July 30, and Chumley had held Gem Three out of the Rainbow trials, although the colt, unknown to Trent, was improving rapidly with carefully spaced gallops every other day and care around the clock.

"She'll be in there about three o'clock. Got it?"

"Okay. Three o'clock tomorrow. Does she have motel reservations?"

"You're to take care of that, too."

"Hack, you know the best places are taken this late in the season."

"Just the same, you get her a nice motel."

"I'll do my best, but don't expect the royal suite."

"And I want you to show her around some, Chumley. Show her a good time. She's got class. I don't mind telling you that she's been on my tail lately. I'm giving her this trip to keep peace on the reservation. Savvy?"

"I savvy," Chumley replied, wondering what sort of woman could put pressure on the old boy.

"Furthermore, keep your cotton-pickin' hands to yourself," Trent said, his gravelly laugh grinding in Chumley's ear.

"Don't you know I'm a gentleman?"

"Nobody's a gentleman when there's pussy around," Trent growled. "Now, about the trials. Where do we stand?"

"Bad news and good news, Hack." You always led off with the bad. "Bunny Barbara's got a problem with her ankle. Don't see how we can start her Friday. It's the left front ankle and it's got heat in it and she favors it. She's been too good to risk."

"You're positive about the ankle, now?"

"I am and so is the vet. As for Hula Moon—" Chumley said, withholding Gem Three's report till the last.

"Has she come around?" Trent broke in.

"You mean her behavior. She's still a bad breaker and runs all over the track. I'll start her, sure, but don't expect anything till she grows up, if she ever does." Chumley had to start her as a long shot because she was sound. If she got off right and didn't lug, she could win her trial and qualify. At the same time, he wouldn't brag on a promising filly he hoped to buy cheap at the end of the season and campaign as a three-year-old in the big derbies. "Hey Now also will start, but I doubt that he'll qualify. For this reason—he's developed a breathing problem and that last hundred yards gets awful long for him. I've even tried a mask on him that filters air."

"What about The Gem?" Trent barked.

"That's the one good news, Hack. The Gem is ready. Been looking sharp in workouts . . . wants to run. The way he looked just before the Sun Country."

"And a race he should've won. Good work, Chumley. We're getting somewhere. You know how this pleases me."

Which is a switch for a change, Chumley thought to himself just as Trent said, "Of all the horses I've paid into the All-American, The Gem is my favorite," and Chumley's silent response to that was, If only you hadn't run him in those god-damned yearling futurities. Aloud, he said, "I'm flying in Sonny Delgado from the West Coast for the ride. He'll check in two days ahead to get acquainted with The Gem. He's super and we're lucky to get him."

"A member of the team, eh?"

"If you want to call it that," Chumley said, wincing. "Will you be here for the trials?"

"I'm tied up on a deal. But you can bet your boots I'll be there for the All-American—and I'm not saying *if* we make it."

"We have a shot, a good shot if The Gem continues the way he is. Meantime, I'll meet the little lady for you." He started to say something in addition about Gem Three, but Trent had hung up, as discourteous as ever.

The boxcar lettering on the silvery hide of the twin-motored aircraft read: TRENT ENTERPRISES, INC. The lone passenger descending the steps didn't fit Chumley's touristy image of the woman he was to meet: slacks, gaudy blouse, low-heeled walking shoes, wind-blown hair, probably on the plump side and in her vague forties. Someone harmonizing with Trent's sloppy appearance and raw taste. This shapely woman was petite and much younger than Trent, eye-catching in a tailored western suit of light tan, a hand-painted belt at her slender waist, her feet encased in chocolate-colored cowboy boots. A slim-look western hat touched off her amber hair, which fell to her shoulders. Trent was absolutely right for once: She had class.

Still not quite certain, he stepped forward and tipped his hat, saying, "Pardon me. I'm Melvin Chumley. I'm looking for a Miss Connie Eaton."

Her momentary questioning look vanished. She said, "I'm Connie Eaton," and held out her hand, smiling as she did so.

"Hack Trent called and asked me to meet you. I'm Hack's trainer."

"Yes, Hack said you would. Thank you, Mr. Chumley."

"Call me Mel or Boom Boom—that's my nickname." Looking at her, he realized how little time he'd had for feminine company since training for Trent as far back as April, prepping for the Kansas Futurity. "I've arranged accommodations for you at the Lone Pine Motel. It's not the best, but I know it's clean. This late in the season, especially with the All-American Trials and the futurity coming up, the nicest places are booked up, some as far as a year ahead." No need to explain that he had gone to extra lengths to get the room—fifty dollars worth, passed to the avaricious desk clerk.

"That sounds perfect. This is my vacation and I know I'll enjoy Ruidoso my first trip here." She drew a deep breath. "The air smells so clean, the sun feels so good." She took his arm as he led off for the airport building. "Did . . . did Hack say when he's coming out?"

"He won't be here for the trials, August twenty-fifth, but he will be out for the All-American on Labor Day."

"He told me he would be here for the trials. In fact, he promised me he would."

"He said something had come up. Some business deal he's on."

"That's Hack," she said, leaving much unspoken, and Chumley said silently, Yes, dear lady, that's our Hack. But you did not speak your mind about the bossman in front of his girl friend.

Her extraordinary amount of luggage required two trips to Chumley's pickup, for which she apologized. "I hope you don't mind riding in a pickup," he apologized in turn when they were loaded.

"I think that will be fun."

"It's a high step up," he warned, giving her a little boost, which she really didn't need. Against his arm she felt light and supple, and the brief scent he got of her hair was thoroughly delightful.

His enjoyment of her grew while driving leisurely from the airport on down toward town to the lone traffic light, chatting about Ruidoso and its boomtown growth, brought about by the success of Ruidoso Downs; and let's not forget the climate, he said, the escape it offered from the scorching summers in Oklahoma and Texas. Not that he was running down Texas, his native state.

She listened attentively to each word, or so it seemed to him, and he attributed that to her being a southern woman of manners and grace. She spoke only to exclaim or to ask a question in her soft voice. Hack Trent, Chumley concluded, had stumbled onto a treasure in Connie Eaton, but bullhead that he was, couldn't see the discovery for the mountain of his own vanity.

The Lone Pine, which wasn't far from his lodgings, delighted her, so she said, although he thought Room 64 too small and the furniture decrepit. It was clean, however.

Unloading her luggage, he found himself more on his manners than usual, to the verge of excessive chivalry, wishing very much to please her, meanwhile increasingly puzzled by what she saw in Trent.

"I have to run out to the barns now, Miss Eaton," he said when her belongings were inside.

"It's Mrs. Eaton," she said, "and please call me Connie. Thank you for meeting me. It was a lot of trouble, I know."

"Not a bit," he swore gallantly, and left her his phone number if she needed him. *Mrs. Eaton.* So she had been married, or maybe was still married. He wondered how she and Trent had met, under what circumstances. He felt sorry for her, and the feeling turned him glum.

Leaving, he still could not remove her from his mind. In addition, meeting her had awakened the past. His former wife, Elsie Mae, lived in Abilene, Texas, happily married to a steadfast, church-active businessman. Coming from a strict Baptist background, she couldn't take the horse-racing crowd, the betting, the rough language around the barns, the partying, the "shooting up" ailing horses to run, the nomadic treks from track to track, or being left at home while he was at the tracks.

And so they had parted, yet as friends. No children made the breakup easier; sometimes he wished there had been a kid or two. He'd have gone to hell and back to hold a family together then. On each anniversary of his birthday, without fail, Elsie Mae sent him a card, note enclosed, reminding him to take care of himself and watch what he ate and drank. Hell, he thought, I loved her and I let her go. Why? Because she was unhappy. Because I had to work with horses. Because I didn't know anything else. Because we didn't fit. No more than Connie Eaton and Hack Trent fit now. He truly felt sympathy for her. Poor lady. She deserved better, unless it was money she was after. In that case, you got what you bargained for, the same as he had when he became Trent's trainer.

Listlessly, he drove out to the barns to check on the horses, saw to their feeding and care for the night, shot the bull with a couple of horsemen, and drove back, restless and dissatisfied with himself and his way of living.

He reached for the phone before he quite understood his intent, then looked up the Lone Pine number, dialed and asked the clerk for Room 64.

"Hello," she answered, surprised.

"This is Mel Chumley," he said. "I'm afraid I forgot my manners this afternoon. Would you like to go out to dinner this evening?"

"Why, thank you, Mel. I'd love to."

"That's great," he said, feeling merry. "We'll go to a supper club. New Mexico's finest, no less."

"How shall I dress?"

"Just as you are."

"I could hardly do that," she said, suppressing a quiet laugh. "I'm not dressed."

"I liked that western outfit you had on today. Anything goes out here. People are very informal."

"I think I'd better wear a dress."

"Wup. Don't forget that high step-up into the pickup."

"Then I'd better wear a suit."

"I'll come by in about an hour. That okay?"

"That's fine. Thank you."

He showered and shaved with extra care, donned a flowered

shirt and co-ordinated neck kerchief and a sky-blue, three-piece western suit, dusted off his python-vamp boots, and was ready to go.

Connie Eaton greeted him in another eye-catching outfit: pink pants suit and a soft-looking sweater of creamy white that brought out the blue of her eyes, not to mention her figure.

"You'll get wolf whistles tonight," he guaranteed her. "Sure glad they don't tag dance out there."

"You flatter me," she said, "but I like it." It occurred to her that Hack had never complimented her appearance, no matter what she wore.

Chumley drove to a supper club miles downriver. A lively western band was playing to a packed house of horse people and tourists. He ordered drinks and dinner; in the interim he asked her if she cared to dance.

"I haven't danced in years," she said haltingly.

"Neither have I. Let's see if we can make it out of the gates."

She was easy to lead and light in his arms, her head against his shoulder. Uncertain in the beginning, he found the rhythm of the progressive country music before long and they were going smoothly. Nice holding her. Mighty nice. They danced two numbers. Leading her back to their table, he said, "You're as light on your feet as a spring filly, but I think the ground kinda broke out from under me back there at the break," and she laughed in the quiet way that he liked.

They followed dinner with more drinks and more dancing. They found much to laugh about. Later, quite late, he glanced at his watch and said, "Guess I should get you home. Hack wouldn't like for me to keep you out late, even though he told me to show you around."

The gaiety on her face seemed to fade all at once, and he sensed that he had put a damper on what had been a most enjoyable evening.

"Yes," she concurred, "we'd better go."

The night was starlit and windless, filled with a sweet languor. A time to forget pressures. A time to look up, not down. A time to wander, not run. He drove slowly along the winding river, neither of them speaking. To break her silence, he said, "I look for Hack to come out a day or two before the All-American. That is, if we make it into the big one."

She seemed remote, her thoughts far away.

"He owns part interest in the Happy Hour Courts," Chumley chatted on. "That way he always has a place to stay. Hack never misses a bet."

She added nothing.

For a gal who had flown all the way from Little Rock to rendezvous with a married millionaire, she showed a remarkable lack of interest in his arrival or holdings. Like why hadn't Trent made reservations for her at the Happy Hour? Chumley's guess was that Trent's wife was coming out for the races.

"I've reserved a box for you at the Turf Club so you can watch the trials," Chumley kept on, striving to break her pensive mood. "It'll be a wild scene. Races start early in the morning, go most of the day. World's fastest two-year-olds shooting for the moon. Hope you'll enjoy it."

"Sounds exciting. I want to go."

"Ever been to a horse race?"

"My late husband used to take me to Hot Springs."

He turned his head. "You mean you lost him?"

"In a plane crash in Tennessee."

"I'm sorry. Very sorry. I shouldn't have asked."

"I'm glad you asked," she said, emerging from her mood. "About the trials? How many horses do you have entered?"

"Three. Only one really has a shot . . . Gem Three. Hula Moon and Hey Now are extra long shots, and The Gem's front wheels will have to hold up."

"His front wheels?"

"That's track talk . . . his knees. If we don't get a shot at the big bundle, I imagine Hack and I will be parting company. He demands an All-American winner. That's his goal. His dream. That's why he hired me."

"You mean he'd fire you? That's incredible, demanding that of a trainer."

"I'll put it this way," Chumley said, his tone carefree. "Hack would be very unhappy. See, he thinks racing can be run like any business. Proper management. Putting figures into computers. Positive attitude. Teamwork. You know, burgers and fries."

She had a laugh over that.

"He can't say I haven't made money for him, though. The Gem took place money in the Sun Country Futurity. Bunny Barbara ran second by a nose in the Kansas Futurity, and third in the Rainbow. A sweetheart of a filly. But she's got ankle problems and is out of the trials. Hey Now has won some consolation money. So Hack is ahead of the game this season."

"Sounds impressive to me."

"We could have done a lot worse. Even with a big stable of two-year-olds to work with, trying to develop potential stakes winners, you can have a total crop failure. Sometimes I think maybe the claiming route is the best. You won't run across many stakes horses, though it does happen; but if you're a good judge of horseflesh and a horse has won some pretty good money, you can make it on claims. About half the races run are claims. I may go that route next season, instead of aiming at these rich futurities. Line up several owners and have at it."

"I'm not sure I understand what a claiming race is."

"First of all, the system keeps superior horses from being run in cheap races and winning everything. It's a leveler, an equalizer of competition. It works like this: Say you put a horse in a fifteen-hundred-dollar claiming race. That means you will sell him for that. Naturally, if the horse is worth ten thousand, you wouldn't risk him at that low level. . . . Let's say a horse catches your eye. You follow him for a while, bird-dog his workouts, check out his legs and general health, look up his performances and how much money he's won. You want him. So you get the money behind you and go to the claiming box before the horse runs and fill out a claim card and drop it in the box. The moment the race starts that horse is yours. He's also yours if he falls down and breaks a leg. That can happen, too."

"It sounds like a gamble to me."

"Every race is a gamble."

The firefly lights of Ruidoso and the onset of snarling traffic reminded him too soon that the evening was over. Turning left at the Y, he stopped at the Lone Pine and gave her an assist from the pickup.

At her door she held out her hand. "It was a lovely evening, Mel. I haven't danced that much since I was a teen-ager. Thank you for asking me."

"Thank you for going. That's the most fun I've had since the high school senior prom at Jacksboro, Texas, and, believe me, that was *some* night." He watched her face with a kind of gentle gravity. "I want you to know something, Connie," he said and hesitated.

"What is it?"

"I'd have asked you out tonight whether Hack Trent had told me to or not. Good night."

Chapter 14

Cindy drew into the third division of the elimination trials for the $1,280,000 All-American Futurity. First post was nine o'clock, with 25 heats scheduled for 249 two-year-olds running 440 yards. Each horse would be photo-electronically timed. When the tension-filled day ended, the ten fastest hopefuls would advance into the nationally televised classic on Labor Day. The trials also would determine the fields for the first, second and third consolations of the All-American.

Lee blinked at the purse money reported in the morning El Paso *Times*: $437,500 to the winner, ranging down to $35,000 for last. Disbursements in the three consolations alone totaled $250,000, plus $30,000 in nominating and breeding awards.

Serena and Nancy, who had arrived Thursday evening in the asthmatic Falcon, visited the barn early to fuss over Cindy before going to the grandstand.

"How does she look?" Serena asked Lee.

"We walked her and she was kicking up her heels. I believe she's ready. She likes it out here. You know: Country girl comes to the big time."

"Daddy, she remembers me!" Nancy said, thrilled, stroking the blaze on Cindy's face.

"A filly," her father teased, "always remembers the person who spoiled her the most."

"Well, I hope you haven't been mean to her."

"Terribly mean. Twenty-four-hour maid service and breakfast in bed."

"I want to braid a red ribbon in her mane."

"Go ahead. But hurry. They'll be calling the first race pretty quick."

After the family left, Lee and Cal and Smoky sat around waiting. Doug had gone to the jockeys' room. Momentarily, Lee forgot the race, Serena uppermost in his mind. Should he have told her about seeing Moss at the track? But why worry her and spoil her day, when she was happy and full of hope? And maybe that wasn't Moss, after all. But it was. He knew it was.

"The track is still a little heavy," said Smoky, who had just returned from there. "Makes our nine hole look all the better. Out there where it's high and dry."

"We had a lucky draw," Lee sighed. "If she's not bumped at the break, she's got a chance. All I want is an even start for her."

Cal said, "She's a runnin' horse, Lee. I believe they'll have to catch her if she gets away clean."

"I don't know a thing about the rest of the field," Lee said, frowning. "Wonder who's favored."

Smoky said, "All I heard was Battle Wagon and Misty Maid, the five and six horses."

Lee tried not to show nervousness. Cindy was much calmer, head over the stall door, curiously intent on horses across the way being ponied to the saddling paddock. The qualifying trials, Lee fretted, were more pressure-packed than the finale. Because once you got that far, you knew you had a shot. There'd be no tomorrow if you failed today, and one one hundredth of a second could spell the difference. He turned on Cindy's radio. A man's melancholy voice, backed by listless guitars and banjos, grated on the nerves at a time when you needed composure. He snapped it off and sat down again, worrying over the wind factor. There was a slight head wind this morning. If it switched around later to a tail wind, the times would go down. You could still win your trial and not qualify.

When over the loudspeakers the raspy, impersonal voice called, "Attention, attention. Take your horses to the paddock for the third division of the All-American," Lee fairly leaped out of his lawn chair and reached for Cindy's bridle. The announcer repeated the call.

Smoky laughed. "I believe Lee's ready to run."

Ponying Cindy around the straightaway and along the path to the paddock on Booger Red, the filly frolicking now and then, Lee could feel the tight expectancy flowing from the humming grandstand. In the 9 saddling stall, while Smoky and Cal stood by, he cleaned Cindy's feet with a brush. Turning, he spied Serena and Nancy waving from the paddock fence. He waved back. Serena threw a kiss; so did Nancy.

Other horsemen were walking their keyed-up charges around the paddock. Lee's impulse was to do the same, if that might help her, then decided she didn't need that as quietly as she was behaving.

Now Cindy stood ready and saddled. Lee took another pull at the overgirth. Doug, wearing cerise silks, hurried up. "You got any notions?" he asked, giving Lee an urgent look. "I don't like this head wind. I been watching the flags in the infield." He was tight-lipped, his face grim.

"Just pull the hammer and go like hell. We're running against the clock, not horses. You know what to do," Lee finished, and slapped him on the back.

Doug managed a tight grin. "That's what I figured you'd say. Let's go."

Jockeys up. In moments the bugle was sounding "Boots and Saddles" and they were on the track for the parade to post. Jogging past the stands, listening to the crowd, Lee thought of an enormous swarm of bees. The infield flags stirred to the east. Still that head wind. Glancing at the twinkling tote board, he saw that Cindy was carrying 18–1 odds. Battle Wagon and Misty Maid were about to be bet into the ground.

Behind the gates, watching the loading begin in numerical

order, Lee saw the 1 horse refuse. The starter stood on an elevated platform or tower, in one hand an electric cord that held the gate-release button. His calming voice, low but clear, reached down there: "Tail him in, Dick." Led in front, assisted from behind, the colt moved forward. That 1 hole was tough on a high-strung youngster forced to wait while the rest of the field was loaded.

The two and three horses followed—no trouble. "Grab the tail on the number four horse . . . push it in." Thus four was persuaded. "Keep number three's head up. . . . The two horse is leaning against the side—straighten him up."

Battle Wagon, a handsome sorrel colt, stepped readily into the five slot. He stood quietly, a mass of sleek muscle alert and primed to roll.

Lee's eyes stayed on Battle Wagon another moment, thinking, There might be the horse to beat.

Misty Maid, a brown filly, had other ideas about how to behave. She flat balked. "Get behind her, Phil. Give him a hand, Blondy. That's it. Good." The two gatemen virtually crammed Misty Maid into the six hole, much to her dislike. In rapid order, the crew loaded the seven and eight horses.

Lee nodded approvingly when Cindy walked in, but once inside she pulled against the tailgate. *Move her up, Doug. Quick! Be ready!* As that warning raced through Lee's mind, Doug righted her.

The ten horse went in like a lamb.

A hushed stillness. A rattle of the gates where Misty Maid demonstrated her discontent. Other horses stirred. The whole gate structure was vibrating. Moments. Now all heads were straight. All feet solidly set.

"The flag is up," came the announcer's voice.

The watching starter pressed the button and the bell rang and the gates flew open.

"There they go!"

Dirt flew in a dark rain of bits and clods.

Cindy came out smoking on top, Doug batting her every jump.

Her lane was clear as the eight and ten horses tore straight ahead.

Misty Maid stumbled heavily bounding out, fell against the unlucky seven horse, and both were immediately out of it. Two dreams smashed right there. Gone, a season's high hopes. Maybe the one chance in a lifetime. Battle Wagon, breaking like a veteran campaigner, had shot away as if propelled.

Lee caught the announcer's staccato first call:

"Cindy takes the lead on the outside. Battle Wagon second. Salty Dog third." Third looked like the two horse to Lee.

They streaked away, a bobbing, shrinking wave. Cindy still firing, still running straight, taking to the track. Doug had quit batting her.

The one horse brushed the inside rail, momentarily lost ground. Under his jockey's frantic sticking he made a determined effort to catch the pack.

Second call: "Cindy's leading by a length. Battle Wagon second . . . driving hard. . . . Bar Son third on the rail. . . . Salty Dog fourth. . . . Bright Angel fifth. It's a horse race!"

As the leaders swept past the paddock, Cindy appeared to break stride, even falter. Lee went cold as Battle Wagon closed on her. Doug batted her again. She took hold again, driving, driving.

The screaming crowd drowned the next call. Lee couldn't see much from here. Everything just a blur of horses. But he knew Cindy was up there. He thought, he hoped. He could see the jockeys standing up. It was over.

He held back for just an instant, almost dreading to ride down there. And then, reining Booger Red around the gates, he struck into a gallop, aching to find out.

The vocal stands had dropped off to a guttural murmuring. He pulled up near the winner's circle to look at the tote board. No results yet. Suddenly it flickered alive and a roar soared up from the crowd.

Lee, eyes fixed, became aware of an unlimited joy and pride for his horse when he saw nine on top. Below it five, then one, then eight. Battle Wagon second. Bar Son third. Bright Angel fourth. But the time? Because time was everything today. For a bit he couldn't locate the reading toward the other end of the board. He found it—:21.73. Twenty-one seconds and change on a sticky track.

Lee Banner whooped and dismounted to greet his horse and jockey.

Doug Adams was grinning from ear to ear, jabbering like a schoolboy. "She stepped in a soft spot at about the paddock . . . that broke her stride . . . threw her off. But when I asked her to come on, she went into overdrive. Till she slipped, I thought we already had it won."

Lee pounded him on the back and led Cindy to the winner's circle for the group picture taking. Cindy in the center, ears pricked curiously at the cameraman. Lee holding her bridle. Doug back in the saddle. Serena and Nancy both dewy-eyed. Cal and Smoky as proud as any owner. Everybody beaming.

"I told you she's a runnin' horse," said Cal, nudging Lee when the scene ended. "Smoky and me, we put our money where are mouths are, too."

"How far back was Battle Wagon?"

"About a length."

"He scared the daylights out of me, he got off so fast. Now all we have to do is sweat out the rest of the trials and hope there's no tail wind."

"She's in the big one for sure," Smoky said.

"Twenty-two heats to run yet," Lee cautioned.

Some Okies spilling out of the stands to crowd around the Oklahoma filly and congratulate Lee cut short further talk.

Lee walked her to the test barn, and afterward watered her and washed her down, and went over her legs, rubbing, examining. Except for a superficial cut on her right cannon, likely caused when she hit the soft spot and broke stride, she was as sound as when she had started the race. Everything was cool and firm. This mindfulness while Cal and Smoky hovered around like mother hens.

"It all goes back to that old saying," Cal said sagely. "That conformation predicts soundness. Good withers, a strong back, a long-muscled hip, straight legs."

"And knock on wood," Lee said.

Later, Lee watched the postings at the racing secretary's office. A winning colt named Warrior Way registered a :22.18 clocking in the seventh division, and Easy Injun won his heat in :21.82.

There was the constant commotion of horsemen anxiously checking the postings, of jotting down times, of some venting their feelings. Lee heard a man say, "You have to be crazy to put late-entry money into this kind of gamble. I don't know what's worse: registering a fast time in the morning and worrying about the wind factor all day, or coming into the twenty-fifth race knowing what your horse has to beat to qualify." Another man said, "I figured my filly had a good shot. But she got bumped at the break. She couldn't carry two horses with her and run fast enough to qualify. Let's go get a drink!"

Lee hung around until one-thirty, when he walked alone to the barns to relieve Doug, leaving Cal and Smoky betting every race, Serena and Nancy in the Turf Club. He studied the infield flags. The head wind had dropped a little and certainly the track was drier and faster. He worried. What if a strong tail wind came up and blew a bunch of horses down the track? That could happen. You took nothing for granted, even with a :21.73 clocking.

The afternoon limped by on an alternating sequence: the announcer calling horsemen to bring their charges to the paddock for the next race, a lull, and then frenzied partisans screaming to the heat's conclusion.

The last race was twenty minutes old when Lee remembered that it was feeding time. He was going about that chore, absently, wondering where his people were, when he heard a car groaning up the slope from the road below the barns. He banged the feed bucket down. He'd recognize the sound of that motor anywhere.

Hastening, he saw them getting out of the old Falcon, their

slowness irksome. Nancy from behind the wheel, and Serena and Cal and Smoky and Doug, an overcasualness on their faces.

"What held you up?" Lee asked sharply.

"Traffic," Nancy alibied. "It's like after an OU–Nebraska game."

"Well . . . how'd we do?" he gruffed.

"Daddy!" Nancy shrieked as only she could. "Cindy's in—she qualified—everything's so beautiful!"

They enveloped him then, his women hugging and kissing him, and Cal and Smoky and Doug shaking hands and standing by, the two older men taking hitches at their big-buckled belts.

"She ran the second fastest time," Cal said.

"That track was faster this afternoon and the wind shifted some," Smoky said, his gambler's eyes keen. "Sudden Deck clocked 21.68. Cindy'd beat that if she hadn't slipped."

Lee Banner kept shaking his head in wonderment. That evening he called his Norman banker.

After trying the Houston and Dallas numbers, Boom Boom Chumley located Hack Trent at his Oklahoma City motel. It was past seven o'clock.

"I've got real good news for you," Chumley announced, after Trent's coarse "Hello."

"Who's this?"

"It's Chumley. The Gem made it into the finals this afternoon. Had the third fastest time. Wish you'd been here."

"Now, that's more like it, Chumley. Tell me *all* about it."

"He won the twenty-third heat by one and a half lengths. Ran it in 21.77. I've never seen him look sharper. He came out of it sored up, which didn't surprise me. I've got him on a hoser for those gimpy knees and he's had his Bute."

"By God, Chumley. By God. This is what I've been hoping for for The Gem. Tell me more."

"He got away nine to five on the board, loafed a little at the stretch pole, then ran off from everything. He was pouring it on at the wire, I tell you. Sonny Delgado rode him super."

"By God, Chumley. By God."

"When will you be out?"

"Don't see how I can make it till the day before the race. Myrna will fly out early. She'll stay at the Happy Hour as usual."

"Want me to meet her?" Chumley felt he had to offer.

"Don't bother. She'll call friends out there. I'd come out with her, but I've got a bunch of problems out west of here. One of my deep tests I told you about. Big fishin' job . . . whole string of tools lost at twelve thousand feet. Speaking of meeting people, what do you think of Connie?"

"She's quite a lady."

"Classy, eh?" in a tone that as much as said, Boy, can I pick 'em.

"Very much so."

"Did you show her around?"

"I did. Even took her out to dinner."

"Just remember what I told you about keepin' your cotton-pickin' hands off her," Trent said, gravelly.

"Now, Hack."

"I want that little girl in a proper frame of mind for when ol' Hack gets out there."

Chumley almost choked, conscious of a genuine regret for Connie Eaton and a strange, deepening anger, and again the question bruised his mind: What did she see in Trent? And why was he so damn cautious, so damn guarded, when Trent asked about her?

"I got her a box for the trials. So she saw The Gem run."

"Good. I couldn't have done better. She's heard me talk about The Gem. I have to say this, Chumley. You know how to train a horse, bring him up to his peak. That's planning, Chumley. Planning and teamwork."

Suddenly, Trent hung up without a parting word.

Teamwork, hell, Chumley fumed. You mean luck. The Gem was running on Bute and heart and speed breeding. He hoped there was one good shot left in the colt for Labor Day. Only by the most careful handling—and luck—had they come this far.

He went out and climbed into the pickup and sat a moment, silent, worn out. He always felt low after the phone sessions.

"Hack says he's tied up on a well in western Oklahoma and won't be out till the day before the All-American," he said, turning to Connie Eaton, seeing, as he spoke, the abrupt conclusion of their relationship and he hadn't even kissed her.

"The day before," she echoed. Her voice was toneless. That was all she said, when he had expected to hear her express disappointment.

He was silent again, sensitive to her nearness, enjoying having her with him. Awkwardly, he said, "I'd like to take you out to dinner."

She sat so long without speaking that he took that for refusal, which he expected in light of Trent's coming. To his surprise, she answered him in a greatly altered voice of anticipation. "On one condition. You said this has been your lucky day."

"So far, if I can keep The Gem on the track."

"I'll go if I may take you to dinner? A sort of celebration on making it into the All-American?"

"I had the Inn of the Mountain Gods in mind. That's an elegant resort operated by the Mescalero Apaches. It's kind of expensive." Our farewell dinner, he left unsaid.

"Sounds delightful. Is it a deal?"

"It is," he said, and on impulse leaned toward her, at the last moment thinking she would turn her face away. She didn't. He found her lips. He kissed her, a light, tentative kiss in the beginning that suddenly intensified, hers unexpectedly sweet and giving.

He drew back, not she. Neither spoke. He started the motor and drove off, his head spinning.

Watching the trials, Todd Lawson could feel himself in every race. There wouldn't be much bull going on in the jocks' room today. No time for pranks. It was get-serious day. A sudden death situation. The boys eyeballing the flags, heedful of wind and weather and the condition of the track, alert to any change. Card games, sure, and seats easy to find as nervous jocks, after a few hands, got up to pace off their tension. The top riders were piloting as many as eight or ten horses today, some more, hoping to qualify one. If a man's luck held and he urged more than one runner into the Labor Day classic, there followed the decision of which horse to ride, which horse of the lot had the top chance of winning. He could envy their "problem."

When the last race was over, he worked through the crowd to the racing office to see the postings. Horsemen whose sprinters had survived the trials were whooping and slapping backs and shaking hands. Others, downcast, took defeat in silence. The Oklahoma man's filly was among the ten fortunate ones. A good-looking blood bay. Todd wished them luck. And Sudden Deck was in, ridden by Flip Keller.

He located his pickup among the horde of vehicles jamming the high parking lot just beyond the entrance gate. Slipping into line, he squeezed through choking traffic; turning off past the Y, he parked in front of an adobe house where he had rented a room with an outside entrance from an elderly lady who boasted of having viewed every All-American Futurity since its inception in 1959. Getting out, he noticed a blue Opel he hadn't seen here before.

He found his door unlocked, which caused him no concern. Sometimes he locked it, sometimes he did not. Didn't matter either way. There was little or nothing among his belongings to interest burglars. On several occasions his well-meaning landlady had left it unlocked after cleaning, which included shaking out the throw rug. But this morning he *had* locked the door. Supposing his landlady was again the culprit, he stepped inside, and as he turned to close the door, a voice said softly, "Hello, Superjock."

The mocking words slammed through him, jerking him around. He stared across the dimness of the room, struck speechless, knowing, yet finding the discovery too incredible after the gap of years. She sat in a chair by the bed table, swinging one well-set leg.

"Don't you remember me, Todd?"

"How'd you get in here?" he asked, both angry and strangely depressed.

"Your sweet little landlady. I told her I was your wife."

"So you lied as usual."

She rose, her movements self-assured, and strolled toward him.

Eve was still a very striking woman, always was, he had to admit that: skin still the color of smoke, eyes still dark and piercing. A full, red mouth. Long, lustrous hair that fell in auburn waves, a frame for the taut, masklike face. He determined to find signs of age, possibly telltale lines edging down her throat or crinkling the corners of her dominant eyes—but he saw none. Nor a hint of fat on that honed-down figure, clothed in a suede suit of stylish brown and high-heeled dress boots encasing those elegant legs. An enormous diamond ring on her left hand. On her left wrist a bright bracelet of twisted silver set with pieces of blue-green turquoise. His eyes swept back to her face. This time he discerned a tenseness, and the pupils were dilated.

She drew still before him and presented her face for a kiss, bringing a scent of some sort of heavy musk he didn't like, but that got inside him.

He just stood.

"Not even a peck for old times?" she said, tilting her head.

He said, "How did you find this place?"

"I read the newspapers, you know. Saw where you were still trying to be heroic and ended up in the hospital again. And the moccasin telegraph says you've been at the Villa Cantina, renewing old acquaintances. Furthermore, your doting little landlady likes to broadcast around town about the once great Todd Lawson rooming at her house, and how nice he is."

His voice equally biting, he said, "I see you're as sweet as ever. What do you want? Why'd you come here?"

"Why?" she repeated, taking clicking steps away from him, and turning, gazing back over her shoulder, hand on hip, left foot at right angle to the other—that pose acquired as a West Coast fashion model. "Why? Because I wanted to see you again. Because I never quite got you out of my system. You know: Todd Lawson, the All-American Boy. The jock who wouldn't pull a horse even when he needed the bread."

"You're play-acting now. Why did you look me up? Answer me."

As if dropping any pretense, she strolled back until they were face to face. "I said I wanted to see you again—that's straight. I'd lost all trace of you. I thought maybe you needed . . . well, a lift of some kind."

"I'm doing fine. I gallop horses about every morning. The other day I rode the winner in a quarter horse allowance."

"I missed that," she said, unimpressed.

"It felt great."

"Like old times?"

"Like new times. I don't want the old ones back. Never."

"Look," she said, "you don't understand. Maybe I'd like to make up for the time I walked out on you when you got hurt." With her adorned left hand, she drew a sweeping gesture of disdain. "I'd like to get you out of this . . . this shabby hole in the wall."

"It looks good to me. It's clean."

"I don't mean that. It's just that I want to see you on your feet again. Riding in the big futurities and derbies. I'm doing well, you know. If you'd let me—"

He cut her off. "You look well. Are you married?"

She didn't answer; by that he surmised that she wasn't, just living with some guy. But she said, "My husband is in a lot of things. We live in Dallas most of the time. Come here during the summer season. Yes, Todd, I'm doing well. Quite well."

Eve was a puzzling woman. A chronic liar. Couldn't help it, apparently. In the California days, she'd go out with friends. Tell him she'd gone to the beach. Go to the beach, tell him something else. Sometimes she'd be gone for days and return with all sorts of stories: another beach party, a distant shopping spree, running into "old friends" who seldom turned up afterward. The ones who did, generally a collection of offbeat characters, he didn't like. She had never lacked for company. And thinking about those California days, when he was boozing and riding, and often gone from her, he almost felt sympathy for her. Almost.

"You do look well," he said, and she did, except for the telltale disclosure behind her eyes.

Coming to him, she slipped her arms around him and kissed him on the mouth, her body fully against him, the musk scent between them. She said, barely audible, "You look well, too, Todd. You look fit, you look happy."

"I am happy."

"It's been a long time, Todd. We could make it a real reunion. Make love—right here. Now. Like old times. I haven't forgotten you, no matter what you think. I need you."

He could feel the wanting for her and started to lift his arms, then hesitated. Somehow he did not embrace her and realized that actually he was afraid of her, of himself as well, sensing that through renewal he would be turning back over the long, long way he had struggled to come. Little by little, the emotion left him. He dropped his arms and said to her, not unkindly, "You don't need me, Eve. You never did."

She pulled back. A muscle twitched in the mask. Behind the overwide eyes, he saw an inwardness; perhaps, for once, he also saw honesty. She said, "It's not there anymore, is it, Todd? It's gone."

"You knew that a long time ago. But when we started out, it was there and it was true . . . until the money got too big." He stepped back.

They looked at each other for a space, like the strangers they had been back there, really, not speaking, until she said, "I guess I can understand if you won't let me help you."

"You don't owe me a thing."

"All right, if you say so. But to me it's still a debt. I can let you in on something, Todd. Something big. You can make a great deal of money on your own, and you can make it fast. Big money."

"Like how?" It followed that he didn't believe her.

"I won't tell you unless you say you want to get smart and quit galloping horses for three bucks a head."

"Eve," he said, his weary disgust ripping through, "that last year I couldn't remember talking to you when you weren't on some kind of high. You're on a high now. I can see it. What the hell are you into around here?"

He caught the twitch again.

She stiffened. She flounced to the door and paused, a graceful figure turned just so, her booted feet just so, the mask slightly upturned. "At least I tried to help you," she said, full of pity for him. "I'll see you again, Superjock, after you've had a while to think about things—and the old times." She stalked out.

He listened to the retreat of her quick, clicking steps, and heard the Opel grinding, then starting, and the crunching of gravel, and the car roaring off in the direction of town.

He hoped she was lying again. Belatedly, on that thought, it struck him that she had given him no name.

Chapter 15

Doug Adams had insisted on taking the last night watch. Grinning, he explained that would allow him to make the "evening shift" with other jockeys at the Villa Cantina.

Up early on Sunday after Friday's trials, Lee took black coffee in the trailer house he had rented for the family, and drove to the barns at daybreak. He parked the pickup on the muddy slope below and walked up to the long shed row, expecting to find a sleepy-eyed Doug awaiting him. Doug, however, wasn't up yet. He was still abed on a cot next to the stall. Neither was Cindy poking her blazed face over the stall door, impatient for her majesty's breakfast of oats and hay.

Lee, coming under the overhang, was about to nudge Doug awake when he saw the dried blood on Doug's head and on the blanket. Recoiling, he called Doug's name and shook him. Doug didn't answer. He was out, maybe worse.

As it had that morning at the ranch when Lee found Doc and did not hear Land Rush's familiar racket, that strange alarm sounded again within him and he whirled up and looked inside the stall.

Cindy wasn't standing back in the shadows. Neither—and his relief was momentary—was she down like Landy. She was gone.

He jerked back to Doug and laid an easy hand on his shoulder and called to him. Doug moaned a little. Other early horsemen were stirring around the barns. Lee yelled and motioned, then ran for the phone.

They had to carry Doug down the slippery slope to the ambulance. Lee rode beside him to Ruidoso's Hondo Valley Hospital, holding Doug's hand while the attendant fed him oxygen. On the way Doug thrashed and moaned now and then, but did not regain consciousness.

The dreadful waiting set in.

Cal and Smoky usually ate breakfast at the Whispering Pines Restaurant. Lee called there and Cal came to the phone.

"Got some mighty bad news," Lee said. "Somebody beat Doug unconscious and stole Cindy."

There was a gasp at the other end of the line. A run of stunned silence. "Lee, you've got to be kidding."

"I'm not. Doug's in bad shape. I wish you'd bring the girls to the hospital. I'll call Doug's folks after a bit. He's still in emergency. I'll call the police with Cindy's description so they can start checking. Have them notify state police and the Downs security."

"We'll be right there, Lee. Don't forget to tell 'em about Cindy's blue eye."

Shock was beginning to seep into Lee now. He felt physically sick, his concern for young Doug prevailing over his seething fury. Thus he waited.

Everybody was there when Doug was wheeled out of emergency. The doctor, short, wiry, bespectacled, harried, said, "He's in deep shock . . . severe concussion, broken shoulder, four broken ribs, punctured lung."

Lee became as still as a rock. "Will he make it?"

"Are you family?"

"Friends—mighty close friends. He's our jockey. His family's in Oklahoma."

"His injuries?" The doctor was puzzled. He cut small circles with his right hand. "So many bruises? Did he fall from a horse?"

"No, sir. He was beat up. They beat him, then stole our filly."

"He's young and strong. That much is in his favor. However, I think you ought to call in his family." A nurse spoke and the doctor excused himself.

Lee turned, meeting Serena's eyes, and he saw mirrored there the rollback of his own thinking. The vulnerability of innocent people. The nightmare again. The hurt. The fear. The anger. The helpless anger. The not knowing. Doc and Landy. Now Doug. Now Cindy, gone.

"They did it, didn't they?" she said savagely, accusingly.

In the mildest of voices, Lee said, "I'd better call Doug's folks. Get them out here by plane. Then I'm going to the barns. I want Cal and Smoky with me. I want you and Nancy to stay with Doug."

She nodded numbly. Nancy, pale but unusually calm, took her mother's hand.

Along the shed row, horse people conversed in huddled groups. They became silent as Lee and his friends climbed the slant. A local officer introduced himself: Detective Mike Vernon, head of Ruidoso's Criminal Investigation Division. He reminded Lee of Undersheriff Bob Caldwell back home. Educated, intent, a tenacious face; spoke well. The new breed. All business. Residents near the track were being questioned now, he said. Lee gave him a statement and talked to a reporter, who took Lee's photo standing in front of the empty stall. Lee declined an invitation from a Downs security officer to go to the office of the track's general manager. "Will a little later," he said. "Right now I feel like a sheep dog that keeps hanging around the old homeplace after his family moved off."

Two New Mexico State Police arrived. They said an all-points bulletin was out. Highways were being checked. Lee thanked them, while feeling little could be done. There were no leads. Horse tracks told nothing, for horse tracks were everywhere. He found Cindy's prints and those of other horses pocking the slope down to the road, there to merge and blur and lose identity, obliterated by passing pickups and cars. He tramped back to the stall with Cal and Smoky, fighting the unreality of it all.

As word spread around the Downs, more horsemen converged with offers of help. One was Todd Lawson. Not only did they share Lee's loss, they shared his fury.

Another patrol car stopped below and a local officer ran up to the barns. He was younger than Vernon and dead serious as he looked at his report pad. "I think I've got a lead. Questioned elderly subject who lives across the highway. Around three o'clock subject heard a commotion—voices—a clatter. Subject said he looked out and saw a vehicle about the size of a big furniture van. It was stopped with the lights off. Subject said about then the driver turned the lights on and drove toward the Y. If the horse was in the van, suspects could have gone through town and into the mountains, or taken Highway Seventy to Tularosa."

Vernon turned to Lee.

"And maybe on to El Paso and Mexico," Lee said. "That's what I'm afraid of. I will put up a reward, but I doubt it will be enough to jar loose any leads. We came out here on a shoestring . . . borrowed the money to pay our filly's late entry. If she's in Mexico, we'll never get her back." He looked at Todd Lawson. "Todd, I know you've ridden down there. What's it like?"

"It's a rough go. Lots of big match races. Wealthy ranchers will bet the moon. A hundred-thousand-dollar purse is not unusual. For an Anglo jockey it's a big fee if you win, nothing if you lose. Sometimes it got real hairy. Threats, guns, drugs. Offers to join in on the trafficking because they knew I could fly a plane. I quit riding down there some years ago." His rugged face brightened. "That's a long way to haul a horse. Maybe your filly is around Ruidoso. Plenty of places to hide a horse, but they'd have to stick close to the roads." He was, Lee saw, trying to sound hopeful.

A track official pointed out that Cindy's status was that of a "scratched" horse in the All-American, which meant that Lee would receive the tenth-place money of $35,000.

"I hadn't thought that far ahead," Lee said. "That will help with the reward money."

The track identifier said the lip tattoo system used on American tracks was close to infallible. The numbers could not be blurred or changed. To remove the tattoo, he explained, the lip tissue would have to be removed surgically. Therefore, the filly could not be run in the states on a track approved by the American Quarter Horse Association.

"That points even stronger toward Mexico," Lee reasoned. They were getting nowhere. Going in circles. Talking and sympathizing. He had held back on revealing what had happened in Oklahoma, and when Vernon said, "Mr. Banner, other than stealing a filly that had the second fastest time in the trials, and possibly match racing her in Mexico, I'm puzzled by the motivation," Lee knew that he had to come out with it. He said, "There is another motivation and I'll tell you what it is."

"Would you rather talk about it in private?"

"No, I want everybody to hear it. Maybe that way somebody will run across something. The more people who know, the better."

"Go ahead," Vernon said.

Lee told them the story from beginning to end, to seeing "Moss" near the betting window, and added a postscript. "I don't know what it means, but the name Bruno popped up back there. Like maybe he was the mastermind behind the trafficking." He shrugged. "There it is. Now I'd like to call the hospital."

Serena said Doug was still out. No better, no worse. Doug's parents, flying in this afternoon, would augment the round-the-clock vigil at the hospital. Lee stuck to the Ruidoso police station, where Detective Vernon, through radio, television and newspaper pleas, had asked persons to call in any pertinent information. Lee announced a $15,000 reward, and Ruidoso Downs posted an additional $10,000. Horsemen at the track pledged another $10,000.

A television crew from El Paso interviewed Lee and Vernon and track officials, and took footage of the stall and track. The Associated Press called, United Press International called. The *Daily Oklahoman* called and Lee talked to a sports writer, who kept emphasizing the "Oklahoma angle." Afterward, Lee told Cal and Smoky, not concealing his bitterness, "Quarter horse racing has finally made big news back home. It takes something like this. Wonder if they carried a line when Cindy set the second fastest qualifying time on a heavy track?"

When evening came, Lee drove to the hospital and sat until midnight. Doug's parents would stay throughout the night. Meanwhile, Doug's condition was unchanged.

At ten-fifteen Monday morning, when Lee took a call at the police station, a man's blurred voice said, "I can tell you where your gray filly is." Jukebox music blared in the background. Vernon, who was listening in on the line, smiled and shook his head.

"That's good news," Lee said, going along. "Tell me where she is, you'll get your money."

"Have to see the thirty-five thousand first."

"I have to see the filly first. No filly, no money—and by the way, she's a blood bay—not gray."

The man disconnected.

"The cranks are coming out of the woodwork," Vernon said.

That seemed to fuel a flurry of wild rumors. A bay filly answering Cindy's description had been seen hauled through Albuquerque. Cindy was in Laredo. Cindy was sighted loose on Interstate 10 between Las Cruces and Deming. Cindy was in Carlsbad. Cindy was in Tucson. Cindy was everywhere.

In the middle of the afternoon, a woman's flat voice: "Your horse is in Lincoln. She's here in a two-horse trailer. Bring all the money and she's all yours. We'll be waiting in front of the old courthouse where Billy the Kid made his escape."

"I can't bring you all the money today," Lee hedged. "But if you have my horse, you'll get your full reward."

"How much can you bring?"

"Five thousand."

"Bring it. But don't come in a sheriff's car or police car."

"I drive a green Ford pickup with an Oklahoma tag. I'll be there." He turned to Vernon. "I don't have any faith in this, because why would they settle for five thousand? But let's give it a try."

Lee and Vernon drove through the mountains to Lincoln and parked in front of the courthouse, while Cal and Smoky, following in Cal's pickup, continued on through the village to look. No horse trailer was in sight. Tourists meandered along the broad street, in and out of the historic places; some stopped to buy apple cider and apples and homemade jelly. Cal and Smoky, circling back, parked on the other side of the street from Lee and Vernon.

Two hours passed.

"Let's go," Lee said, disgusted.

"Some crank is having a lot of fun over this," Vernon said.

Darkness caught them on the way back to Ruidoso. Lee drove fast, taking the winding lower valley route, which took them past the Downs' barn area, now lit up like an armed camp.

"You can bet everybody's sleeping with his horse tonight," Lee mused. "Makes you think of the old saying about closing the barn door."

At the police station the desk sergeant said, "Had a nut call you wouldn't believe. A guy in Los Angeles . . . claims to be some kind of guru. Calls himself 'The Celestial One.' Said he'd fly in if Mr. Banner sent him a ticket, paid him five hundred a day and all expenses. Claims he's getting signals from outer space—he calls 'em psychic vibrations—that Cindy is somewhere in Oregon." The sergeant rolled his eyes. "He left his number. There was nothing else."

Lee called the hospital. "Lee," Serena said, breathless, "Doug regained consciousness about four o'clock. He knew us all. Seeing his folks helped so much."

"Boy, that's a relief. Did you tell him about Cindy?"

"Not yet."

"It can wait. I will later."

"I feel much better about Doug now. If only he doesn't develop pneumonia."

"I'll be right out. We had a dry haul at Lincoln."

"Oh, Lee, do you think we'll ever see her again?"

"We have to hope so. We have to keep trying."

Late Monday afternoon Todd Lawson unlocked the outside door of his room and sat awhile, reviewing the busy day. Galloping horses most of the morning. His strength was returning. He was gaining confidence. Horsemen were beginning to believe in him again. That allowance win had opened some eyes. With luck, he might have an agent for the fall season at Sunland. He turned on the little radio which his obliging landlady had left for his use. The six o'clock news was on. Midway through the report he perked up at, "Authorities are still without leads as to the whereabouts of the speedy Oklahoma filly stolen from Ruidoso Downs early Sunday morning. . . . Jockey Doug Adams, severely beaten during the theft, is reported in improved condition at Hondo Valley Hospital. . . . The missing bay filly, named Cindy, established the second fastest qualifying time in the All-American trials and would have loomed among the favorites for the Labor Day classic. . . . Owner Lee Banner, Ruidoso Downs officials and horsemen have posted rewards totaling thirty-five thousand dollars for the filly's return. Authorities fear she may have been taken to Mexico." A detailed description of Cindy followed.

Todd turned off the news, reliving the incredible theft. By trying to do the right thing, Lee Banner had crossed ruthless people back in Oklahoma. A horseman's luck. Now here. Made you mad as hell. Made you wonder if organized hoodlums were moving in on the southwestern tracks.

He showered and shaved, preparatory to having dinner at Babe Younger's, and was dressed to leave when there was a knock at the outside door. He didn't know why, but he knew Eve would be the caller before he opened the door, and he knew before he let her in that he should not. All she could mean was trouble.

"Hi," she said, as if they were accustomed to seeing each other every day, trailing that heady musk scent. She wore a swishy, rose-colored pants suit and she had changed her auburn hair to that stylish new tight curl, done in ringlets.

"What is it this time?" he asked.

"Todd, why be so uptight every time I see you about what happened between us?"

"You read me wrong. I'm not in mourning. I just want to be left alone. I made that clear the first time."

She feigned hurt. "I'm only trying to help you."

"I made that clear, too. I don't need or want help."

Uninvited, she took the chair she had previously and rested an indolent left arm on the bed beside her leather purse, displaying the eye-popping diamond ring and the distinctive silver bracelet, while she swung the provocative leg. Todd continued to stand, at a loss how to get rid of her other than throwing her out, though puzzled why she had come back.

"I still can't get over how well you look," she said, her eyes frankly approving.

"Simple. No booze. No pills."

"I shouldn't have left you."

"Why not? I was down and broke."

"You make me sound mean and mercenary," she said, appearing hurt again. "I guess I deserve that." She turned her head just so, seeming to gaze off in retrospect, which highlighted the mask-like perfection of her face as he knew she intended. "But I am not without feeling or conscience," she said, tossing her head for emphasis when she turned back to him. "There's so much you could have again and all you'd have to do would be to wiggle one little finger, like this, like now."

He ignored the invitation, his voice amused. "You mean the debt thing?"

"If you choose to call it that. I still feel guilty, always will. And, like I told you, I never got over you. That's part of it." She lowered her eyes just so, and when she looked up at him after some moments, her eyes, made deeper and darker by the long lashes, had the wide-open innocence of a child's. Almost, he caught himself. God, how she could put on. And, he saw, she was on a high again. "That's why," she said softly, "I came here tonight to tell you how you can make yourself five thousand dollars at a crack, real easy like."

"Just an honest day's work, eh?" he scoffed.

"Less than a day. Only a few hours. All you have to do is fly an airplane a few hundred miles once a week."

Understanding took root, suddenly burst. So that was it. He might have known. "Once a week," he said. "Like south of the border?"

Her smile: maybe yes, maybe no.

"Like to Oaxaca and back?" he persisted. "I fly the stuff in, land at some desert strip, a truck is waiting? About then the Border Patrol descends?"

"There would be nothing to fear."

He didn't understand himself. Why was he listening to her? It wasn't money. And he wasn't fool enough to trust her if it was. An odd sense, something dim but groping, broadened within him as he said, "I haven't flown in years. Not since before I got hurt at Bay Meadows."

"You could retrain. You were very good at one time. You used to say flying's like swimming. Once you learn how, you don't forget."

This had gone far enough. He was on the point of telling her flatly to count him out, to forget it, and yet here he was saying, "I'd have to think about it."

"You will? Good!" She seemed surprised. Getting up, she embraced him quickly.

"I said I'd have to think about it, Eve."

"Of course. I want you to think about it. No hurry. Before we carry this any further, too, I want you to talk to my husband. You know . . . the details."

"Where?" And still no name, he thought.

Her hesitation was not prompted by evasion. He divined that. She hesitated because she wasn't wholly sure of him—not yet. And then she said, "There's a place up in the mountains," and checked herself.

"There are mountains all around us."

"Just say it's between here and Capitan. I'll get back to you later about when and where. I'm glad you're getting smart, Todd. There's so much we can make up for along the way." She lifted her left hand to caress him. As she did, the silver bracelet took his eye. Without thinking, he caught her hand and studied the bracelet, made of intricately twisted silver wire set with nuggets of bluish-green turquoise. His mind ran back. "This," he said, "looks like extra fine Navajo work. Something Web would have liked."

"Web?" Startled, she jerked her hand free.

"Yes. Web Parker. Who else? Remember how he went overboard for turquoise? The high-priced quality stuff, the old pawn? Remember how he spent money? That was Web. When he went in for anything, it was all the way. Never halfheartedly. Remember when after just a few lessons, he bought that Cessna?"

Her face twitched, that infinitesimal sign of tension.

He would have thought nothing more about it had she not lost her poise for an instant. Had she not, although no explanation was necessary, let go an outpour of depreciation. "I bought it here. It's nothing much. Really nothing. Nothing at all."

"Then you made a lucky buy. It looks like something out of a collection."

She turned to the bed and picked up her purse. Facing about, she regarded him searchingly, coldly, short of suspicion, it might seem. There was that tenseness about her face, an obscure suggestion of hardness. At last, he thought, she looks older. But, gradually, her expression returned to that convincing smile which he remembered she could summon whenever she wished. She moved to the door and said, "You will think about that now, won't you, Superjock?"

He found himself nodding, not unlike they were playing mere roles.

"I'll be in touch before long," she said, and flung him a vague little wave.

He watched her go out. She was lying again. Something had happened. Something was wrong. Strange woman. Unpredictable. Either on a high or a low, never in between, on a level where life was really lived. Long ago he had thought of her as beautiful, and she was, then. He doubted that he would ever see her again.

That dimness he could not connect kept bothering him as he drove to Babe's Place. Customers stood lined outside and the parking lot was full. He left the pickup a block away and took a place at the end of the line. After a long wait, he shuffled inside. Babe was at the order window, talking to Estela. Now and then Babe glanced at the line. Seeing him now, she sent him a radiant smile, and when his turn came, she led him to the rear dining room, where a girl was clearing a small table.

"You look tired," she said.

"Nothing that seeing you won't fix."

"You mean Estela's cooking."

"I mean you. But I'll take both. I'd like an omelet, Mexican style, and some cornbread, if that's okay, and black coffee."

"You Texans and your cornbread. I'll see what I can do."

After dinner, he lingered over coffee until he felt guilty, watching the tide of hungry tourists and horse people continue unabated. Babe was at his side when he rose to go.

"You're frowning, Todd. You're not worried about anything, are you?"

"I keep thinking about that filly that was stolen. I've seen her work. She doesn't run, she flows. Second fastest time in the trials . . . on a slow track, too. Now she's gone. Ruidoso's changed, Babe. Big money everywhere. And money brings all kinds of people. People not interested in horses. Here to take what they can, any way they can." More tourists shuffled in from the outside. "They're starving," he said, finding a grin for her. "You won't get out of here till midnight, and I've got to get up at five o'clock."

"You're all right?" she asked, not convinced.

"I'm the luckiest man alive. I found you."

"That's one half of it. Tomorrow night I'll close at ten o'clock if I have to turn people away." She looked about self-consciously and said, low, "Todd, I miss seeing you during the day."

"That's another half," he said, smiling at her.

He paid his check and left. He was approaching the adobe house when his latent unease suddenly steered him on. He circled and headed back, driving slowly, looking; when he saw no Opel, no strange cars, only the pickups of the other two roomers, he turned in. He got out and cut his glance around, realizing that he half expected somebody to come charging out of the darkness at him. His feeling deepened. Inside, he snapped on the light and locked the door. Turning, he breathed the heavy musk scent again, evoking the uncanny sensation that she was still here, sitting over there, mocking him, suggesting.

Sleep, which usually came moments after he lay down, eluded him until late. After a few hours, something woke him up. He imagined it was the rumble of Ruidoso's heavy nocturnal traffic on Sudderth Drive. A different awareness, like sudden light, broke upon him as he sat up. He rolled out of bed, thinking, no, it couldn't be. It was too farfetched, too improbable. But, an inner voice countered, so was stealing an All-American filly. He went back to bed, but couldn't sleep. His mind kept sorting out, rejecting, accepting, denying, swinging back, firming. No. The more he tried to stifle the possibility, the more it refused to let him rest. He slept no more.

At daylight he started looking for Lee Banner.

Lee had not passed through the check gate at the Horsemen's Entrance, nor was he at the little cafe on the highway close to the track where horsemen often stopped for early coffee. At eight o'clock Todd called the general manager's office at the Downs.

"No, sir, Mr. Banner isn't here now, though he's expected to call in later. Mr. Banner and his family are staying in a trailer house downvalley, but he has no phone." Todd started to hang up.

Of a sudden the feminine voice sharpened alertly. "Sir, is your call about the missing filly?"

"It could be."

"Then please call the Ruidoso Police Station immediately." She read him the number.

Todd dialed and quickly had his man. "Lee, this is Todd Lawson. Something came up last night I feel I ought to talk to you about. It may concern your filly, it may not. It's a long shot if there ever was one."

"Want me to meet you?"

"No, I'll come there. I'll hurry."

They huddled in Mike Vernon's cramped office, away from the bleating of the police radio.

Jerkily, in haste, Todd set forth what had taken place, from Eve's offer of "easy money" for one flight a week to Mexico and back, the return landing not designated, to meeting her husband, unnamed, in the mountains to work out the details, leaving out only Todd's reference to Web Parker, which he thought unimportant.

"Where in the mountains?" Lee asked.

"Between Ruidoso and Capitan."

"Whew. A lot of places between here and Capitan."

Vernon, arms folded, frowned in negation. "I can't see the connection between all this and Lee's filly."

"It's drugs," Todd replied. "Drug traffickers killed Lee's stud back in Oklahoma because he was going to testify against them in court. Now Lee sees this guy Moss at the track. Moss must have spotted Lee, the way he disappeared so fast. Moss connects Oklahoma and Ruidoso."

"I see that," Vernon said, "but I can't connect Moss to your former wife, Eve."

"I ransacked my brain most of the night trying to figure this out from every angle. It's just a hunch . . . but it makes hard sense, if you knew Eve. She wouldn't trail with some guy unless he was top dog. The kingpin, in this case. Only a kingpin would be flying in stuff from Mexico. Not some small-time guy working the streets."

"The kingpin back in Oklahoma was called Bruno," Lee put in. "Probably a cover name."

"What if Moss doesn't figure in this at all?" Vernon went on.

"Even if he doesn't," Todd said, "and it's another kingpin, it was drugs in Oklahoma and it's drugs out here, and drugs lead to Eve and Mexico, and drugs and Mexico can lead to fast horses and high stakes in match racing."

"Let's go back to Cindy," Vernon theorized. "Stealing a filly is taking a big risk. If Moss engineered it, would he do it for revenge alone?"

"It would have to be profitable, too," Todd reasoned. "That

filly is extremely valuable. She outclasses horses I've won big money on in Mexico. Mind you, I'm talking about match races. She could make a Mexican rancher wealthy. They like to bring in an unknown runner and clean up. When they can't match a lightning-fast horse anymore because it's too well known, they sell the individual in another state in Mexico, or peddle the horse in South America. I know. I've seen it done."

They pondered their own thoughts in silence, broken when Vernon said, "We could chew this back and forth all day. There's no doubt about the dope traffic in southern New Mexico. The Federal Drug Enforcement Administration, in co-operation with this department and the sheriff's office, has an undercover investigation going on now. We think Ruidoso is a distribution point, but so far we can't prove it. Just a few street arrests up to now. No kingpin." He looked at Lee. "What do you think? We'll do what you say."

"It's the only lead we have. Let's check out the country between here and Capitan."

"I pretty well know what's between us and Alto. I'd say it's from Alto on where we'll need to start looking, from Alto to Fort Stanton. . . . The county will want in on this. So will the state police, only they're working a wreck near San Patricio at the moment. So will the DEA."

"We can't wait around for everybody," Lee said, rising.

"Neither can we afford to go off half-cocked. Drug traffickers don't surrender meekly. They shoot it out. I'll gather up what men we can here."

Lee called Cal and explained. "Do you and Smoky want to go? You're not obligated."

"We'll be right there."

"Better pack your thirty-eight."

Chapter 16

Inside twenty minutes they were driving into the mountains, Lee and Todd in Vernon's patrol car, Cal and Smoky together, two policemen in Vernon's personal car, and an off-duty sheriff's deputy riding with a DEA agent.

Past Alto, Vernon pointed to a road slashed through the pines, and Lee said, "We'd better look for a shed or barn."

The road ended abruptly before a small cabin. A young woman sat on the sunny porch, overseeing two children playing in the yard. A yellow station wagon bearing a Texas tag was parked by the porch.

The detective stopped, leaned out and said, "Morning, ma'am. We're trying to locate a Springfield, Illinois, family. It's an emergency call. Illness back home."

"We've just moved in," she said, coming to the edge of the porch. "Renting through Labor Day. There's another cabin on this side just off the main road. You might ask there."

Vernon thanked her and drove out, took the next road and they found a family of vacationers and another Texas-tag car. No shed, no barn.

Deeper into the mountains, bouncing over a little-traveled road, they approached a house of once lodge-like pretensions.

Now the boards on the front steps showed gaps, the porch sagged, and a hanging shutter exposed a broken windowpane.

"There's a good-sized barn back there," Todd said.

As they drove up, a man appeared on the path leading from the house to the barn. Suddenly he darted for the woods, his progress obviously labored.

"Let's go," Vernon said, and they piled out, all carrying pump shotguns.

Vernon intercepted the man at the edge of the woods. "Sir, we'd like to talk to you."

"What about?" he hacked. He was a whippet of an old man, slight but rock-jawed, unshaven but clean, wearing faded jeans and shirt. Eyes, rheumy but aggressive, regarded them without fear. He conveyed an air of independence. He was unarmed.

"We're looking for wetbacks," Vernon said. "We'd like to search your barn."

A sly smile gullied the leathery face. "Go right ahead."

"We'd rather you came with us, sir."

The same smile. "Don't mind."

With an exaggerated show of obliging, he led them to the barn and inside. There a brown saddler of advanced age was nibbling hay.

"My old mare, Belle," he cackled. "You won't find any wetbacks around here, young man. Best place to look is down in the valley where the horse ranches are."

"Why did you run when you saw us?" Vernon questioned.

He looked down, digging the tip of a scuffed boot into the abundance of barn litter. "Well, I'll tell you. I'm way behind in my taxes on the old place. Tourists used to flock in here. When my health failed, I couldn't keep it up. You can see for yourself how run-down it is. Folks quit comin' so much; then they quit altogether. I ran because I thought you boys were from the county assessor's office, come to nag me about my taxes." His watery eyes narrowed on Vernon. "Wetbacks, you say? You're no border patrolman. You're a city officer. What're you after way out here, anyway?"

When Vernon seemed reluctant to explain, Lee said, "Let's

tell him, Mike. I will. Old-timer, we're looking for a filly stolen at Ruidoso Downs. Maybe you can help us, you're a horseman. She's a two-year-old blood bay. Blaze on her face. Left eye a pale blue. White socks on her hind feet. Stands fifteen hands. She's a finalist in the All-American. Stolen early Sunday morning. They also beat up our jockey. He's in bad shape."

"Nobody with a filly like that has come by here." In the same breath he exploded with, "That's one of the worst crimes there is —stealin' a man's horse. I'd shoot the son of a bitch."

"Any new people moved in around you lately?"

"Nobody I know. When tourists come up this road, they take one look at the house and turn around. Wish I could help you."

"If you hear or see of anything, call the Ruidoso police department."

"You bet 'cher boots I will. I'm Ned Donaldson." Introductions followed; everybody shook hands. They walked to the yard, where the other cars were drawn up, and drove away. Glancing back, Lee saw Ned Donaldson waggle a detaining hand, hastily break into a run after the car, waving both arms.

"Hold on!" Lee yelled at Vernon. "He wants us to stop."

Vernon jammed on the brakes. The old man ran up, hacking, "I just remembered. Three guys came here . . . wanted to rent the place. Looked it over good—everything—walked over the land."

"When was that?" Vernon asked.

"Few weeks ago. They offered me more money than I'd seen in years. I turned 'em down. Wouldn't have 'em on the place."

"Why not? You said you needed the money."

"They wanted the whole layout. Said I'd have to leave. Belle, too. I told 'em to go flat to hell an' back. Belle and I stay. I've got a room in the back. That's the only way I'll rent. Her—she's all the family I got left. I raised her from a foal. No, they said Belle had to go, too."

"You mean," Lee said slowly, "they wanted the barn, too?"

"That's right—the barn—everything."

Lee looked at Vernon and Todd, then back to Ned Donaldson. "Old-timer, can you describe the three men?"

"Looked like tourists you'd see in town. Sport shirts. Big, dark sunglasses. Baseball caps. One guy stayed behind the wheel. Never got out. He looked good-sized is all I can tell you. The other two . . . one was heavyset, looked forty or over. Other one was younger. Slim. He did most of the palaverin'. Both clean-shaven. They left when I got frothy."

"Were they driving a green Mercedes sedan?"

"Son, I wouldn't know a green Mercedes from a bullfrog. I ride Belle to town for groceries. Fetch everything back in a gunny sack." He rubbed hard at his forehead. "Guess that was too far back to mean anything, though."

"Old-timer," Lee said, "maybe you've helped a good deal. Much obliged. Let's go, Mike." But as they sped away, Lee said, "He's right about the time element. It fails to jibe. Since Cindy didn't run till last Friday in the trials, why would they want to rent a place with a barn some weeks ago, before they saw her run?"

Nobody spoke until they reached the main road. "Because," Vernon said, "because they were already going to steal a fast horse for delivery in Mexico."

"Why not Sudden Deck, with the fastest time in the trials? Why Cindy? Why not Gem Three or Easy Injun?"

Todd said, "Because she's not only a class racehorse, one that came within a few split ticks of the clock of running the fastest time on a slow track—but because she belongs to Lee Banner. That links up with Moss again."

Lee fell into a brooding silence.

On the off roads in the next two hours they questioned old and young summer visitors enjoying the cool pines, some hardy year-round residents, and looked into empty sheds and barns and others that housed riding horses. By eleven-thirty they weren't far from Fort Stanton and Lee's hopes were low.

Another road wound off through the tall ponderosa pines, rising steeply. They took it. From the long spine of a ridge they looked down upon a two-story, ranch-style log house. Behind and below the house rose a shed and an empty pole corral. Nothing moved down there. Nothing.

"Looks unoccupied," Vernon said.

Lee, who had been eyeing the road, said, "If that's the case, why is the road so hard-used? Look at the car tracks. Been some heavy travel through here. Tracks look fresh. See where they've run off the road when they made the downhill turn?"

"Want to go down and check it out?" Vernon said.

Lee sat a moment longer, just looking. He said, then, "We can't see the whole layout from here. Instead of busting on down there, let's scout around on foot."

Vernon agreed and they waved the others to stop. With Lee and Vernon and Todd leading, they started a flanking descent to approach the house from behind, following the rough course of a dry arroyo. In position, they climbed to the arroyo's rim and looked.

Instinctively, Lee first sought the corral and the shed. The corral gate was closed and so was the shed door. Looking onward, he went rigid when he saw the van parked next to the house. A red furniture van. Past it, likewise close to the house, a clutter of cars. Everything hidden from above.

"You fellows see that big van?" Lee asked needlessly, and then in a tone of dread, "If Cindy's not in that closed shed, that means they've hauled her to Mexico and come back. Well, I know how to find out real fast."

Vernon warned, "If we rush the place and she's in there, they'll come out shooting."

"I don't mean that—yet. I've got another way. A game we used to play. If she's in there, we'll know in a moment."

His eyes on the shed, Lee raised himself up higher on the arroyo's rim and sent a long, shrill whistle, and waited.

Nothing changed down there. No sound.

His doubts mounting, he whistled again—this time an even longer, urgent, high-pitched signal. As he held the piercing notes, he heard something. A thumping, a clattering and banging. Meaning exploded simultaneously with Todd's "She's down there, Lee! She's tryin' to kick her way out!"

Feeling ripped loose in Lee, a wildness, a pent-up burst of emotion. He couldn't hold back any longer. He scrambled up

and ran toward the sounds his horse was making, the pump shotgun pointed like a spear. Behind him, ignored, Vernon's shouted,
"No—Lee—no!" The shed and corral were some fifty yards away
now. Lee could see the shed door shaking under the onslaught of
kicking.

He was within a rope's throw of the corral when a man ran
out the rear door of the big house, head swiveling. He waved an
automatic rifle. It was the man who called himself Moss. The
bearded Moss seen at Ruidoso Downs.

Moss's attention, fixed on the clattering at the shed, switched
suddenly to Lee. Moss wheeled, swinging the rifle. Lee gave him
a blast from the shotgun a fraction before he heard the crash of
Moss's weapon. Lee felt nothing. Seeing Moss staggering but still
on his feet, Lee pumped and fired again and pumped. Moss fell
screaming, rolling, kicking, clutching vainly for his loose rifle.

Lee had never felt more alert. When a second man bulled out
of the house, rifle ready—a chunky-bodied, balding man wearing
a gray sweatshirt—Lee fired again and pumped. The man took
the charge around his thighs, the shock springing his mouth
wide open. He crumpled with a bellow, clawing insanely at the
rifle. His heavy body bounced when he hit the ground. His rifle
clattered free. It was, Lee saw, the man who called himself
Dolan.

By then Vernon and the others were rushing up. Lee said,
"There should be another guy."

At his words he heard feet pounding across gravel behind the
van.

Vernon and the two policemen and the DEA agent tore that
way. Cal and Smoky pulled up beside Lee.

There were two quick shots beyond the van. No cries. Just
shouts. In moments, two handcuffed figures, closely herded, appeared around the corner of the house. Lee didn't know the
woman, but the man was the one who called himself Green, rec-
ognizable even without his Fu Manchu. He snarled at Moss,
writhing on his back, "What d'you think now, Bruno? You said it
was like a bird's nest on the ground out here."

Bruno couldn't answer.

Lee went over to Dolan, said, "You're the one that beat up our jockey—left him for dead. Well, he's gonna make it. Maybe you won't."

Dolan kept clutching his bloody thighs. "Go to hell," he mouthed.

"Full circle," said Lee, loathing, and turned his back, walking away, aware that he yet gripped the shotgun. With great care, he leaned it against the pole corral, and opening the gate ran to the shed and flung open the door.

His eyes fell on Cindy haltered to the manger.

He untied and led her out, his dread rising as he roved his critical gaze over her. Rope burns on her neck, rope burns below her knees. Her proud head was down, the head that so reminded him of Landy's. She looked gaunt, she looked ragged.

Lee Banner choked. His eyes filled.

"She's not limping," Smoky Osgood managed to say.

"She's still a runnin' horse," Cal Tyler said.

After calling Ruidoso for an ambulance, Detective Vernon and the DEA agent searched the house. When they came out after some minutes, the DEA man said, "This is it. Their distribution point. It's a warehouse of marijuana . . . and that's not all. We found about fifty pounds of high-grade cocaine, worth ten million on the street if it's worth a dime. All packaged, evidently flown in."

Todd Lawson, listening, let his mind run back. Suddenly everything became cruelly clear. Everything. As Vernon hustled the two handcuffed prisoners to the patrol car, Todd said to him, "I'd like to speak to Eve alone before you take her in."

"Go ahead."

She looked at Todd without seeming to see him, even now on that distant plane of hers where she chose to wander alone, needing no one.

"Eve," he said, "you're the last person I wanted to find here. I want you to know that."

The masklike face bared no expression. Today she wore the rose-colored pants suit, elegant in every detail. Except for her luxuriant hair, ruffled somewhat during her capture, he thought she looked like a woman one might find on the cover of a national magazine. Poised. Taut. Slim. Sleekly groomed to perfection. A woman of the times, to be compared or imitated. Yet not beautiful. Not really. Not anymore.

It had to be said now. "Web fell in love with you, didn't he? He gave you cherished things. You used him as you tried to use me, here. He worked for you. He flew stuff in from Mexico." Todd broke off, awaiting her denial. She said no word. He went on. "Web got in over his head. He wanted out, didn't he? A good and decent man. But you were afraid he'd talk. . . . Web didn't take his own life, because he loved life too much. It was arranged for him, wasn't it, Eve?"

Turning as if on a stage, she strolled evenly to the open door of the patrol car. There she paused and gazed back at him, just so. Her face twitched slightly for part of an instant, no more, and then it smoothed, leaving no trace, and she entered the patrol car.

Chapter 17

Boom Boom Chumley's appreciation stood forth in his eyes when Connie Eaton answered his knock at Room 64. She wore tailored navy jeans, an open-neck equitation shirt of a pretty floral pattern, matching vest and the chocolate-brown boots.

"I'm late," he apologized. "Had the vet take another look at Gem Three, but he's okay. Still a little tender up front. Didn't even gallop him this morning. Just walked him around in the sunshine." He paid her another full look. "You sure look nice," he said. "Exactly right to inspect that little horse ranch with me over by Carrizozo. I've brought sandwiches and there's beer in the ice chest."

"Mel," she said, setting the slim-look western hat on her amber head, "you make me feel like a woman."

"Well, you're sure that, Connie."

Their eyes met and clung until, at last, he said, "Guess we'd better get going," and taking her arm escorted her out and into the pickup.

When massive Sierra Blanca bulged into view, looming over them, he asked, "Do you ski?"

"In Little Rock?" She laughed.

"Neither have I. Afraid I'd break a leg and they'd have to shoot me."

She laughed. They both seemed to laugh a great deal when together. At Capitan, he turned northwest on a scenic two-lane highway and soon they were descending the western slope of the Capitan Mountains, Sierra Blanca brooding loftily on their left, below them undulating folds of grass country where white-faced cattle grazed.

"Look at that," he said. "Looks like a picture postcard."

Thunderheads were gathering, forming cloud shadows, making teasing passes over the mountains and the broad Tularosa Basin below, now and again blocking out the dazzling sunshine.

"This is what they call the rainy season in New Mexico," he chatted. "Some places would hardly notice, if they got this little. Rain is good for everything out here except horse racing. That's Carrizozo down there, and beyond is the *mal país*."

"The *mal país?*"

"That black stretch down there. Lava beds. *Mal país* means bad country in Spanish. It's called the Valley of Fires. It's a state park now."

"It awes me, yet I like it."

Before long he turned off toward a fence line, rattled over an iron-pipe cattle guard, continued some distance to a rise, stopped and turned off the motor. Beyond, dwarfed by the vastness, lay a low-slung adobe house, a silent windmill, a barn of weathered gray, a tangle of empty sheds, pens, corrals.

"That's the place I was telling you about," he said, leaning forward to look. "The original ranch has passed on to heirs and been cut up. Just a few hundred acres left and the old house. I've paid down on it with an option to buy. If The Gem lights up the board, even show money, I can swing the deal."

"I hope you get it, Mel."

"It's just a little dream."

"The way you talk about it, it sounds like a big dream."

"If it doesn't pan out, I'll go on to another one. You have to do that with dreams so there'll always be one out there you want to happen."

"I believe they call that positive thinking."

"It's a kind of self-hypnosis. You develop that as a trainer. You have to think this colt or that filly will be a runner. More times than not they don't. I've had some lean years. But you keep on." He sighed. "Regardless of how we come out Labor Day, I'll be quitting Hack, though he doesn't know it yet. I've just made that decision." He hadn't intended to bring up Hack Trent during their ride—that had slipped out—or Trent's pending arrival, which, now, he would be on guard not to mention.

"Why?" she asked.

"Guess I'm too independent. I don't make a very good trained seal for rich men who can't understand why their horses don't always win. It wears on you."

"I can see why you want this ranch. It's lovely out here."

"New Mexico gets to you. In time it's got you. Think you'd like it well enough to live here?" He hadn't meant to say that either, but he had.

She flushed, taken back. "Mel . . . I . . . I don't know what to say."

"Wasn't fair of me to say that, was it?" Still, he said further, "The winters would be harsh. Lots of snow. Cold. But when spring comes, summer and fall, you can't beat it."

She was silent, an expression on her face he couldn't begin to define.

"Just a thought," he said, in a tone of dismissal. "How about some lunch, fair lady?"

"I'm ravenous." She took off her hat.

He laid a sack of sandwiches on the seat between them, opened the ice chest, and pulled rings on two cans of beer. "It's also hard to keep the figure out here," he said. "The good Mexican food, combined with the taste of beer in a dry climate." He was talking too much. His big mouth. Connie, never open about herself, seemed withdrawn as they munched ham sandwiches and drank the beer. He let time pass while he studied the cloud build-up.

They had finished the sandwiches and a second beer when rain dappled the windshield. "We'd better go," he said.

"Mind waiting a minute, Mel? I want another look at your dream ranch." He waited, and after a briefness she said, "What would you say if . . . if I made the money available to you to swing the deal, as you call it? You see, my husband left me—"

"I couldn't do that," he said before she could finish. "Thank you. Too much of a gamble. It's—"

A salvo of thunder boomed directly over them. Wicked lightning, snaking, writhing, did an Apache fire dance. Jerking, she leaned into him and he flung his arm around her, saying lightly, "That's one thing I forgot to mention. Sometimes they also have a little lightning out here." He continued to hold her, aware that she gave no indication of disengaging herself.

All at once the rain let down, dropping a greenish curtain between them and the ranch house.

"Lightning frightens me," she said.

"This is the best place we could be. The worst is out on horseback or under a tree."

"I like it here. It's a different world." She leaned her head against his shoulder.

"We'll be late," he said presently.

"It doesn't matter to me, unless you have to get back."

"I don't." No, it doesn't matter, he told himself. Hack's not due in till Sunday. He rubbed out the reminder.

Something wonderful was happening. He could sense the same in her, he thought. He was supremely happy. He stroked her hair ever so lightly. When he touched her again, his hand caressing the curve of her face, she turned to him with a look of absolute pain.

He drew her to him, kissing her gently, wanting to erase her hurt. She was hesitant, her body resisting. But just as he was about to release her, she slid into his arms and, closing her eyes, gave him an astonishingly warm kiss.

"Connie," he said, "I love you. I want you to marry me."

The hurt was still there as she turned her face away. To his dismay, he discovered that she was crying quietly. A woman's tears he could not bear, and he turned her about and held her, patting her shoulder, reassuring her, saying, "Sorry I upset you.

But it's the truth. I love you. It's probably the only honest thing I ever said in my life. That's from Melvin B. Chumley, voted Most Likely to Succeed at Jacksboro High School, class of fifty-seven, and the one that sure didn't." Smiling at her, he brushed tears from her cheek. "It's not that bad, now. I'll drop the subject."

"It's not that, Mel." Her face was still wet. She looked straight into his eyes. "You must know about Hack and me."

"I know he told me to meet you. Of course, I know he's married." Why tell her he knew the rest?

"I've been at Hack's beck and call for three years. I'm his mistress . . . one of them."

"That's in the past, Connie."

"I wish it were."

"I'm thinking about the future."

"I can't do this to you, Mel. I can't."

"Are you trying to drive me off?"

"I'm trying to be honest."

"You are. While we're on the subject of honesty, let me tell you about that Melvin B. Chumley from Jacksboro. I'm just coming off a year's suspension by the New Mexico Racing Commission. One of my horses showed a positive test for Ritalin. Won a stakes race at Sunland. The Commission also accused me of stealing the test samples before they could be shipped to the State Racing Chemist at Albuquerque. Did you know that?"

"No . . . and I don't want to hear any more."

"There's still more to the story and I'm going to tell you. I went before the Commission and denied everything. Oh, I was eloquent. All the time I was guilty as hell. Get it? Guilty. And they found me guilty."

"You didn't have to tell me."

"You didn't have to tell me about Hack, but you did." It's over, he thought. He took his arms from around her and slumped back, his dejection complete, hoping she might say it didn't matter. She didn't. It *was* over.

"I think," she said, after a short while, "we should be getting back."

He started the pickup and turned around. The shower was passing by the time they drove to the highway.

They had hardly spoken when he stopped at the Lone Pine and saw her to the door. They stood an irresolute moment. She said, "Thank you, Mel, for everything."

"I believe you're telling me good-by."

She regarded him without replying, her expression set and drawn.

He tried to think of something further to say, something carefree, but there was nothing left. It was over. Hack was coming. He said, "Good night," and stumbled out to the pickup.

Closing the door, she took off her hat and vest, conscious of an utter aloneness, and a wrongness, too; overcome, she fell upon the bed and burst into unbroken weeping, in her ears the fading roar of Mel's pickup.

Lee Banner, slipping quietly into the hospital room, found Doug Adams sitting up. He took Doug's hand. "Hi, pardner."

Doug's eyes lit up. "You got Cindy back. Serena told me."

"We did."

"Tell me . . . tell me everything."

Beginning with Todd Lawson's lead that took them into the mountains, Lee related each bit in detail.

"What shape is she in?" Doug worried.

"Lost some weight. Sored up, but sound. We're doctoring the rope burns. Started walking her as soon as we got her back to the track. She loosened up and seemed all right. We'll gallop her lightly in the morning."

"I can't get over her tryin' to kick that shed door down when you whistled," Doug said, his chuckle producing a flinch of pain. "And what about those three?"

"Green is in federal custody. The other two took a lot of buckshot. Moss, or Bruno, will be lucky if he walks again. Right now they're both under guard in an Albuquerque hospital. They won't see outside daylight for a long, long time, with what's against them. They've been wanted in Albuquerque since a year ago, when they jumped bond on heroin charges. The one called

Bruno—and he's got half a dozen aliases—was sentenced on six counts of trafficking to a sixty-to-three-hundred-year prison term. The other two got sentences from twenty to a hundred years."

"No wonder they jumped bond."

"Besides that, there are the Oklahoma charges, and charges of plane theft in Tucson and Las Cruces against Green, or whatever his real name is. And the one called Dolan is wanted in El Paso for a couple of drug-related murders. He was their muscle man, their enforcer. The DEA people say Bruno was the kingpin in southern New Mexico . . . using the Ruidoso airport as a staging area for interstate shipments of heroin and cocaine and marijuana."

Doug's face darkened. "Who killed Landy?"

"He won't admit it, but it has to be Bruno. He was a jackleg vet back in Kentucky. The Thoroughbred people ran him out of the state."

"I don't quite understand all of it," Doug said, his voice tired. "Why did they steal Cindy? There are other good horses."

"Dolan is the only one doing any talking. Wouldn't you know, the self-styled tough guy? He says the plan was to trade her for drugs in Mexico—a million dollars' worth. Match racing is still big down there among the wealthy ranchers. That she was our filly no doubt added to their motivation. On the other hand, if she'd run slow time in the trials, or hadn't qualified, I don't think they'd have touched her. First of all, they had to have a fast horse. One they could say had run top time on a recognized track."

A faraway look dulled Doug's eyes, and Lee sensed his thoughts before he asked, "Who'll ride Cindy in the All-American?"

"I've got Todd Lawson."

"He's a pro, all right."

"I'm sorry it's not you, Doug."

"I'm glad it's Lawson, though, since he helped find her. I won't forget that. I'd like to thank him."

"You can do that in person. He told me to tell you he's coming to see you."

Doug's smile was wan. "Maybe I can tell him a few things about Cindy that will help." He looked so sad, so young, that Lee hurt. "It was always my dream to ride in the All-American," Doug said.

"I know . . . and I want you to remember something, Doug." Lee took Doug's hand again. "Cindy wouldn't be in the All-American if it hadn't been for you. You got her there. You helped bring her along after she got hurt. Your ride in the trials was perfect. I'll never forget it, Doug. Will you remember that?"

"I'll try," Doug said through misty eyes. "Good luck in the draw."

The drawing for post positions in the All-American Futurity was scheduled Friday morning in the Turf Club high in the grandstand. With owners and trainers, track officials and the press looking on, finalists were assured impartial gate assignments.

When Lee arrived, the racing secretary was calling for quiet, and when the chatter subsided, he said he would explain the drawing procedure. Pills numbered one through ten would be shaken in a plastic bottle and dropped out one at a time and matched to the shuffled names of horses written on slips drawn from a box.

"Hell," a horseman grumbled to Lee, "if the track's as heavy Monday as it is today, all this will amount to is a lucky draw contest, with the outside horses having the advantage."

Quiet reigned as a young woman shook the bottle, poured out a pill and called in a tense voice, "Number eight," and another young woman drew a slip from the box and read distinctly, "Johnny Jet."

Immediate shouts. Two men shook hands, obviously owner and trainer.

Lee scanned his list of the finalists and their qualifying times. Johnny Jet had run :22.07 to enter the classic, his clocking the seventh fastest.

"Number seven."

"Triple Charge."

A ruddy-faced man whooped, then chortled, "I dreamed last night we'd draw the seven hole. Man, that's great!"

Lee recalled that Possumjet, a beautiful chestnut filly from Blanchard, Oklahoma, had stormed out of the favored seven position to win the 1972 All-American on a slow track when the distance was 400 yards. A lucky draw for Triple Charge, whose time of :22.23½ was the slowest of the ten horses. Records showed more winners had started from the seven and nine holes than any other positions.

"Number five."

"Gem Three."

"I'll take that any ol' day," said a rangy man wearing a fawn-brown hat and heather-colored western suit.

"I'll swap you, Chumley, if I draw the one hole," a man cracked.

"No, you won't."

"Number four," the young woman called.

"Battle Wagon."

Lee eyed his list. Battle Wagon, second to Cindy in the third division, had checked into the finals with :21.98. The colt could run. Lee respected him. His reading was the fifth fastest.

"Number six."

"Easy Injun."

The colt, winner of the Kansas Futurity and second in the Rainbow, had the fourth fastest sprint with :21.82, only five one hundredths behind the speedy Gem Three.

"Number ten."

"Warrior Way."

A woman squealed and hugged a Marlboro-looking man, and the grumbler next to Lee said, "Plumb tickled, ain't she, to be on the outside?"

Warrior Way's :22.18, Lee saw, was the ninth fastest, which didn't mean much. Every horse had a shot. Going down the list, Lee began to sweat. Only four positions were left unassigned: nine and the three inside holes. As the race now shaped up, Gem Three, Easy Injun and Battle Wagon—holders of the third, fourth and fifth fastest clockings, respectively—had drawn fairly favorable positions in the middle of the track.

Lee was hoping for the remaining outside gate when the woman shook out a pill and called "Number one." Her counterpart hesitated a fraction after drawing a slip, then swallowed and announced, "Cindy."

Lee was conscious of sympathetic eyes turning on him. There was a heavy hush. Seeing that he was expected to say something, he pulled on his ear and said, "This filly's never had anything given to her, unless it was one time—that nine hole in the trials. Even then she stepped in a soft spot and broke her stride, but came on, thanks to a great ride by Doug Adams, who is still in the hospital. Right now, after everything that's happened to her, I'm just grateful to have her back and sound. It's an honor for her to be in the All-American, and I know she'll run with heart. She always has. Thank you, folks, and good luck."

He stepped back self-consciously, hearing a surprising swell of applause. He knew he was flushing. A man stuck out his hand, saying, Texas drawl, "Pardner, I'm gonna buy you a great big drink when this confab is over."

"I'll need it." Lee laughed, shaking his hand.

On the next call, Little Brother, whose :22.16 dash was the eighth fastest trial, drew the coveted nine hole. Then:

"Number three."

"Dial Me."

Lee's list showed the filly had registered the sixth fastest sprint in :22.05. That left the last draw for Sudden Deck, the top qualifier with :21.68, breaking from the two hole, next to Cindy.

Then the racing secretary introduced a representative from the All-American Network, "who has some words for you owners."

"As you gentlemen know," the network man lectured—academic brown beard, open-collar sports shirt showing a gold neck chain, tan suit of stylish cut—"we shall be telecasting the World's Richest Horse Race from coast to coast on some one hundred and fifty stations. An estimated thirty million viewers will see the race. So one of you will be on national television." He appraised them a moment. "For you to project the modern image of the highly successful quarter horse racing industry . . . er—that is—to make a good appearance . . . we suggest that you dress well and have something appropriate to say over the air. It need not be lengthy, but fitting. Some well-chosen words. Comment on the race, of course. In addition, don't forget to thank the advertisers—we can furnish you their names—and thank the management of the Downs for making this spectacular telecast possible. . . . Are there any questions?"

The owners, some in old Levi's and soiled western hats and shirts and buckle-heavy belts, had turned unnaturally orderly, buffaloed by the all-seeing electronic eye.

"Hell's fire," Lee heard Battle Wagon's owner say, "sleepin' with my horse, I'll be doin' good to come up with a clean shirt. And tell me, how could a man remember all that folderol?"

"Well, thank you, gentlemen," the network rep said after an empty pause. "Good luck to all of you. We'll see one of you in the winner's circle."

As the relieved crowd poured out of the club, Lee stood aside, mulling over the luck of the draw that had placed Cindy in the toughest position on the track—next to the rail, a length's handicap, some horsemen said, when the track was heavy. First thing I have to do, he thought, is to put new mud plates on her.

Somebody slapped him on the back and the Texas voice drawled, "Pardner, let's have that drink. You're gonna need it in that one hole."

Hack Trent's first bit of business when he flew into Ruidoso Sunday afternoon, the day before the All-American Futurity, was to call Myrna at the Happy Hour Motel. She wasn't in; not that he expected her to be. That meant she was at the races, which she never missed unless ill. A check with the desk clerk provided further confirmation. Elated, he then called Connie at the Lone Pine. She said she was expecting him.

He took a taxi to the Happy Hour, left his luggage, all except a bottle of Chivas Regal, which he took to the taxi, and directed the driver to the Lone Pine. Fare from airport to town was five dollars, and when Trent paid the Mexican driver five twenty-five, the man said, *"Muy señor mío,* I drive you from the airport, wasting no time. I wait for you at the Happy Hour and drive you here, to the other end of town. *Señor,* did you forget something?"

"That's it, Chico," Trent growled, and marched for the Lone Pine, thinking, That's the trouble with the country today. Too many people looking for handouts.

He knocked expectantly on the door at Room 64, miffed that she hadn't sounded eager to see him when he called.

Connie opened the door and stepped back for him to enter.

"Hello, doll," he said, and waited for her kiss.

Turning away, she went to the center of the room and faced him. Trent followed eagerly and would have kissed her on the mouth, but she avoided his clumsy advance. "Hey, doll, what's wrong? You always give ol' Hack more'n that."

"I have to talk to you," she said.

"Plenty of time for that." He plopped the bottle down on the dresser and looked for glasses. "Hey, doll, where are the glasses? How can ol' Hack fix you a drink without a glass?"

"I don't want a drink," she said.

"We have to have a drink. Where are the glasses?"

"There are some in there by the wash basin. Fix yourself a drink if you like."

Catching an approving glimpse of himself in the mirror—white trousers, purple shirt with a silver bolo tie, checkered sports coat and potato-chip hat—he straightened the bolo and said, "What's wrong? You been lonesome again?"

"Hack," she said, resolved, "I've finally made up my mind."

"About what?" he said vaguely.

"I'm not going on like this any longer. We're through."

"What! You know I can't do anything. Myrna's got me tied up."

"It's not you, it's me. For the first time I can stand back and see myself. I know who I am. We're through."

In the act of pouring a drink, he almost dropped the bottle. He put it down and swung toward her, broad, formidable, his face working, hungry for her, forcing her backward against the bed.

"Aw, doll," he said, "you know how I feel about you. Ol' Hack's been settin' on a well in western Oklahoma for days. It's been a long time no see. I'm lonesome for you." He lifted both heavy hands for her shoulders to pull her to him. She slid quickly away, saying, "You don't understand. We're through—we're finished. That's why I came out here. I knew you wouldn't come to see me in Little Rock."

"What the hell you tryin' to say?"

"I just told you. We're through."

"I don't believe you."

She stepped to the dresser, opened her purse and handed him an envelope.

"What's this?" he said, his voice hollow, looking down.

"Open it, please."

He did so and pulled out a bundle of checks, thumbed through them rapidly, said, surprised, "I wondered why these hadn't been cashed."

"I've been working for some months. Back at my old job as a legal secretary."

He adopted his familiar attitude of penance. His voice had an injured tone. "This is all the thanks I get?"

"I've paid my dues, Hack. You can't say that I haven't."

He advanced toward her, his face roughing, his voice hardening. "Maybe so—but there's gonna be one last roll in the hay with ol' Hack."

She dug deeper into the purse. Her hand flashed. She gripped a tiny automatic of steel gray. She spoke, mouth set, calling on all her strength and calm. "Don't come any closer, please!"

He stared at the handgun, at her. His jaw dropped. He raised his bulky shoulders, a gesture of pretended tolerance. "Aw, doll, put that plaything away."

"It's not a plaything. Now I want you to leave. I don't want to see you again."

Raw anger soared into his face. "You know what this means, don't you? Ol' Hack won't take you back. You're cutting yourself off for good." He waited, confidently anticipating her usual capitulation.

Seeing that, she also saw herself in her former light, and she replied, "Please go, Hack," apprehensive lest she say the inciting word and he should charge across and wrest the automatic away and throw her upon the bed. She held her ground, meeting his eyes. Time seemed to stand still.

She was about to scream at him to leave when, as if seen in slow motion, he turned toward the door, his face a meld of anger and amazement. He opened the door and paused, for almost always one must say a final word or have a final look at that point of departure. He stared at her for so long that she feared he was coming back.

Another infinite moment.

Then, to her bursting relief, he clomped out of her life.

The instant he left, she locked the door and leaned against it, her breath coming in tight little gasps. She was trembling violently and she still gripped the automatic, which she carried for protection against intruders when traveling. Regarding it with revulsion, she wondered what she would have done had Trent not held back, since she had carefully unloaded it after he had called from the airport.

Chumley kept thinking of things he didn't like. Trent would be there by now, had been for some time. Miserable, Chumley took two of the white pills and washed them down.

When the phone rang, he was loath to answer it, assuming he would hear Trent's aggressive voice asking about The Gem's condition. He picked it up on the third ring and said, "Hello."

"Mel, this is Connie."

"You . . . are you all right?"

"Yes. I feel wonderful. Hack is gone. I sent him away. Now I can tell you what I felt I couldn't that afternoon. I love you, Mel."

Chapter 18

Somehow there was a difference about All-American Futurity
Day from any other race day. Something sensed. A restlessness
out there in the muddy darkness. A waiting. A banked tension.
Sleepless since two-thirty, Lee Banner noticed it when he rose at
five o'clock, when he gulped bitter coffee, when he rolled a
brown-paper cigarette that tasted flat, when he cut himself shaving, when he drove to the barns to relieve Smoky Osgood.

"She had a good night," Smoky reported. "Three stretches of
layin' down and three of standin' up."

"Afraid you didn't get much sleep."

"Who needs sleep today?"

Lee dumped a light feeding of grain into the new rubber
bucket bearing Cindy's name, a gift from Nancy. Other than a
few sips, Cindy would get no water past midday. He wanted
her feeling light and quick, hungry and sassy.

Taking a lawn chair, he sat down to endure the long suspense.
The All-American, the twelfth and final race of the day and last
of the season, would be run late in the afternoon. As the early
morning murk dissolved, he marked a further change about the
day: the stillness here. With many horsemen on the way home
with their hopefuls, the shed rows were quieter than usual.

He considered the sky. After the hard rain of last evening, a clear day was in prospect. Been afternoon and evening showers for a week. During the rainy season at Ruidoso Downs a horseman worried about the draw with ample reason. Cindy had drawn the number one worry hole. A man also worried about the "hump," that rise where the oval on which the Thoroughbreds ran joined the straightaway. There was quite a drop from the hump to the inside rail. A horse coming off it might stumble or break stride. The track drained toward the inside, making the first five lanes heavy, but the mud was deepest along the rail. A man could worry himself sick. But, Lee rebuked himself, a man ought to look on the bright side today. Doug was going to be all right after a long convalescence and Cindy had a shot at the All-American. He felt grateful beyond any words.

At ten o'clock, when the air was keen and warm, Lee took Cindy for a walk in the mud. Clearly full of herself, she squealed and kicked and perked up her ears at the surroundings. "You gawk like a country girl at her first county fair," he said, laughing at her. Back at the barns, he hosed off the mud, removed her leg bandages, examined her mud shoes with the bar plates, nailed on Saturday morning and still tight, then rubbed her down from head to tail. By eleven o'clock she was back in her quarters, where she would stay until race time, her activity limited to sticking her head over the stall door and being petted.

Post time today was eleven forty-five, and shortly Lee heard the call come over the loudspeakers for the first race.

Serena and Nancy brought his lunch and a new western shirt with slash pockets. "Believe it's kinda fancy for me," Lee balked.

"Now, you put it on before you take Cindy to the paddock," Serena told him firmly. Lee didn't argue.

Cal and Smoky arrived after lunch, plus some horsemen coming by to wish Lee luck. The conversation dwelled more on the weather and condition of the track than the race and the favorites.

"Don't figure it'll rain today," Cal predicted cheerfully, eyeballing the clear sky. "The forecast is for afternoon showers, like yesterday, but I never go by what the weatherman says."

"An Okie just sniffs the wind and takes it from there," Smoky said. "Cal, you remember back in the early days when just about everybody had storm cellars behind their house, and the women-folk would grab the kids and run for the hole?"

"What do you mean, the early days? We still use ours. When the telephone poles start bending double, Maude and I head for cover."

"If it's gonna rain," Lee said, "it would help our filly if it comes down about two o'clock. Just enough to make the track sloppy. That would even things up a bit. But I agree with Cal. No rain today. The track will be heavy."

When Todd Lawson joined them, Lee introduced him to the horsemen as Cindy's jockey. "Think the hump will bother her any?" Todd was asked.

"We've worked her across it and it didn't seem to. I know she doesn't mind the mud like some horses."

"She's used to muddy pastures," Lee said. "If that means any-thing."

One by one, the horsemen wished everybody luck and left. With only the family and friends around, Lee said, "Way the track is, Todd, it'll be difficult to jump her out enough where we can angle off outside to better footing. What do you think?"

"That would be asking too much even of a good-breaking horse, which she is. There's too much speed in this race to get her outside from the one hole. I want to settle her and let her run her race as much as possible. Doug says she always runs a straight course. If we can just stay out of early trouble."

Smoky, looking troubled, said, "I hear Sudden Deck has a tendency to drift inside."

"That's what I mean. Staying out of early trouble."

After Todd took his leave, Serena and Nancy combed and brushed Cindy's mane and forelock, and then Nancy, making a ceremony of the occasion, commenced braiding a red ribbon into the black mane. "It's her lucky ribbon," Nancy said. "The one she wore in the trials. It's also the color of Mr. Lawson's silks."

"Gosh," Lee teased, "I didn't know that. Did you, Serena?"

"Now, Daddy!"

That accomplished, they all sat around, conversation at low ebb. Now and then they would look at Cindy. Lee glanced at his watch: two-seventeen. He got up and rationed Cindy a sip of water, only a sip. "Don't want her loggy," he said, catching his daughter's frown at his niggardliness.

A lassitude set in. Lee turned on the radio, got weary banjos and plunking guitars accompanying a moaning-voiced male singer.

"That's really pretty gross, Daddy," Nancy said, sounding very universityish.

"You can't get Tammy Wynette every time," Lee said, snapping it off. "That's who Cindy likes."

There followed a discussion about country music, during which Cal let drop that Smoky used to fiddle for country dances back in Pott County, Oklahoma.

"Back then we'd play for two or three bucks a night and a few snorts of moonshine. Or maybe we'd just pass the hat. Nowadays, these fellas are all millionaires and when they play the same old tunes we did, they call it a concert," Smoky sniffed.

At three twenty-one a telegram arrived. Lee signed and opened it, exclaiming, "It's from J.B. He says, 'Good luck in the All-American. We're proud of all of you. Sorry I can't be with you. Your country banker. J.B.'"

"Now, there is a good ol' boy," Lee said.

Cindy seemed to doze.

The raspy voice over the loudspeakers called horsemen to the eighth race.

At three-forty Serena and Nancy made ready to go to their reserved seats in the grandstand. Serena fixed her husband with a look both questioning and wistful.

"Lee," Cal spoke up then, "I'd like to make a suggestion. After we pony Cindy to the paddock and she's ready to run, why don't you go sit with the family, where you can watch the race? You know you can't see much from behind the gates. It may be a once-in-a-lifetime sight, watching her run. Let Smoky or me pony Cindy around. You watch the All-American."

Lee's impulse was to refuse. But what could he do that they

couldn't? Therefore, thinking of all these two old friends had done, and of the fast Bug colt that Cal had lost, and of Smoky's tough luck with Buzz Boy, he nodded and said, "Believe you're right, Cal. It's a good idea."

"I think Cal should pony her to the gates," Smoky said. "She's more used to him."

"Whatever you want to do," Lee said.

Beaming, Serena told Lee, "We'll wait for you at the paddock."

When the eleventh race was called, Lee sponged Cindy and wiped her face, and rubbed on her and talked nonsense to her, while Cal and Smoky saddled Booger Red for his pony horse duties.

Waiting for the final call seemed an eternity to Lee. No one spoke or moved, just sat. Across the way, Lee heard the start of the eleventh race, a mile claiming feature, and the announcer's calls as the leaders changed, and the rising roar of the crowd as the horses charged to the finish.

At last, like a summons, the matter-of-fact voice grated over the loudspeakers, "Attention in the barn area. . . . Take your horses to the paddock for the twelfth race."

Lee was on his feet as the call was being repeated, opening the stall door and leading Cindy out. A pause now while the three eyed her back and forth, critically, as if they might have overlooked some small detail.

"This young lady's ready to run," Smoky said. "I've never seen a quieter horse. But when she gets on that track, she's gonna turn into a bomb. You bet she will."

"She knows what to do," Cal said, "She's a runnin' horse."

Those two like coaches, Lee thought, peptalking an athlete.

"Let's go," he said, trying to sound calm.

Todd Lawson put off coming to the jockeys' room until the very last, knowing from experience how it would be there. Everybody uptight, everybody attempting to act cool. He had gone to bed early, hoping to sleep late, but instead, had waked up early. After visiting the Banners and their friends at the barn, he had tried to nap in his pickup; that, too, was unproductive. No way, he knew, before the All-American.

The eleventh race was being called when he walked in.

"Just getting ready to send out a search party," a concerned Art Yates said. "You all right?"

"Feel like an apprentice before his first ride."

"It never changes, does it? Well, luck to you."

Todd went to his locker and started undressing, his mind on the blood-bay filly and the sticky footing out there and the hump. The tote board, which earlier had the track rated "muddy," now said "heavy." Ironic, he thought, that the slowest qualifiers had drawn the favored outside positions where the track was driest and fastest, while the top speed horses were inside. There was one leveler for his filly. Campaigners like Sudden Deck, Gem Three and Easy Injun likewise would be running in deep muck. As for the hump, all you could do was work your horse over it in advance—and hope for good luck.

A voice, more taunting than inquiring, broke in upon his projections. "Say, Pop, have you seen the money lines on all the finalists?"

Here we go, Todd thought, turning around.

Flip Keller, dressed in white silks, was holding a newspaper at arm's length. When Todd didn't speak, Keller said, "Says here that Easy Injun has run up over a hundred sixty-five thousand from six wins in eight outs. . . . Gem Three, ninety-five thousand—four wins in seven outs. . . . Sudden Deck, a hundred seventy-five thousand plus. Of that, a hundred fifty-four thousand came when he won the Rainbow. . . . Let's see. In five outs, he won four and ran second. Never out of the money. . . . Even Dial Me has pocketed over forty thousand. Won the West Texas Futurity, y'know."

"So what?" Todd said.

"Just wondered if you'd seen the breakdown?"

"I have, and my filly is at the bottom of the list. Less than twenty-five hundred won on Oklahoma bush tracks. None of that means a thing. Today's another horse race."

Keller's reaction was to move his lips in that irritating manner of his.

Todd said, "What all this blow means is that she's the horse to beat and you know it. Meantime, you'd like to grind on the old bird that will be in her saddle—in case he's lost his guts. Well, let me tell you something, *Macho*. I was riding winners before you got on your first stick horse, and I haven't changed a bit."

The room had stilled—the rustlings, the muffled voices. From the corner of his eye Todd saw Yates half rise from his chair, then sit back down as Keller, with a little jiggle of his head, said, "Just a point of interest, was all. Didn't think you'd get sore, Pop," and ambled away to his locker.

But, Todd sensed, it wasn't over yet. Dressed, he reported to Yates and weighed in. Today each horse would carry 120 pounds. Todd passed the time trimming his whip and resting. By now the sun was lodged far down and the grandstand was casting shadows. Even in here the drone of the crowd was distinct, like a pulse throbbing. At the break it would burst into a roar, rising to a crescendo, whooping, shouting, screaming, unbroken until the race was done and hopes rose or fell. Before long he heard the nervous rustling of the horses coming to the saddling paddock, and soon the voice of Yates—the signal to go out and mount. Keller was already at the doorway, flicking his whip, the image of the cocksure rider. As Todd started to walk past him, Keller's lips moved. "Wasn't it the rail at Bay Meadows, Pop?"

Todd wheeled, his anger tearing free, and with his left hand took Keller by the front of his blouse. "You'll have to outrun her. Keep that in your craw, *Macho!*"

Yates was between them at almost the same instant, breaking them apart, snarling at them, "Get out there—both of you!"

Todd didn't argue, thankful for Yates. Another moment he'd have slugged Keller with his right and maybe popped his shoulder. Ended his race right there. *You damn fool, Lawson! Cool down!*

Going out, Keller's smirking face still before his eyes, feeling the churned paddock mud beneath his boots, Todd was conscious of a powerful undertone, as if he breasted a rising swell, and of a lake of faces and people waving and milling. And that other Todd Lawson, that leading rider years ago, mounting from this same paddock, seemed another person. He was, Todd thought, he was.

Lee Banner threw him a wide smile of encouragement, shook his hand and said, "She may lean against the tailgate. She did in the trials. But Doug had her standing straight before the break."

"I'll be ready for it. And I'll holler in her ear to cut down the crowd noise. It's unbelievable out there." He looked at Lee's face. "Anything else?"

"Just ride her."

"Boots and Saddles" was sounding.

Lee gave Todd a lift aboard, Cal led away on Booger Red, and Lee hastened across the paddock to Serena and Nancy and they worked their way through the crowd to their seats on the sun deck.

Watching the horses circle out on the track for the post parade, Lee felt his throat thicken as the strains of "America the Beautiful" floated slowly over the loudspeaker. Being the number one runner, Cindy was first behind the colorfully garbed rider leading the procession on a striking copper dun quarter horse. Cal was allowing her sufficient slack so she could move with ease. She kept arching her neck and dancing and occasionally glancing at the chattering crowd. Behind her danced Sudden Deck, the red sorrel whose qualifying trial was five one hundredths faster than Cindy's. The book on him: sometimes a bad gate horse. Sometimes he drifted in. Exceptional early speed. Dial Me, on Cindy's right, could be another bad actor in the gate.

The twinkling tote board was changing every few seconds. At the moment it showed Gem Three and Easy Injun, 9–5. Sudden Deck, though in the two hole, 5–1, Battle Wagon, 15–1, Dial Me, 17–1, Johnny Jet, 20–1, Little Brother and Warrior Way, 25–1, and Triple Charge, the slowest qualifier, 30–1. Although the newspapers termed her the "sentimental favorite," Cindy was a 15–1 long shot.

"What do you think, Daddy?" Nancy asked.

"Every horse has a shot. I just hope she gets out where she has a fair chance to run."

The grandstand's mass of voices seemed to draw breath. The horses passed and took their warm-up gallops.

"They're approaching the gate," the announcer said.

A short pause.

"They're at the gate. Now post time."

Figures moved purposefully behind the weblike structure of the gates to begin the numerical loading, two handlers to a horse.

Lee, watching through binoculars, saw Cindy step in without argument. She stood mannerly and today did not lean against the tailgate. Still, Lee worried. She had until the last horse loaded to work herself into a nervous state, every flounce of a thousand-pound body touching off rattles that resounded the barrier's steel length.

Sudden Deck went in, all business. Dial Me, a tempestuous mahogany bay, took an abrupt dislike for the three hole and refused. Two handlers put her in, anyway. Battle Wagon, eager to run, wanted right in there. Let's run.

Lee glanced back at Cindy. She still hadn't leaned, but now she turned her head curiously toward the other horses. *Straighten her, Todd. Be ready!*

Gem Three, a bright chestnut, and the seal-brown Easy Injun, both battle-tested pros as two-year-old colts, entered with little urging. Triple Charge, a beautiful gray filly, threw an unappreciative fit when escorted toward the favored seven hole, whereupon her handlers, apparently on signal from the starter's tower, waited on her for later loading. Johnny Jet flounced before eight, then gave in to pressure from behind. Little Brother and Warrior Way as much as said, "Let's go."

Now the handlers led a quieter Triple Charge into the seven position.

Lee took a last checking look at his filly. Her head was straight. A hush blanketed the entire track and grandstand.

"The flag is up."

The bell shrilled, the gates flew open and the crowd screamed.

"There they go," said the announcer, sounding remarkably calm.

To Lee's alarm, Cindy broke a nick late behind the pack. Seemed to be slipping a little when she left. Now, quickly, above the crowd's roar, he heard the announcer's staccato first call:

"It's Easy Injun on the lead—Gem Three second—Sudden Deck third—Dial Me and Battle Wagon running fourth—Little Brother fifth."

Cindy wasn't in contention yet, two lengths behind Sudden Deck, who had got away cleanly. *Tap her, Todd.*

All at once the filly Dial Me started weaving an erratic course. She lunged to her right just as Battle Wagon was gathering steam. She knocked him off stride, straightened, then bumped him again. Suddenly both horses were out of it. Lengths behind. Lee winced. Battle Wagon—that good-looking colt—wiped out.

Now Lee saw Cindy moving up on Sudden Deck. Todd not whipping her yet. Just settling her, letting her run her race. On the far outside Warrior Way mustering a bid under frantic sticking. The announcer's call:

"Gem Three takes the lead by a neck—Easy Injun second—Sudden Deck half a length back in third—Cindy fourth—on the move—Warrior Way fifth on the outside. It's a horse race, folks!"

To his right, like flying objects through the hail of mud, Todd Lawson saw Dial Me collide with Battle Wagon, shear off, heard the thud of horseflesh as they collided again. Saw them drop back. Cindy was taking hold of the track by now. He could feel it—that visceral communion between jockey and horse—as she lengthened stride, running lower, running faster. As he tapped her left-handed, asking for more, Sudden Deck drifted in a bit toward the rail—or was Keller slyly cutting them off just enough to crowd her? With that length and a half lead, he could get by with it.

On instinct, Todd took her around to the right, into the gap left by Dial Me and Battle Wagon. As he straightened her, he switched the stick swiftly and whipped her right-handed and she moved up again. Sudden Deck very close now on Todd's left. At that moment he felt the filly's rhythm change as they flew up and over the hump. Yet not breaking stride, not stumbling as they came down off it.

As she settled herself, taking hold once more, Todd hollered in her ear and took dead aim at the head of the pack blitzing down the middle of the track.

Serena and Nancy were screaming like demons and Lee was whooping for his horse when Cindy, ears laid back and coming like hammers, swept up alongside Gem Three at about 350 yards. Todd Lawson just a low shape, hand-riding her, letting her go on her own. The announcer's call lost in the wild roaring. A four-horse race now. Gem Three and Easy Injun firing head to head. Sudden Deck digging in on the inside. A blanket would cover the middle horses.

Lee saw Easy Injun charge to the fore by a head. Gem Three's rider went to the whip and the colt closed with a powerful surge. Cindy matching him stride for stride, still coming on, coming on. Easy Injun now a jump off the blistering pace.

Just before they flashed across the finish, Lee glimpsed a blazed face stuck out in front. So it looked, or was it wishful hoping?

Around him the roaring tailed off like a passing storm. Everybody was standing.

Lee, watching the tote board, saw the photo signal flash. Serena took his hand. Nancy held her mother. No one said a word.

While the stewards viewed the picture, people swarmed to the finish line in anticipation or shock.

Suddenly, brightly, the board twinkled happily. Lee dared look. At the top of the results he saw 1, below it 5, then 6, then 2.

He whooped. His women screamed and hugged him.

Down there the horses were trotting back, Todd Lawson waving his whip, Cindy still full of herself. For the strangest flick of time, Lee seemed to see a big bay colt with black points, and then a kind of misty blur clouded his vision. When he blinked, clearing his eyes, the big colt was gone, and Lee Banner and his family began making their way through the noisy crowd down to the winner's circle.